DOOM 94

by Jānis Joņevs; translated by Kaija Straumanis

DOOM 94

by Jānis Joņevs

ISNB: 978-1-903110-53-9

First published in this edition 2018 by Wrecking Ball Press.

Copyright: Jānis Joņevs

Cover design: Reinis Pētersons

Typeset by atomluft.com

Supported using public funding by
ARTS COUNCIL ENGLAND
LOTTERY FUNDED

I went sledding down a hill Wednesday. The hill was big, but not really long. I didn't fall off. I went down it a bunch of times. But I wanted to fall off just once, at least someday.

Guntars. Diary. 4th grade.

The following story is based on true events.

I
THE SH●T

8

1

It's 1994. Men in plaid flannel shirts walked down the street. Jelgava hummed silently. I stood in the library doorway, waiting for them to pass by.

I was a little afraid of them, like I was of everything. After waiting a moment I went out and saw that the sky was bright.

It was April 5th, 1994.

I took two steps and looked over to see them stopped in front of the grocery store, taking up the entire sidewalk. No, I wasn't afraid – I just didn't want to offend them by overtly crossing to the opposite side of the street. So I decided to turn left and take the shortcut home, through several interconnected courtyards between apartment buildings. Usually I stick to the streets, leaving the obscured spaces to the footballers and other declasse elements. But today I strode confidently into the first courtyard.

There was a strange object in the courtyard directly behind the library – a smallish brick cube with an unknown purpose; maybe it was the ventilation shaft for Hell's coatroom or something. And directly on top of this cube sat a second group of guys. The school bully – a kid a few years older than me named Ugo (that was just his nickname; every bully needs one) – and two others just like him who I didn't recognise. All three were smoking.

I tried to think about something else and get by them unnoticed. It didn't work.

Ugo called to me:

– Nice glasses!

One of the others chimed in:

– Don't run away. Come talk to us.

I stopped and turned to face them, the books in my hands feeling pathetic and vulnerable, but provoking.

Ugo noticed them and asked:

– What're they about?

But the second guy barked:

– Spit it out, what're they about!

Several clever answers sprang into my mind, but I went with a quiet:

– All kinds of things.

My two interrogators turned to the third guy. He gave me a look which probably only I perceived as strangely nervous, and said:

– Give us your smokes.

At the same time, far away, thousands of kilometres across the ocean on another continent, a hand slid over a 20-calibre Remington pistol, pulled back the magazine, checked inside – yes, it was loaded.

But here, I shook my head, and not out of malice or because I didn't want to share; I just didn't have any cigarettes. The third guy didn't seem too upset and said:

– Then give us a lat.

I replied:

– I don't have one.

And to show my regret I spread my hands open wide, sending the books tumbling to the ground. He signalled to me to stop as I bent down to pick them up, leaving face-down on the Jelgava dirt the man who in his time believed that he would rule the world, and continued:

– Give us fifty santims.

I again showed them my empty hands. His tone turned modest:

– Twenty santims.

This time I lied with the same gesture, and he said:

– You've got some nerve.

He got to his feet.

There, far away, at that exact moment, the 20-calibre Remington was cocked with a click, just like in the movies, ready to fire. The barrel was brought to a temple.

Here, the third guy took one step to close the gap between us. I saw his chin up close and a siren went off in my brain; I wanted to be anywhere but here.

There, far away, the bullet hit its mark, shattered the skull, tore through tissue. The shot barely, just barely rippled the surface of the water in a nearby pool, but neither the neighbours nor the people on the adjacent street heard a thing.

But I felt something. The siren went silent, and something like music took its place. It felt like something had happened, only I didn't know what. And it felt like something else would also happen, but I also didn't know what. I even had the sudden desire to get beaten, I mean, for someone at least to hit me, because maybe that would start this *something*. I tilted my head to one side, looking past the group of guys and scratching my forehead, as if I was trying to remember something.

Ugo had jumped suddenly to his feet, and was gesturing frantically as if wanting to say something. Later he'd tell me that he had heard the shot loud and clear.

The second guy who had been sitting next to Ugo would later say he'd heard a strange three-chord combination and had felt happy, so happy that he'd almost started to cry. The cigarette he was holding fell from his fingers and burned his shirt, but he just sat there with a dumb grin on his face.

The third guy, who was standing in front of me, was the only one who didn't hear anything. That's what he'd say later, spitefully. He was thrown off by my sudden meditative expression, and turned to his friends to show them my stupid face, but found Ugo with his arms raised in a 'V' and the other giggling while his shirt smouldered. What pissed him off even more was when the first two helped me pick up the fallen books, while I picked up the still burning half-cigarette and slowly savoured my first ever drag.

None of us understood any of it.

I went home feeling drunk, the books no longer seeming interesting. I put them on the table, didn't speak to my family, didn't watch *Saved by the Bell*, but instead stared out of the window at Jelgava, and drummed a random beat on the glass with my knuckles. I knew that I no longer wanted or needed to do my homework, though I didn't yet know what I did want and need. That night, I sat at the desk in the dark for a long time. I didn't have my own room, so the only light I could choose not to turn on was the desklamp.

A few days later Radio SWH announced that the lead singer of Nirvana, Kurt something or other, had been found dead. The first reports said, of course, that it was suicide. The radio DJ expressed his sympathy and respect, and immediately followed that up by saying he hoped that this tragic event wouldn't result in an unnatural increase in fans, as had happened when Freddie Mercury had died.

Ha, ha, ha, ha, ha, ha.

Freddie Mercury nothing, mister DJ. A bottle of cheap Merkurs brandy is worth more.

The DJ's wish didn't come true. He could hang onto it until November 1997, when the INXS fan base didn't increase after the charmingly poignant death of Michael Hutchence. But back then, in April 1994, was a turning point in our lives.

It would take a few more days for me to understand it. For me to find vindication in the intuitively collected newspaper clippings on countless shady-looking musicians, the theoretical and self-depreciating interest in drugs, the intuition for depressing aesthetics and the mapping out of our stomping grounds. But for now I just felt strange. Different.

2

Up until then I'd been a good kid. I listened to my parents without question, to my teachers too, was a good student and dreamed of a good future career as a lawyer or president, where I'd bring order to the world and do away with all the negative people. I wanted to become smart, rich and famous. It was all part and parcel – if you were smart, you were generally good, and for that the world would, naturally, reward you with money, fame, and happiness. Probably also with beautiful women, an area I currently had zero luck in. I didn't believe in being smart but poor, good but unhappy, and the lonely. The world had to be right, and I wanted to be right within a right world.

Then, suddenly, I found myself on the other side of a barricade. As if I had spent the past fourteen years not gathering knowledge about life, but gathering strength to grieve and long for something inexplicable and nonsensical. Why, why would anyone want to be Kurt, to spend a lifetime depressed, depressing others, to marry some ugly skank and then shoot yourself? Wouldn't it be better to be one of the guys from Take That, who smile, are adored by beautiful girls and even make some money? But suddenly there was a whole crowd of us (no, not a crowd, we were the handful outside the crowd) who hated those who succeeded and who idolised the damned.

I was sitting in the shrubs by the school, facing the Gypsy House – a long wooden building with fake windows painted on the sides (whole generations of gypsies really did live in there, and when I was little I was told you should never show a gypsy your teeth). Alunāns Park loomed a ways off, along with a colourful cluster of trees locally referred to as the Shittery. I was smoking with Ugo and a few other guys. There were a handful of thugs there too, all sullen and pretty well known. There was Ghost, one of the three or five brothers who lived an alternative lifestyle, and Nose, his brother, who didn't even go to our school but came to sit with us in the shrubs. DJ was there too, a handsome but scary guy. He tended to get up in my face. I was absolutely terrified of him, so I always acted indifferent and jumpy around him. There were three more guys there too, whose names I didn't know, all with longish hair (at that time no one had truly long hair yet); one with blond, one with brown and one with greasy hair.

Nose was talking. He was old, at least two years older than the rest of us, so when he spoke you could hear the life experience behind it, but his tone of voice conveyed light-hearted sorrow.

– Some idiot in America took a shotgun, stuck the barrel in his mouth and said, 'I'm like Cobain!' and the gun shot itself off.

– What happened to him?

– Died.

– Shotguns are super sensitive.

Nose looked sadly at the guy who had offered this superfluous information.

– A ballistics expert, eh.

The guy scratched his greasy head.

– What about balls!?

Everyone grew thoughtful for a minute. I had a question too:

– How could he talk with a shotgun barrel in his mouth?

And I was immediately embarrassed. I couldn't silence the logic in my head. I had to stop it. DJ sneered and said:

– Cobain spent his whole life singing with a barrel in his mouth. You wouldn't understand.

Then he pointed at the school:

– Fuck you!

Everyone was silent for a moment. I could hear the wind carrying 'Something in the Way' from the direction of the Shittery.

The blond guy (I'd seen him around outside school) lit half a cigarette and said:

– Cobain lived in a cardboard box. He had stomach-aches his entire life. That's why he did drugs.

This set off DJ again. He threw his hands up in the air and hissed:

– And he was right to! All of us should do that. Because they – and here he again pointed to the school – say that we shouldn't. But we're with Cobain. At least I am.

The greasy-haired one mused:

– Where do you get them?

DJ gestured dismissively and secretively to the Gypsy House.

Nose added:

– You can drink too. Vodka.

DJ nodded in agreement, but then Nose's brother said in earnest:

– It's hard to drink vodka straight.

Here everyone perked up and offered his suggestions:

– You can chase it with a cigarette!

– You can mix it with Yuppi, the blond guy said.

I took mental note of these recipes. Yuppi, by the way, was a popular powdered drink mix in the early 90s; you'd mix it with water to get lemonade. I added:

– Vodka's real great if you drink it through a straw. You put the bottle in your inner jacket pocket, a straw in your mouth and drink up. It's wild, the best way to get lit.

I was talking in an unnaturally natural voice and about things I had never done. At that time my only contact with vodka was on my dad's breath when he drank it. The trick with the straw was something I'd gotten from my sister, who'd told me stories about the boys in her classes. As I was talking I thought to myself – what kind of straw is long enough to reach from an inner pocket to your mouth? I was lying, and my new, unfamiliar friends, haters of lies and hypocrisy, would unmask me and ship me off to the teachers' pets, and punch me in the glasses as a farewell.

– What kind of jacket? DJ shouted in challenge, lifting his arms to demonstrate his own tattered jean jacket, which was graffitied in ballpoint pen with 'Hate', 'Incesticide' and 'Fuck'.

My mother and father would never let me wear something like that.

Ghost chimed in:

– I still think beer tastes better. I drank it once – something made him glance over to the Gypsy House, and he continued on, louder – I drank a lot of it once . . .

There was a girl standing there, looking in our direction; long hair, short skirt, heavy boots. DJ jumped to his feet and ran over to her. She kissed him deeply, and then they both left, just like that, hand in hand. She had a tiny backpack on her back; those were in style back then.

Ugo broke the silence, announcing suddenly that wine was also good. I remembered the lunch the old Duke of Richelieu had, where he had secretly served the king of Sweden tokaji; the beverage had glistened in the glass like liquid ruby.

– Wine is super expensive!

I just blurted it out. Ugo smirked once, twice and then pulled a bottle out of his pocket. He blew off the dust and showed us the label which clearly read: 'Riddle' Wine. Everyone said:

– Mmm! Ooh! Well, c'mon.

Ugo offered to pass the bottle around. We agreed. But my heart started to pound. Class was about to start. Students have to go to their classes. I'm a rebel in my soul and in appearance, and I smoke, so do I honestly have to do anything more? Let me go to class, dress nicely and listen to my parents, because I'm there with you in my heart of hearts, which at the moment is pounding anxiously.

But there was alcohol in the bottle, and I'd always been secretly intrigued by it, as I'd been with stories about maniacs, despots, catastrophes. A few years ago some girls in my grade had copied out descriptions of torture from the history book and had read them aloud to the rest of us. The interest in pain and heightened emotions made sense to me – somewhere out there was life, *the* life that just had to get started. Alcohol was the same way; it glistened in the bottle like liquid pain.

And girls like guys who drink (so writer Rūdolfs Blaumanis said). At least, for sure, those girls with heavy boots and slender legs. Girls from Kurt's world. I reached out my hand. Ugo asked:

– Anyone got a corkscrew?

I, along with everyone else, felt around my pockets as if a corkscrew could magically appear in one of them. No-one had one – well, that's too bad, stupid even, but nothing to do about it, so we might as well go back to school. Then Nose spoke up, saying you could open a bottle of wine by forcing the cork down, in the opposite direction. You just needed a good enough tool, even a key would work, a strong twig, a pen. We all turned immediately to the bushes to look for a pen, but the unfamiliar greasy-haired guy spoke up:

– Eureka! I'll run to the cafeteria. There should be one in the kitchen!

And he ran off to the school. I watched him go and thought how there might not be a corkscrew in the school kitchen, and even if there was, what were the chances that they'd let a suspicious student have it; he was just running away, running away from sin, from degeneration, from the "riddle" left among us. I was a bit jealous of him, but also felt somewhat light-hearted – he had executed the standard fear and betrayal that had been meant for me. He had just opened the heavy door to the building, we could hear the bell ring, then the clipped sound of the door closing – and then nothing more.

Years later, a lifetime later, not long after this book was published in France, I received a letter:

'I read your book, yes, and I remember that day we were drinking wine in the bushes by the school, and I'd like to make a correction to what you wrote. It went like this. I was the one who ran to get the corkscrew that day, but I didn't run away. I had a lot of connections with the cafeteria and kitchen staff; I was sleeping with all the cooks and monitors, and we all drank together regularly. Not everyone at school knew that, just the in-crowd. I'm writing you from Nancy, where I work in a company that makes hair products, and drink two bottles of Bordeaux Champagne a day, if you know what I mean.'

3

At some point I did go back to school. It smelled like floor wax and chalk-covered rags. And they told us how to act and live. Sometimes you'd get whacked upside the head. Everyone just ran around yelling.

I did well in school, except for physical education. In short, I was a nerd.

Those distinctions were made clear in school. Nerds had the good grades, but were afraid of everything; the thugs were strong and athletic, but stupid. Girls were either pretty, or just non-existent.

Jurġis and I were in the nerd crowd. We lived in the same building, went to kindergarten together, and had shared a desk since first grade. At home we hung out all the time, built ships out of dining room chairs, set up toy-soldier battles on the rug and later, in school, just tried to get by.

And then something changed.

One day Jurġis and I were sitting in the front hall behind a palm tree, scheming something. We had a piece of paper in front of us and we were drawing out some kind of plan. Then, per usual, one of the thugs came up and snatched the paper from us and crumpled it up to throw it away.

Today the thug was Ugo.

When he saw it was me, he put the crumpled piece of paper back down and said:

– Hey!

– Hey!

That's what I said back. Then Ugo gave a half-wave and left, without even calling us dumbasses.

I swelled with pride. See, the mould could be broken! The world was changing! Long live Kurt! He had protected us. We were saved by a perfect chord and a gunshot.

I looked to Jurġis to share in the moment.

But he goes:

– You hanging with them now?

His expression hurt, betrayed. I go:

– What? Everything turned out good!

– So you're good with them? You smoking and sneaking wine in the bushes with them, too?

Would he rather Ugo gave us each a Charley horse in the shoulder? Is he jealous of my victory? But he keeps going:

– You're crazy.

Then what did that make him? I say, casually:

– Alright, enough planning. It's time to start taking over the world for real.

He goes:

– It was just a game.

But no – it was never a game for me.

I ask:

– Don't you listen to Nirvana?

He goes:

– I don't like them. It's just screaming.

And there it was. Life had split in two. And somehow I'd ended up on the other side.

It didn't sound too bad, though – me, crazy. Isn't that what everyone wants? To break out of the everyday, out of normality and get confirmation of your existence. Hadn't Kurt been crazy? And I was, too. I could be like Cobain.

That's how I lost a friend.

And a teacher.

I wrote 'Kurt Cobain 1967–1994' on my desk.

Ms Raudupīte saw it and said:

– Jānis, not you, too? But you're a good student.

She wanted to keep me on that side. Up until then I'd been somewhat of a teacher's pet. I helped the class place commas. Meaning – Raudupīte would dictate a text for us to transcribe; she'd read the sentence once, then twice, so everyone could get it down. During her second read-through I'd tap my pen on my desk to mark where the commas should go. A quick, precise tap, like Dave Grohl – who I didn't know existed at the time. And everyone else would write in a comma at each tap. Then Raudupīte would read the entire text through once more, and I'd again tap my desk at each comma. They had to figure out the semicolons and ellipses on their own. It was exciting to be kind of a secret Judas right under her nose.

Teachers don't really need to be that good. I remember our first-grade teacher, Ms Lielkalne. She was almost famous for how kind and mothering she was. My parents said:

– You're so lucky! Now, if you kids aren't good for a teacher like her...

Damn. Lielkalne was like out of a children's book. Whenever we acted up, she just sat with her face in her hands. We felt awful. And based on the stories she told us, we were the most awful bunch there ever was.

A person has the right to be bad. Transgressions and their respective punishments should be calculated like prices in a store – one murder costs a death sentence, and a graffitied bathroom stall costs a grade percentage. A clean transaction and zero tears.

This prohibition on being bad wouldn't have been allowed in Kurt's day. And then the fates delivered us Mrs Burkova. Her husband was a public prosecutor. She had a sharp voice and a boyish figure. Best of all, she was cranky, unfair, and ridiculously easy to offend. We had regained our right to be bad.

No, I was done being a good student. But I couldn't give it up completely, either – I'd catch Hell at home if I did.

Enough of Burkova. Right now Raudupīte was the one yelling at me. But I didn't hear her because I was busy with the Walkman travelling from desk to desk, and which was now in my hands. The cassette in it wasn't mine, either. I'd never heard it before. Pearl Jam's *Ten*.

I had made it to the main song. I listened to it, stopped the cassette, then took the cassette out and rewound it using a pen cap. To not waste the batteries. I listened to the song again. It was about me. I, too, am quiet and sullen, and spend time 'at home drawing pictures', everything fell into place, except that I wasn't 15 yet. I could wait. If no-one could understand me by then, I'd blow my brains out in front of all of them, then they'd see. It would also be a nice tribute to the song itself. Then they'd all see how important it had been to me. The whole class.

Jeremy spoke in class today.

And I'd want the song to be playing quietly in the background. It was so good. Though, maybe it was too good?

Someone tapped my shoulder, and without looking I knew someone wanted the Walkman back. Get lost, go learn where to place commas. But the tapping didn't stop, and I started to mutter to myself using some choice language. But muttering can turn out to be rather loud, especially if you're listening to 'Jeremy' at full volume.

Raudupīte, our teacher, was standing right there, right in front of my desk. Her expression sorrowful. She had been lecturing me for minutes, but I'd heard none of it. I'd only been saying words. The entire class was thrilled. Everyone except Jurģis.

I was kicked out, and told to come back with my parents. For something so stupid! As if the rest of the class hadn't done worse shit. But this was my first time.

I stood alone in the hallway. Then a little kid came careening down the hall and slipped—they didn't wax the floors here just for the smell—then scrambled back to his feet, looked to see if I was laughing and then disappeared into the bathroom.

I'd lost a friend and a teacher. But I wasn't at all sorry. There was a whole new group of friends and teachers right on the horizon, all crazy loners. That's what I stood there thinking while some little kid was taking a dump.

4

I switched on my desk lamp. It was an old lamp and used to be my sister's. She had plastered the lamp with stickers from bananas: 'Ecuador', 'Colombia', 'Costa Rica'. I didn't like them, but I felt bad tearing them off. I didn't have any stickers of my own. So I wrote 'I feel stupid / And contagious' on a piece of paper, licked it and stuck it onto the lamp.

I opened the black Crown cassette player. My dad had brought it back from Finland several years earlier. It had worked like new for years, but in the last few months it had started to wear out. I put in a cassette, closed the player, hit play. Nothing. I opened it again, took out the cassette (which was hard because they always caught) and saw that one of the teeth one of the tape reels had popped out. I pushed it down, but it popped out again. I took the piece out and discovered that the spring hidden under it was at fault. I threw the spring away, put the tape reel back in, put the cassette back into the player and hit play. This time it worked. I had the golden touch back then.

Nirvana's *Incesticide*, their enigmatic 1992 album. I sat and listened closely. 'Sliver' seemed so different, so un-Nirvana. And what was it they were singing about in it, about lost childhood or something? Then there was 'Molly's Lips', and I was afraid to love it because it almost sounded pop-like. 'Polly' was so strong and juvenile compared to the version I knew from *Nevermind*. Back then I thought the song was about a parrot or a cat. 'Polly wants a cracker'. I didn't know it was about a terrible real-life event. I'd thought – how original, a song about a cat. The last song, 'Aneurysm', was the most beautiful. 'Love you so much, makes me sick'. Those were the only words I could make out, but it was all I needed to understand how beautiful the misunderstood were. I couldn't help but turn up the volume.

My sister came in from the other room.

– What are you listening to?

– Nirvana.

– Again, huh. Listen to something else. And quieter.

I couldn't argue with my sister because she was going to have to go talk to Raudupīte with me. The last song was over anyway, so I took out the cassette. Now what? Kārlis had given me his copy of Therapy's *Troublegum*. In it went.

It was no Nirvana – absolutely not. But I should still listen to it. 'My girlfriend says / That I need help'. Total lies; I didn't have a girlfriend. What else. 'My boyfriend says / I'd be better off dead'. Better. 'I'm gonna get drunk / Come round and fuck you up', much better. Damn, I can't get further into the lyrics than that. 'All people are shit' – that's pretty profound stuff. Most importantly, sullen and without compromise.

My dad came into the room and turned on the TV, sat down on the couch. The couch was somewhat lopsided and broken; my sister and I jumped on it a lot as kids, but that was a long time ago. I turned the music up a notch so I could hear it over whatever sports my dad was watching. If our TV had had a remote control, he would have turned the TV up a notch as well, but instead he just said:

– Turn that thing of yours down.

There wasn't a whole lot to Therapy anyway. Nothing wild. I took out the cassette, put Nine Inch Nails in. Yes! *The Downward Spiral*. More on-point. I'd read about the band in the *Evening News*. Trent Reznor had talked about how all his friends had committed suicide, and so on. Then I'd spotted the cassette at the market and had raced home, excited to learn about the best way to kill yourself.

It was something wholly different; it was perfect. There was clanging and banging – it was beautiful. It was industrial music. 'Black and blue and broken bones / you left me'. When would someone leave *me*? 'Nothing can stop me now / I don't care anymore'. Exactly. No one was going to stop me.

– Turn it down. Or off. You can't possibly like it anyway. What's there to like.

That was horrible. I felt like the last bastion of a fragile, true art form. So, of course, I didn't turn it off. Now they sang: 'I want to know everything / I want to be everywhere... I wanna do something that matters'. See, dad. I want to do something. And I'm doing it right now, here, by the stereo. Fighting against you.

Then 'Hurt' came on. It was so beautiful that for a moment I forgave the world, and turned the volume up to share it with everyone else. You can't not like a song like that. Everyone who hears it understands it. 'You can have it all / My empire of dirt'.

And my dad said nothing; I felt that the beauty of the pain had overcome him, and made him happy.

The cassette ended. Now what? My collection wasn't that big yet. Stone Temple Pilots. A homemade tape. Play.

My dad shifted in his seat.

– That's too much!

He had no idea that this wasn't nearly wild enough; I didn't even know it yet. Fine, fine, I turned the volume down. I leaned closer to the stereo and immersed myself.

My mom came into the room, an apron around her waist.

– Dinner's ready.

Neither of us said anything, and I have to admit it was rude of us. Back then I didn't know that politeness was likely the most valuable thing you could have.

The cat sauntered into the room, looked around, and went back into the kitchen.

– Not even the cat can stand that stuff you call music.

I got up and went into the kitchen and sat down to eat potato pancakes. I took one at a time, but now and then my mother would come over and pile a stack onto my plate. I'd told her multiple times I didn't like it when she did that. I ate all of them, but my emotional balance was ruined. And then she tried to get me to eat the pancakes with lingonberry jam – she said I didn't understand anything, that I was letting the good parts of life pass me by.

I don't want all your good parts of life, you can't make me eat lingonberry jam! The battle was on.

And then it came to me – I had to listen to Ministry! I hurried back to the room. Ministry was a genius idea for a band name. I'd seen a music video of theirs on RBS TV where they were crashing cars. This music sounded like crashing cars. I put my face close to the stereo and listened.

– Enough, enough. Go to bed.

– Just the last song.

I had to turn it up. My god, the sound! The thundering of the drums! The guitars! How could anything be this beautiful?!

– Jānis, I said that was enough.

My entire family was standing there, looking at me.

– Jānis, think about the rest of us.

But Ministry shouted:

– What about us?

What about those of us who don't want to go to bed?

Then my sister added:

– You tell him, he won't listen to me. He just listens to that garbage and gets weirder and weirder.

They were all angry with me, me, the good kid. My dad, from the deepest, most beautiful part of Latgale, his little brother lies dying, sobbing, the doctor is too far away, the Germans set up a cannon in the yard and give round candies, later he served on the other side of the arctic circle, where airports dive up from underground, then work, work, only honest work; my mom, still beautiful, just like back when she didn't listen to her teacher's command to cry when Stalin died, when she went to the barricades and made my dad go with her; my sister, my saintly sister, who would soon stop speaking to everyone and live only in her quiet dream world, writing strange poems that many people will like.

But, 'What about us'?

I turned it off, off. And hid my sneer as I climbed into bed.

5

Ministry were glorious. So were Jesus Jones, and Sonic Youth, and KMFDM, and Psychopomps and Temple of the Dog. This is what I learned from Kārlis, a classmate of mine since first grade, until now just an uncultured punk who once kicked a soccer ball into my stomach. We'd recently started talking again for some reason, and he lent me a few tapes like they were a drug, a weapon, a mystical entity. Usually they came from his brother. Kārlis said that he and his brother had been listening to Nirvana well before 5 April 1994 – can you believe that?

Nirvana. It was still the best there was. Even better than The Cranberries, better than Dolores O'Riordan's lake-green eyes.

– She drinks, by the way.

This comment came from my friend Pūpols, a unique character. The nickname meant 'pussywillow', but he only resembled the fuzzy bud in shape. His personality was angled, thorny and incomprehensible. Earlier we'd been talking about Assyrian archers and *The Corsican Brothers*. I remember how talked on and on about them – and to continue the conversation I walked with him to his house, and then he walked me back to mine. Now we had moved on to music and the musical lifestyle.

I already knew that the name "Riddle" wasn't meant to characterize the legend of this brand of wine, but rather its origins, contents, and consistency. We drank it often in the newly built but abandoned mansion that was probably meant to be some young couple's future wedding chapel. And now we were there with our wine and cigarettes. When I told Jurģis about it at school, he repeated:

– You're crazy.

And I liked it. But in moderation. You could be a little crazy, but not too crazy. Girls supposedly liked that. Though it wasn't working at the moment. But it didn't matter because I was used to it. I'd lived long enough to know that girls didn't like me. But I was crazy. Only a little, crazy within reason. Don't worry, friend.

Pūpols, in turn, was of the strict belief that we had to drink a lot. As much as possible. Because the goal was to get drunk! Kārlis was the only one of us who had succeeded in this. He'd even thrown up on the way home, and his eldest cousin had said:

– You're a man now, son.

But we hadn't been able to get drunk. We drank beer, almost two full bottles, then split a bottle of wine between five of us, and a bottle of vodka among a whole group of our friends – but still, nothing. When I got home I sat down next to the stereo and blasted Nine Inch Nails, trying to see if something in me had changed. It hadn't.

The group that met at the abandoned mansion had been joined by two real-life adult women, eighteen years old. The girls had gotten successfully drunk for the first time ages ago and had already earned their stripes, so they were able to give us tips:

– Don't eat beforehand. It'll hit you sooner on an empty stomach.

– Mix alcohols, if you can. You won't be sorry.

Eva worked as an art teacher; she looked at me and was saying something with her eyes. I treated her presence like that of a ghost – you'd seen one now and again, but they weren't real. But I remembered their suggestions.

That Thursday I skipped the school dance. I always skipped them, to be honest, but this time I had the feeling I was missing out on something. Friday morning, the whole school was buzzing with news. Things at the dance had gotten interesting. Our classmate Artis had achieved the dream – meaning he'd gotten piss-drunk and passed out in the middle of the gymnasium. And he had passed out so hard that not even the school director was able to wake him up. Smelling salts being the extent of our school's emergency first-aid kit, the school called for an ambulance to take him to hospital. Stuff always happens to everyone else.

Pūpols had made the most of his Thursday night, too. He can't remember who else was there, but he drank half a litre of vodka and then headed home. His body gave out on him right in front of his building, and then out of nowhere a group of our classmates wandered over and helped him up to the fifth floor and handed him over to his father. His father was our history, poli-sci and German teacher. He listened to the group as it announced:

– We found Pūpols out here...

His father carried him to his room. The next day, Pūpols' little brother raced to school to tell us that when their father had interrogated him that morning Pūpols had held his ground like a man:

– Where were you drinking last night?

– I wasn't drinking!

– Wasn't drinking. You threw up everywhere last night!

– I didn't throw up!

When I told Eva the story, she purred as if in a trance:

– I like the scandalous ones...the bad boys.

That day I went out on a mission. In two or three other neighbourhoods throughout the city my friends left their parents' houses the same way, saying they'd be back late, begging with their eyes that they don't wait up for them. The Jelgava wind whistled clearly: tonight, boys, you get drunk.

Full of determination, Friday night I grabbed three lats and walked with Kārlis to the Fifth Line. There we met up with a weird group of friends who were supposedly big drinkers. Half an hour later we came to Cips' house. He came out to meet us, sleepy (he was always sleepy), and said he could come with but first he had to go to Jelgava to get cash. Thirty-five minutes later we were back in Jelgava, where Cips went to talk to someone, and mysteriously came back with ten lats, saying:

– Now let's go drink!

Kārlis gave up and refused to walk any more. But Cips was one to keep his promises. So he and I walked on back toward the Fifth Line. Forty minutes later we and another Fifth Line goon stopped at a kiosk on the Fourth Line by the name of 'Bordertown', where we bought a bottle of champagne and a bottle of beer. We hunkered down in an abandoned building and drank half the champagne; then we topped up the bottle with the beer and kept drinking. The townie goon said:

– It's weird. Bitter and sweet.

I drank in silence and concentrated, waiting to get drunk. Nothing. When the bottles were empty it was time for me to hurry to the bus stop so I could make it home on time and not get into trouble. The road back took us past the kiosk, where we were ran into the townie goon's brother. He convinced Cips to buy a bottle of White Stork cognac. Then they all walked me to the bus stop. Once there the bottle was opened, but curiously enough Cips and the townie goon didn't want to drink. The goon's brother and I emptied the bottle fairly quickly, and finished it right as my bus pulled up. As I climbed onto the bus I thought:

– Again, nothing.

But it didn't bother me anymore. I couldn't get comfortable in my seat. It wasn't me who was sitting there, it was me in a movie about myself, and I watched as I shifted uncomfortably in the seat. The movie wasn't all that interesting, but I'd never seen it before, so I watched it for a while with apathetic interest. The bus had reached Jelgava. I started to think about having to mobilize the puppet-version of me to get off the bus, when suddenly I had a moment of clarity and it occurred to me:

– Is this it?

Was I finally drunk, had I finally opened the door of my consciousness and entered another world?

The bus pulled up to a stop, the second to last before mine. I noticed a water pump on the side of the street. Eureka! I just needed to splash some cold water on my face, and it would be like taking a mask off. I got caught in the closing doors, but managed to squeeze my way out.

The setting sun was blotting out this movie about Jelgava; it descended from the sky and drowned the apartment buildings, the abandoned mansion, the massive tower of the Anna Church. It slowly dawned on me that I didn't have to go anywhere, that this moment was never going to end. I bent over the water pump like a little robot, grabbed the handle and pumped, pumped, unleashing a deluge onto my face. My filmed face, dripping with indifferent water.

6

I won't bore you with the details, but I decided never to drink again. Because of my night of revelry my parents made me cut my hair – which had just grown past the standard length – and banned me from the opening night of Jelgava's Junkyard, an alternative club. So my social life was ended and locked up. I had to look for another road to the underground.

The answer wasn't far. It had a slim waist, curvy hips and a g-string. And five others. The guitar.

Kārlis' brother told us about one of his legendary friends who played the guitar, and who did nothing but play guitar until the day he was called up into the army. One day his Lieutenant had everyone stand at attention and barked at them:

– Does someone here play the guitar?

– I-I do.

– Can you play Nirvana?

– Yes, Lieutenant!

– Then let's go, you're going to teach me.

And they went to practice in the best barracks, while the rest of the soldiers stayed behind to weed creeping thistle in the minefield.

If you can play something by Nirvana, not even war can touch you.

My mother bought me a guitar for eight lats in the hopes of channelling my mounting restlessness into something at least halfway constructive.

I picked it up, emptied my mind, immersed myself in Nirvana and let my heart do the talking. And yet, the guitar didn't sound like my heart did. It turns out it hadn't been tuned.

I put the instrument in a linen tote bag and went to see my friends. Most of them recommended someone named Ģirts or Edvīns, who could tune a guitar so well that all you had to do was brush the strings and they'd play 'Bohemian Rhapsody'. But somehow we managed to tune it without them. Everyone who tuned it would immediately play through his entire repertoire. Kārlis' brother could play the beginning of 'Come as You Are', supposedly the beginning of 'Plateau', and a few accidental chords from some INXS song. Kārlis could only play the beginning of 'Come as You Are'. I couldn't play a thing. Back at home I'd sit with the guitar for hours, waiting for it to speak to me. But it didn't say a word. I was happy with how great a single string sounded when I plucked it on its own, but as soon as I added a second string, chaos ensued.

It took me a lifetime to piece together the beginning of 'The Man Who Sold the World'. Then I partially learned a few Beatles songs from some sheet music. Someone also taught me Eric Clapton's 'Tears in Heaven', a song that let you mess around for twenty seconds like some melancholy virtuoso.

– I've got it! Man, I'm like some kind of prince of guitars.

The strings started to listen to me. I combined the chords I knew, made up some of my own, and original, achingly beautiful compositions came to life beneath my slender genius's fingers, along with the songs my idols played, songs everyone knew. My parents heard me playing and said:

– Go to bed.

I got better and better. Familiar and entirely new classics drifted forth with each touch. I did an experiment – I plucked each open string in turn. Out came Nirvana's 'Where Did You Sleep Last Night', expertly played. Confused, I went to bed.

The next day in school our homeroom teacher introduced a new student. She was blonde, her curves not unlike those of a guitar and she had a goofy smile. As it turned out, her name was, appropriately, Milēdija – *milady*. The silent howling of wolves flooded towards her from every boy in the room.

During break everyone crowded around her, not looking at her and talking:

– I made the sickest three-pointer at basketball yesterday.

– Sure you did, fat-ass.

– We beat up some gypsies the other night.

– You're the gypsy.

Kārlis said nothing and just stared openly at Milēdija. I didn't give in to that kind of unhealthy obsession; I didn't follow the crowd.

I put on a stoic smirk and thought about the Crusaders besieging Constantinople. No, about Kate Moss, who had seen Jesus at a Nirvana concert. What had Kate been on? And where could I get some? I'd heard it helped play guitar.

The crowd of admirers started to jostle one another, and tall, stupid Edmund shoved me hard. I went to sit back at my desk, away from the world.

Not the best move. Having finished giving each other a hard time, those jackasses turned to me with an unspoken, uniform decision to target me with their displays of machismo.

– What're you sitting for? Sing us some Nirvana!
– What do you guys do out there in the bushes anyway?
– You're all freaks, aren't you? Right, you're not normal?

To be honest, these were all good questions, and I would have been happy to answer them if only she had asked me herself, not these jokers trying to show off. I ducked my head and started looking through my backpack for my Uzi, or some other automatic weapon. But then the bell rang, and the honourable Ms Raudupīte came in and calmed everyone down, though it meant she grew increasingly more agitated.

The class was full of idiots. Or daydreamers slumped in their desks, who were just as useless. But Milēdija spoke up without having to be encouraged. In the first class of the day, and intelligently, at that. Like some kind of know-it-all. If you're so smart, then tell me something about the guitar. Tell me how to get rid of the false sense that everything I play sounds amazing. How do I get on the difficult path, the true path?

Then Raudupīte called on me to talk about the Latvian poet Jānis Ruģēns. Ruģēns was actually a rather likeable guy, and quite eccentric. Once he made a fool of the local clerk by showing him off like a monkey to a rich farmer from another county.

– Listen, do you want to see a monkey?
– Of course I do, who wouldn't?
– He's in there, behind a glass window.

The farmer went into the municipal building and there it really was, a monkey sitting behind the glass window (the clerk was an incredibly hairy and bearded man). The farmer was delighted and began to poke the clerk with the handle of his whip, laughing:

– Look, he doesn't like it when you poke him! He's just like a person!

But now, as I re-enacted the story in front of all my classmates, these farmers who weren't listening to me, just laughing, I felt just like Ruģēns' monkey.

After class I wanted to talk to Kārlis about Pearl Jam. I wanted to regain my footing, return to mankind, validate my existence with the coolest kid in class. But Kārlis was talking to Milēdija.

What could they have to talk about?

I went to leave the classroom; when I reached the door she spoke to me:

– Do you like Latvian literature?

– What?

The entire school hurried past us. Milēdija smiled:

– Grab the bull by the horns!

And she smiled again and the whole world cracked in two.

– It's kind of a joke, a saying, though not really literary. I'm from the countryside. But listen...

I let my suspicious gaze wander higher than her lips.

– You don't really like Nirvana, do you?

I didn't understand what she was getting at. Was this a test? Who are you working for, lady?

– I do.

– Strange. You look like someone with more refined tastes.

And she turned and left, her skirt fluttering after her.

I wandered around after school. I wasn't afraid of courtyards anymore, instead heading straight into them. This lessened the risk of one of my mom's co-workers catching me smoking. I stopped by a rubbish bin to light a cigarette, then looked up at the sky and said:

– Don't let anything happen between Milēdija and me, don't let it. It's not what I need. I'd rather learn to really play the guitar!

Why do we act like someone has to take note of and execute our personal requests? When I got home and picked up my guitar, I wasn't able to play anything at all. When I got to school the next day, Milēdija didn't even look at me.

7

Although I had new friends and interests, I did retain some of my old habits. I still read books. I mean, I know the time for *Ivanhoe* had long passed. Now it was time to read something non-standard. Like Camus' *The Stranger* and *The Plague*. Then I could talk to Milēdija about them if we managed to have a few minutes by ourselves during break. Eva lent me Salinger's *The Catcher in the Rye*. At that time I was most taken by the fact that this was the book Mark Chapman was reading after he shot John Lennon and was waiting for the police to arrive. I still liked Lennon, that was allowed – even Kurt had liked him. But it didn't stop me from feeling giddy about his murder; it had happened the year I had been born, and Salinger's book fit into all of it. The book itself was rather interesting, too. In it Salinger's protagonist contemplates whether he'd want to be able to talk to Maugham or Hardy. Did I want to talk to Salinger? I guess, yes. What would I ask him? I don't know. I'd want him to listen to me.

And as one observant girl had already noted, I like Latvian literature too. Back then I devoured books by Andris Puriņš. He wrote about regular things. His protagonists sometimes would end up meeting ancient Aztecs or aliens, but he also wrote about alcoholics and punks. Students who pined after things, got over them, who drank and listened to a lot of music. And who didn't like school either.

But someone should talk about the thing Kafka wrote: 'Beyond a certain point there is no return. This point has to be reached.' Where was that point? We're not yet truly free, we're still so close to falling backward. What step do we need to take to really break away?

We didn't read Kafka back then. But a different book offered an alternate suggestion. It was a fairly popular book – Czech author Radek John's *Memento*, a didactic work about the detrimental effect of drugs. Though for me and many other nerds, *Memento* became a sort of bible lauding the amazing powers of narcotics. Yes, Michal's girl and friends died, and he himself lost his mind, but that was life. It's what we all longed for – not to be a prude. That said, if I wanted to live, I needed drugs.

Where could I get some? The newspapers said we were surrounded by drugs, that they were easier to come by now than ever before. But then where were they? Eva said she had a friend who could get us some weed. Gatis used a pen to demonstrate how you were supposed to smoke weed, but he didn't know where to get any. The crime report on the radio said that some pills had been confiscated from a group of students, but the students claimed they'd found the pills on the street. I kept my eyes on the road, but found nothing.

Those who lurked around the Other School and smoked on the basketball court said that all the good stuff had been left behind by the Soviet army. In the abandoned bases, in the medicine cabinets and gas-mask pouches in the bunkers, you could find tablets with the label 'FOV', which were to be used in the event of poisoning. A girl had taken one with her coffee one morning. For the rest of the day she thought she was being followed by two creatures: one was a long, bendy and segmented pipe and the other was just round and furry. Inguss from the Other School had eaten handfuls of them. When he got home he took a hammer and put it in the phone cradle.

– It needs to charge.

Parafin had ground up half a FOV pill with the end of a lighter and then snorted it. Soon he was gushing blood out of both nostrils and he was certain he was going to die. It was beautiful.

But I never wound up finding a FOV pill. Yet they were apparently all around me.

Parafin knew of some easier to find substances. Once he went into the hardware store and approached the sales associate:

– I need five tubes of Moment glue!

– Why so many?

– Because it's my birthday today!

Apparently you could even get high off bananas. If only I knew how, I'd try bananas for sure. Glue was strong stuff, it could give you a headache.

One day we were sitting on the asphalt by the Other School. I was talking about drugs. My knowledge was rather unsystematic, but broad.

– Sometimes you see a huge, pulsating flower. It pulses–

– Where?

– Right there on the floor... Out over half the room.

Salt chewed a straw and corrected me.

– It makes you giddy, hysterical. The pills, if you can get them, make your whole body go stiff.

– Even your dick?

– Not yours.

Tiny bits of quartz glinted in the asphalt. I wondered what they'd look like if you were high. They'd turn into tiny planets. Planets where little fairies lived.

Then a gypsy started to walk towards us. My entire body froze in fear. It was normal to be afraid of gypsies. He greeted Ķīselis and joined us, crouching down in a typical thuggish pose, and spoke softly. Then Ķīselis pointed to me. The gypsy stood up and waved to me to step aside with him.

I was afraid of gypsies the same way I was afraid of dogs.

I stood up. Warning bells were going off in my mind. The gypsy took a few more steps and I followed him. He stuck out his hand. He had a weak handshake; he just clasped my hand briefly and then let it drop.

– You need plasticine?

He asked me this but stared hard past my head. I liked plasticine just fine; back in the day I used to make all kinds of animals out of it, particularly hippos, my favourite. But why would I need some right now?

I'll teach you how to roll it and smoke it. And I'll show you where to get Belamors.

I understood less and less of our conversation. So I said:

– Excellent! All set.

His stare moved closer to my face, but still looked right past me.

– How much do you need?

I still had no idea what to say, so I answered:

– It'll be enough.

The gypsy glanced around quickly. I did too. The guys were still sitting in the same spot on the asphalt, not looking at us. They were playing rock-scissors, where the loser was subjected to Mercy. It worked like this: the winner would put a hand palm-down on his victim's head, then pull back the middle finger and let it snap back down. And so on and so forth. Salt was exceptionally good at it; it was my luck that I couldn't participate.

– Meet me back here in two days. Eleven o'clock, when no-one's here. Four lats.

We went back to re-join the group. No one said anything, and the conversation went back to normal. But I knew I was party to a crime. I was going to buy drugs.

It would be fine if I could share the experience with someone. I ran into Gatis as he was wandering around. He seemed like a harbinger of our futures – he was always on the outskirts, always quiet, a little mean and annoyed with the rest of the world. He believed he had to walk a different path. I decided to tell him what happened.

What he didn't say was:

– My goodness! Don't do that! It's all downhill after gypsies and drugs!

What he did say was:

– Great!

He nodded approvingly and added quietly:

– It would be cool if you shared.

That's exactly what I wanted to do – share. I was so moved that I forgot to invite him to come with me.

And so I went to the meeting place by myself. I was making my way around the Other School when I ran into Milēdija. I played it cool, and offered to walk with her for a bit. I couldn't think of anything to say. Then she asked me:

– What are you doing out here?

I tried to think of something unusual to tell her, but all I could think of was the truth:

– I'm going to buy weed from a gypsy.

She responded with the sweetest word in the world:

– Crazy.

She said it as gently and archly, as always. I added that I might get my ass kicked, and she smiled. Milēdija looked at the headstone carving workshop and laughed lightly:

– The whole class is saying we're together.

I laughed too, what would our wonderful class come up with next. Like they were high or something.

I walked with her until the kindergarten building and then headed back to the Other School. Even I had to think – what was I doing there?

Soon the gypsy showed up; he held out his hand to shake and asked:

– One?

It was like in a movie. He motioned to me, and we walked until we had reached the centre of the gypsy quarter. It was a rough neighbourhood – it was isolated, a city built from nails and painted boards, and felt like a foreign country to any passer-by because all around you just heard their strange language. Several men approached us, of different heights and sizes. The gypsy said:

– Don't be scared. You're totally white, but don't worry, I'm here.

Suddenly he looked straight at me.

– You're a normal kid. Your hair's normal.

That tore open the wound. As mentioned previously, I'd had to cut my hair after the first time I got drunk, and now I just looked *normal*. The gypsy continued:

– We're at war with that crazy long-haired group.

He pointed out toward the outskirts of Jelgava:

– Their base is at Uzvara Park. A bunch of our guys went to fight them.

Holy Kurt! He was talking about the underground club, about the inaugural and, for now, only huge party at the Villa Medem manor, the one I didn't get to go to. I'd heard there had been a big fight with the gypsies.

– The place was packed with them! We were by the door, on the front steps. At first we were winning. But then the doors opened and, like, a hundred of them poured out! Every one of them with long, shaggy hair.

The gypsy threw up his hands in a wild gesture, his brown eyes wide. Well, far as I know, there couldn't have been a hundred.

– The first one had an iron bar!

It had been a broom handle – that's what the victors had told me.

– Good thing we were able to get out of there. But we'll be back. Do you know when their next thing is?

I didn't know. We had stopped next to a small wooden shack.

– Give me four lats.

He said this both hushed and business-like. I gave him the money and he went into the shack, just like that, without knocking. I waited outside for a long time, and started to think about how I didn't want to be here, in this gypsy quarter, when it got dark. I understood, I'd fallen for a classic trick, I'd learned a lesson – and for four lats was a fair price to pay for it.

Back then, four lats was a lot.

But then he came back out of the house. They didn't have any today; I should come back tomorrow.

I headed home, free and happy, without my money and without the weed.

The next day I returned begrudgingly to the wooden shack. The gypsy's brother, I think, came out holding a big monkey wrench. No, Dolārs wasn't here. Relieved, I again headed back home. I didn't see the gypsy by the Other School. Just like in a book – I'd been conned in a drug deal, so to speak.

But not for long. One day Ķīselis came right up to me and whispered:

– From Dolārs.

And he stuck out his hand; he had something balled up in his fist. I reached out my hand. What was he going to give me? The coveted plasticine? But no, it was just my four lats.

– He can't get any right now, so he gave your money back. Said he was an honest gypsy.

It was unbelievable. Everything, all of it in this situation had turned out wrong.

But no matter, we had our poor-man's ways of getting high, too, and we didn't need money or gypsies to do it. The group from the Other School did it by the brick wall, over there by the bushes.

Voldiņš volunteered and crouched down next to the wall, taking seventeen deep breaths (everyone counted out loud). On the last one he held his breath, stood up with his back against the wall, and the leader of this so-called ceremony and his assistant applied pressure right below Voldiņš' solar plexus. And Voldiņš, the volunteer, passed out. His head lolled onto his chest and his body slid down the wall and slumped over, his face slowly coming to rest on the asphalt. Immediately, they lightly slapped him awake and he relayed what he had seen:

– Devils. Some kind of devils, with horns and pitchforks. The devils are singing. Women with bloodied nipples are licking the floor. Monsters fly around, vomiting. Okay, screw you guys, I'm going home.

I wondered whether Voldiņš' imagination was really that wild. I reminded myself that nothing what he said was original, it was all from fairy tales, fairy tales, fairy tales. Now I know that Voldiņš hadn't been making things up; he'd seen the future. Everything he said he saw soon came true.

8

Jelgava echoed more and more resolutely with grunge, alt-rock and an indescribable genre of music that was likely the truest form of underground. I wasn't doing as well in school anymore. Pūpols kept hanging around and amassing shadier and shadier friends. Eva was treading on thin ice at her new job.

I had my guitar, and planned on starting a band. There was no clear concept yet, though, and I had no idea how to play that block of wood. Just the one Nirvana song, 'Sappy'.

Though it turned out that there were already some bands in Jelgava. More and more people talked about having practice and cutting their fingers on their guitar strings. There were even concerts.

Tonight, almost all of Jelgava's underground scene poured into the Jelgava Art School.

Imbecile Hog – our classmate Ugo's band, the punkest of the punks.

With Cut – the best band to come out of the Other School. Mareks on drums, Ēriks on vocals, Gints... They were famous, Jelgava-grunge.

Shiny Hairless – the city's underground legend. Later they'd become the pop-like Herlis and Citruss, but for now they were purists.

Frontlines – Šolis' band, amazingly depressing. Thanks to them I later gravitated to Joy Division.

I was in the bathroom, smoking by the window. The smell from the cigarette didn't overpower the smell of the paint so many students had washed out of their brushes (the style back then was to rinse them out in the toilet, not the sinks). The sounds of the first band warming up drifted through the door, and I was filled with a sense of greatness: history was being made here. Just like in their time Nirvana or the Pixies had played at their schools.

Someone called to me from outside the window. I looked out and saw a few guys I'd never seen before. One of them asked me:

– Are you already in?

I nodded and took a drag of my cigarette.

– Do you know how we can get it?

The main doors were easy to find and access; but there was a doorman there asking one lat per person for admission. I felt a flood of generosity:

– Go around the corner, I'll meet you by the other window, I said and pointed, taking another drag.

I knew about the secret hallway and stairs that led down to that window.

They were waiting when I got there. I opened the window, which was close to the ground. All four of the guys pulled themsleves up with some difficulty, especially the one who was holding an open bottle in one hand. He hurriedly offered to me. I tipped it back, and immediately spit out the mouthful – one of the guys had frantically unzipped his pants and was pissing right there on the wall. Though pissing was an understatement: he was practically assaulting the wall like he'd been holding his bladder for a year; he reeled, pissing over the entire wall and the stateliness of the concert. The rest of them howled with laughter, and one of them asked:

– How much you got in there?

Now that the mood was shot, it occurred to me that he may have been too embarrassed to go outside in front of all the passers-by. He was just a bit shy, this kid who had defiled the art school's walls. Self-consciousness had been the reason behind this orgy. I feel like a lot of the stupid things we did back then were born of our being overly sensitive and weak.

Once the shy stranger had zipped his pants back up, we all headed upstairs. Imbecile Hog had already finished their set. It was 90s Jelgava punk rock – sharp and quick.

I found Eva and her friends in one corner of the room. They were passing around a 1.5-litre bottle of Fantastika lemonade. Baiba passed it to me and said:

– It's spiked!

Believe it or not, I was still naïve enough back then that I actually peered into the mouth of the bottle, wondering just how a spike would've gotten in there.

Kārlis and his friends came in. They had a Mangaļi mineral-water bottle filled with a brown liquid. Two seemingly innocent things – mineral water and cola. They came up to us and said that Gatis couldn't get it because of the same one-lat problem. I went outside to find him.

I could show him to the back window, but I didn't want to take my refined friend through piss-stained halls.

He was standing outside, sullen and irritated.

– Well, can you get me in?

I thought a moment. No other ideas came to me. Gatis said:

– Let's try copying the stamp.

He had a pint bottle in his pocket. The back of my hand that had the admissions stamp was soaked with some vodka. Then Gatis pressed the back of his hand to mine. A strangely intimate moment. Then we both inspected his hand: there was no stamp, just a ghost of a rosy blotch. I looked at my hand: my stamp was completely gone.

Gatis sighed, sniffed and headed straight for the main doors. I followed.

He just walked past the guard at the door. The guard looked after Gatis and said nothing. With his long hair and otherworldly gait, he must've looked like he belonged there. The guard eyed me a bit longer, but I instinctively gestured toward Gatis – I'm with him – and slipped inside.

The school auditorium was thumping with sound. With Cut had launched right into their hit single, without keeping the audience in suspense, without waiting for the audience to chant for them:

I don't see you, don't see me,
Hell is burning all around us.

Then there was a run of indistinguishable words, and then the chorus:

Fire – Fire!
Fire – Fire!
Fire – Fire!
Fire – Fire!

A few fans jumped around in front of the stage. The majority of the audience sat on the floor, their backs against the walls. My group was sitting right by the door so they could more easily take care of the need to smoke or puke, and passed around their bottle of brown drink.

With Cut was thrashing out their next song:

They had life!

They had weed!

Well Jesus shit, of course they had life with weed. But where was I supposed to get *my* life? I watched Gints closely as he screamed into the microphone, wondering if he knew he was envied, a rock star preaching the painful truth?

We live,

and don't know why

we kill each other.

Kill our brains and minds,

we don't know how to exist together.

I went toward the stage and joined the group of fans. It wasn't hard to get to the front row. I jumped around with my newly-acquired dance moves and inconspicuously watched the others. This wasn't regular jumping around, but a kind developed in a secret Garnier-type laboratory to cater to those who until now had spent their entire lives embarrassed about their dancing abilities. I jumped around and felt closer to the entirety of alternative culture, to all the people around me, especially to those who hadn't made it out to the art school tonight. I thought warm thoughts about them and jumped higher than everyone around me. But then the song ended and I got self-conscious.

I went to re-join the girls. Eva put her hand on my shoulder and handed me the bottle of spiked lemonade. To me, a neurotic teenage boy, this gentle gesture was annoying. Some meaningful lyrics sounded from the stage:

There's no future. No Future.

I want to live, but I can't.

Eva was from Nākotne – a city whose name translates to 'the future'. Nākotne was just outside Jelgava. But With Cut had clearly said it: there is no future. So I decided not to hang out with Eva anymore, and instead devote myself fully to rock and roll.

With this last song the Jelgava grungers finished their set. There was no encore; it wasn't custom back then. If the audience didn't shout "Go home, you cows!" during your set, then the show was considered a success. With Cut's guitarist Gatis had received a special ovation, and was headed toward us now with a grin on his face. He said:

– This girl told me that I played the loudest.

Our Gatis, however, was sceptical. He simply replied:

– With Cut plays nothing but shit.

And he left to go talk to them. He always knew everyone. I stayed behind, thinking about shit. How did he figure? They were a real band, real underground, true Jelgava grunge. How could it not be good?

Eva and Baiba suggested we climb up to the roof. I called my friends over to join us. The metal ladder streaked our hands with rust; the sky was already dark. The two groups, who otherwise didn't know each other, immediately lit cigarettes. I did too; I was the one common denominator here. It was a beautiful but cold night. And although it wasn't at all comfortable sitting up there, no one made to leave.

Weren't they worried that the next group had already started its set? Was I the only one who cared about the history of rock and roll in the city of Jelgava and the surrounding region? I wasn't going to say anything, though, wasn't going to remind them of the band. I wasn't going to tell anyone to come see shit bands. I wasn't jealous of them any more.

I didn't want to play in just any band, or whatever band anymore.

I wanted to at least play in Nirvana.

9

We went up on roofs whenever we had the chance. We liked it up there. Often we'd climb back up onto that same unfinished art school roof. A non-world from where we could clearly see the world. From above. No one could see when we'd smoke up there. Sometimes we'd work through a "Riddle" or two.

The nearby nine-storey apartment building had an even higher roof. The building was in the neighbourhood called Žukova, or simply Žucene. Here you had to look out when you climbed up out of the roof door.

But it was worth it. You could see everything from here – the unfinished chapel, the unfinished school – and feel like you'd made it in life. The view on one side opened up to Lielā Street, which snaked through the centre of town. Along it were three identical buildings, a single word displayed on the windowless wall of each, respectively: 'Work', 'Peace', and 'Freedom'.

Down below you could see a cafe that was famous for shootings and gang arrests. Back then people said that stuff about any place, but I'd seen it with my own eyes at this cafe: the cafe was surrounded, then a van pulled up with a bunch of strangely-dressed cops inside, each of them with an Uzi, and soon they were walking someone out of the cafe, his hands bent far behind his back and his head hung low. Doing the airplane.

Those were rough times. The Jelgava Central Prison was under the reign of the infamous Ivans Haritonovs. During his time there, he learned Latvian, learned how to use the computer, read and played sport. His friends would stop traffic along Garoza Street and pass all manner of goods over the prison fence to him, and there was nothing the police could do about it. The situation was even worse at the Pārlielupe Prison. That's where Juris' brother was locked up, who'd once asked me to borrow my stereo, but I'd said no. How could I have lent it to him? He found a stereo somewhere else and drank away the money he got for selling it, while I ended up with a dangerous enemy.

On the other side of the apartment building Lielā Street turned into Dobele Highway, leading all the way to Nākotne – which I had sworn to steer clear of. Although Eva was right there next to us on that same roof. What was she, a beautiful young woman, doing hanging out with a bunch of teenagers on a roof? At the time I didn't ask, not myself or her. At that time I thought the rooftop was the only place in the world where someone could want to be. The worst place in the world.

Gatis, Sīnis and Kačaks were there, too. We had two litre-and-a-half bottles of beer with us. You could get them refilled at the bus station for fifty santims to the litre. The beer tasted good, especially when it was cold. But by the time we made it to Žucene from the station the beer would have warmed up, so we never knew just how good it could taste. We also had a pack of Hollywood cigarettes and a yo-yo, that popular toy from the mid-nineties.

Sīnis went to the edge of the roof and looked down.

– If I weren't afraid, I'd jump from here in a heartbeat!

Then he looked over at us. Then back down.

– Life has no meaning.

Eva answered, her voice low:

– It's fun when it doesn't.

She looked at Sīnis.

– Don't stand so close to the edge.

– It's fine, I'm scared anyway.

– Sīnis, c'mon, get away from the edge.

– In which direction?

– Stop it, please.

I jumped up and ran to join him. I stood with the toes of my shoes over the edge and gently leaned forward. It was a game I'd invented. You had to lean forward just far enough so you could see the ground floor. Standing on the edge of the rug at home, the motion of leaning forward is barely noticeable, but up here you definitely noticed. I stood there leaning forward and no one called me back, and I still had to lean further and further. Good thing Gatis finally drawled:

– Want a drink?

Almost like the poet Eduards Veidenbaums, I traded death for beer. I straightened up, feeling the strength in my legs, and went back to

Gatis. I made it two steps before my feet got tangled in something and fell over, hurting my arm. Everyone burst out laughing, except Eva, because she didn't have a sense of humour. I looked down – it was the string from the stupid yo-yo.

I sat up and began to untangle my shoes.

– What's this dumbass thing even doing up here?

Yo-yos were very popular then, and so, obviously, dumb.

– Which one of you jerks put it there?

I persisted. Sīnis was the only one to react:

– Why're you asking me? I've never touched one of those my entire life!

I looked to Eva and Gatis. She turned her face away, offended, he smirked and took a swig of beer, which I still hadn't gotten my hands on.

I looked down at Jelgava. A grey, sombre scene. Fifty years ago the city had been reduced to rubble. Everything crumbled and burned down. Then the city was rebuilt – five-storey buildings, prisons, warehouses. When driving through Jelgava once, musician Dambis of Inokentījs Mārpls commented that nothing was going to come of buildings like these. People here didn't have ideas.

– What should we do?

No one had an answer. There was no more beer left, but no one wanted to leave. There wasn't really anywhere to go.

– Well, what should we do?

Sīnis was getting restless. Gatis answered slowly:

– Stop fidgeting. Play with the yo-yo.

The toy was still lying on the roof floor between us. Sīnis took the opportunity to reassert his earlier claim:

– I've never touched that piece of shit before in my life!

– So do it now, maybe you'll like it.

Sīnis picked up the poor toy and chucked it over the edge of the roof, right where he himself had been tempted to fall over earlier. We all froze, waiting for it to land.

And then – the sound of glass shattering, followed by loud cursing in Russian. It had gone right through the windshield of a car. At least we assumed so – no one went to the edge to look. We could hear the voices clearly down below. They quickly figured out the yo-yo had come from the roof, and they swore they'd kill us.

Kačaks asked Sīnis why he'd done it.

– What? This is awesome, we knocked out some *gopnik's* windshield!

– *We* knocked out?

– Fine. C'mon, friends, throw me over!

The voices down below kept shouting. Now they were requesting the homosexuals on the roof to kindly show themselves and come on down for a chat. No-one moved.

The voices down below then said they were going to come up to the perverts on the roof instead. We whispered amongst ourselves:

– Do you think they noticed exactly where that thing fell from?

–Who knows. How could they have?

The voices down below announced that they'd spotted us and were on their way up. Suddenly the roof wasn't that welcoming anymore. I didn't want to be up there. Or down there, either. So where, then? Far away, at home with my mom.

The voices downstairs were quiet. A very pronounced quiet.

– They're taking the lift up.

– Let's get out of here!

Sīnis once again headed for the edge of the roof.

– No, with the lift.

– But they're in the lift.

– There're two. We have to leave *now*.

We scrambled down through the roof hatch. To get to the elevators we still needed to make our way down a rusty ladder.

– C'mon, hurry!

They pushed me through the hatch and I grabbed onto the rungs. Two steps down it occurred to me how impolite it had been to climb down before Eva. How did it go – my mom had once taught me there were two options when climbing up or down a ladder: for one of them you should let the girl go first, for the other the girl went second... Which one was for climbing down? I looked up and Eva was already climbing down, her panties were green, then she stepped right on my face and I kept climbing down, my adrenaline now doubled.

One of the lifts was clearly in use. We could hear it humming as it drew closer.

– To the other one!

The other lift was in use, too. Either our murderers didn't fit in a single lift, or some old lady was coming home with a bag of dumplings.

– The stairwell!

We clattered down the stairs, and around the seventh storey clearly heard a thug-laden elevator pass on its way up.

We stopped at the door, but only for a second, which was enough to smell the gamut of fresh-to-stale of urine in the hallway. Eva pushed open the door and we went out into the street.

And there really was the car, its front windshield shattered. A man in a red jacket stood next to it, along with three others wearing tracksuits. They watched us with uncomfortable intensity. We said nothing and turned to leave, but because we hadn't made a plan, we all started off in different directions. Eva and I even collided, her nose crushed against my cheek.

The man in the red jacket called to us:

– Oy!

It was the same bloodcurdling voice we'd heard from up on the roof. The men, of course, had never gone up to find us.

– Come here!

My knees buckled. No-one else moved. It didn't make the man in the red jacket any less suspicious.

– Who're you?

From one of his hands swung the damn yo-yo.

– Is this yours?

None of us hurried to deny the toy was ours. Suddenly one of the guys in a tracksuit spoke up. Probably the brains of the bunch.

– It's not them. These dumbasses only play with pills and razors.

He came up to us and kicked Gatis:

– Get a haircut!

Gatis was the only one with long hair. The rest of us only had ripped-up jeans and sad eyes. But it was enough to recognize our kind.

– Get lost!

And we left. It was the first time that I felt I belonged to something, to something other. And this otherness had saved us.

I looked up to where we had just been, and saw and felt everything take off.

10

You may ask: I've talked about rock and roll, about drugs – but where's the sex? Wasn't it, after all, a time when the world was free and girls would write "Rape me" in permanent marker across the backs of their jeans?

Yes, it was also around that time that they we started health classes in school. Our teacher was flustered and smiled like her face was paralysed. She explained that it was time for us to learn about sexuality, about the reproductive system and kissing. When the first lesson came to an end she announced:

– You have an assignment for the next class. Draw me your best wood!

The room went silent. I for one was silent because I'd Freudianly misheard her. Some of my classmates had, too; I asked them about it afterward. It had surprised me that a teacher who had up to then been so respectable had used such direct slang, but I supposed that's what happened when you started to learn about sexuality. Be that as it may, how were we supposed to do our homework? I wasn't yet that familiar with the subject in question that I could accurately draw it. And did she mean for us to draw it to-scale, or... Several shocked voices spoke up:

– What? What are we supposed to draw?

– Wood! W-o-o-d!

– What? What, what?

– A wood, a forest, trees – a wood!! W, as in welcome, wallet, water.

The assignment would up being a kind of psychoanalysis. The woods we'd draw would be analysed, and each of us would basically find out of he was born for sex or a lost cause, or just gay.

We weren't learning for school, but for life. One night Gatis and Edgars went to the bus station bar. They sat down and quickly drank their money away. Then they sat there, not knowing what to do next. The bartender took pity on them and gave them each a cola and brandy, on the house. The guys drank them happily, and the bartender made them each another. Back in the nineties, some people were nice like that, or else rich. Soon enough Gatis and Edgars were the only customers left. The bartender started to close down the place, but invited them back to his place for another drink. And of course, they agreed. They didn't know the bartender, but they could get to know him, and he'd shown himself to be an upstanding person. So the three of them headed to the bartender's place. The bartender kept his word and served Gatis and Edgars drinks, and what's more, a selfless person would, drank little himself. Our boys didn't pay much attention to their host, but enjoyed themselves until they'd both passed out.

Edgars woke to someone unzipping his fly. He opened his eyes to see the host with his hands on his waistband. And instead of making up some claim about helping his guest out of his clothes so he could sleep better, he staggered away theatrically, pretending to be completely drunk and out of it.

Society wasn't as puritanical back then as it is now. Lesbians strolled with their wedding parties past the Freedom Monument and elicited only kind or curious smiles from passers-by. Edgar, however, decided it was time to go home to his parents. He couldn't wake Gatis up, and so yelled in his ear:

– Wake up, Gatis, or you'll get it up the ass!

That got Gatis moving, and they left the bartender's house without saying goodbye.

They walked home half-awake and still drunk, in an existentially strange place. By the time they reached Rainis Park, Edgars' anger finally caught up with him. They passed another group of late-night wanderers, who cracked some joke about their long hair. Edgars, his anger taking over, replied harshly. Immediately, a handful from the other group rushed to hold down Gatis, while two more gave Edgars a black eye.

Those were the sexual escapades of my wonderful friends. But me, I had nothing.

I could sit at home and read books. I could go visit that same Edgars to watch a movie. He was always watching movies, usually horror films. But maybe it would occur to him to put in one of those secret movies *about relationships*. I'd never ask him to, but maybe he'll think of it himself, and there'd be gorgeous women, so sorrowful and mysterious, so affectionate and loving.

But Edgars wasn't home. On the way back, for whatever reason, I stopped at Eva's. She lived in the cheapest neighbourhood, almost a shantytown, which people called 'kurjatņiki', or chicken coops . For the most part the apartment buildings were abandoned or condemned. But some of the buildings were still occupied. I met Eva in the courtyard. She said:

– C'mon, c'mon! Inga will be here soon too. She picked up some kind of liquor.

So I went. I don't know how it happened, exactly, but after she unlocked the door Eva left the keys in the lock. As we stepped inside, I closed the door behind me, the deadbolt clicked into place, and we were locked in – classic. We turned to bang on the door, but soon understood there was nothing we could do. It seemed this was the only inhabited flat on this floor.

– What now?

Eva's voice was distraught. She fell onto her bed, symbolizing mankind's helplessness in the face of fate or accident. There really was nothing to do, so I looked at her. The hem of her shirt was hiked up and I could see her stomach; it was flat and fit. The other side of the exposed strip of skin was bordered by her jeans. We all wore the skinniest jeans we could find, to set ourselves apart from the rappers, who were also gradually establishing themselves as a clan and wore the widest-legged pants possible, so-called 'tubes'.

Eva's jeans were particularly skinny, they material pulled tight over and between her thighs and, suddenly imagining what lay beneath the denim, I felt a heaviness, a pressure. And not around my heart.

I sat down next to her on the bed and, to comfort her in this unfortunate situation, I kissed her. We'd kissed a couple times before, but this time we were in a bed. I hadn't forgotten Milēdija, and I also hadn't forgotten that Nākotne didn't exist, the Future didn't exist, or how annoyed I'd been by her touch that time at that concert. But this here and now was a moment separated from the world, and it belonged only to us. I was too shy to put my hand on the exposed skin of her stomach, so I put it on her breasts instead.

She looked at me, not dismayed or captivated, but surprised. This young woman, who was eighteen years old – of course she was surprised. What does anyone know at eighteen? At fourteen, maybe something yet, but at eighteen – absolutely nothing. She looked away, but didn't move; the breasts beneath my hand rose and fell. The ground beneath my feet moved with them. I was anxious.

But why was I anxious? What could possibly happen right then? Only what was meant to. As promised, Inga showed up with her liquor and unlocked the door. Eva rushed out to meet her, thanked her for saving us and explained what had happened with the key, my hand and I left alone in the bed.

Inga had not only brought liquor, but also Baiba, some young artist with long blond hair, who was called Bon Jovi behind his back, and some other guy I didn't know. Then the long-awaited liquor was poured and everyone had a great time. I hunkered down by the stereo. I played Nirvana, Nine Inch Nails, Stone Roses. Eva kept asking for Penguin Orchestra or something like that. Some kind of intelligent, artistic music, some sort of real, beautiful music of life.

But enough about that.

11

I was walking and eating sweetbriar fruits and ended up far behind the market grounds, back to the ends of the earth. I looked at the unfamiliar trees, the indeterminable path of undergrowth. In short, I got lost. But I just walked on ahead, calmly, waiting for the spirit to move me back in the direction of home.

Then I heard a familiar song playing. It took me a few seconds to make it out, to get past the desperation of only knowing that it was something I knew very, very well. And it was, it was 'Sappy'! The only Nirvana song I knew how to play on the guitar. I'd play it over and over, distancing myself from my worldly concerns.

Even though the song sounded a little off, I followed it. Obviously it would lead me to good people, even if a little strange. Who knows, maybe it would lead me to where real life was happening.

I walked out of the woods along a row of garages. The song stopped, and a familiar-looking gypsy came out of one of them. I turned to leave, but he called after me:

– Hold up, dude, don't run off.

I wasn't at all afraid, so I stopped.

– We've got some business to discuss, dude.

He grabbed my sleeve and led me to the open garage door.

– You look like the type.

I stepped into the half-dark alcove, ready to be drugged to the gills and for my organs to be sold on the black market to banana merchants exhausted by the melancholy caused by the dreary neighbourhoods. The garage was filled with sweet-smelling smoke, but I could still make out a cluttered bookshelf, a kid's sled, a motorcycle in an infinite state of repair, a drum set and in the middle of it all two guys sitting in camping chairs, each holding a bottle, not of alcohol, but of iced tea.

The gypsy introduced me:

– This is great, I've been looking for a while and look, I finally found one. This dude.

One of the guys sitting looked me over and asked:

– Can you play the guitar?

His resemblance to Krist Novoselic was uncanny. Jesus Christ! It *was* Krist Novoselic.

The gypsy answered, his voice sounding offended:

– Of course, of course, he knows German too.

And the gypsy was the one and the same Pat Smear, whom I'd seen play hundreds, no, thousands of times in the Unplugged concerts. Dave Grohl spoke up from behind the drums.

– Patty, we're out!

And he raised his left hand; a nearly invisible object was smouldering between his fingertips. Pat growled: – Well, shit – and gestured in understanding, then nodded his head and hurried out of the garage.

– We'd offer you some, but we can't because we're out, Krist explained.

Somewhere in my addled brain I noted how, once again, weed had evaded me.

Woeful and distracted, Krist picked up a bass guitar and played a few bars from 'Sappy'.

– Biu, bim, bim, bim, bim, bim, biu. Wanna play with us?

Dave jumped out from behind the drums and walked over to me: – What're you scared of, sit down! And he pushed a cardboard box over to me. I sat right through it, somersaulted backwards and almost cried out, waiting for them to laugh at me. But they didn't; they just stared at me. I sat up.

– Guys, aren't you forgetting something? You're all in Seattle.

Then they cracked up. Krist explained (Dave started to drum a quiet rhythm):

– What d'you mean Seattle, stop, are you kidding? We're just a bunch of Jelgava boys, we've played together for years, played everything, so to speak. Once we signed up for this contest, but they told us – we don't accept groups from Jelgava. That's how it all started, we made up the part about Seattle and it stuck with us. No-one thought it would get this far, oh, shit, shit, shit.

We sat in the silence of the garage; my mind was blank. Dave struck the cymbal, I fell over again, and again they didn't laugh, and then they opened a bag of crisps.

Krist said:

– We have to play one more show. It may be the most important one. For the truest fans, those who refused to believe the concert scheduled for Saint Alice's Day is cancelled, and we have to give them this ghost concert.

Dave answered through a mouthful of crisps:

– It's all true, y'know.

Krist nodded.

– And we need Kurt. For this one concert, we need Kurt back.

The garage was silent except for the crunching of crisps, the pounding of my heart and the cooing of pigeons outside.

– So we've been looking for him. We found a few guys who look the part, but there were two issues. Either they're not one of us, or they can't play guitar. You sort of look right, and you seem like one of us and you can, apparently, oy, oy, oy, play the guitar.

Dave was sitting back behind the drums and counted off with his sticks – one, two, three, four – as if to say, let's play.

I shook my head.

– What's wrong?

– I can't play guitar.

They both waved their hands at me in rock-and-roll-ish distaste:

– Man, stop. It's going to be more like a gig, a house party, you don't have to be a genius! We promised to play 'Sappy', we'll pull it off somehow. We've got Pat, too. Afterwards we'll smash our guitars, jump around, hit the snack table and then – adios!

I was already standing up to leave, still shaking my head 'no' so intensely that I even started to drool.

– No, I don't know how, I can't, it's not my thing...

Then I slapped my hand to my forehead: – Oh, right, I just remembered, I have to... I glanced down to check my watch, but I wasn't wearing one. But I still hurried out, calling apologetically behind me:

– I have to get home, the kittens are about to open their eyes.

Outside I almost collided with Pat, who was on his way back, carrying something in his cupped hands as carefully as if it was a butterfly. He leapt out of my way, saying:

– Yow, Speed Racer!

I headed home, and found a familiar street right away. I even made it back in time for the RBS Tops.

12

Nirvana was always number one in the Tops. Just like in the previous weeks. Oho, what a beautiful and momentary misunderstanding, I thought. 'About a Girl' was a really good song. Of course, I preferred the album version from *Bleach*, where he shouted, oh how he shouted! But even the Unplugged version of the song was undeniably good. But why was it at number one? I didn't get it.

The next day at school people were passing around the delayed memory book. The section "Your Crush" didn't interest me anymore (how long was a guy supposed to wait for his name to show up, I was tired of it). There weren't any interesting poems anymore like there used to be, either, such as:

Life is just dark

Without a sweetheart.

Now I turned to the section 'Your Favourite Music'. And was surprised. Nirvana after Nirvana, regardless if whoever wrote it was a punk or a shy, straight-A student. Kurt's name was carved into each and every desk. At least the teacher didn't start incorporating him into her lesson plan, thank God.

Saturday I went to the market to buy pancakes to pickle them later, and what did I see? His blue eyes staring back at me from every T-shirt, his face, smiling or grimacing. And what did I hear? 'Smells Like Teen Spirit' or 'In Bloom' playing in every kiosk, sometimes even 'Sliver'. From a few I even heard 'Zombie' or 'Self Esteem'. The shopkeepers-cum-DJs were fat old women, moving their hips totally out of rhythm. And the people came and bought it all.

I went to find Kārlis. He wasn't home, but Pūpols was in the front hall eating croquettes. I told him what I'd seen.

Pūpols bristled:

– But who told me that Nirvana was just a bunch of idiots and druggies banging around like cavemen? That it was negative music, shit, if it could even be called music?

I asked him, full of infuriated interest:

– Who?

Pūpols' face turned red like a pussywillow in the sunset, and a big chunk of croquette flew out of his mouth as he sputtered:

– Who said that it was all just some kind of new, destructive fashion statement that nothing good could come out of? That it would be better for people to stick to positive messages and listen to Michael Jackson who, by the way, can dance better too?

– Who? Who!?

– And those same people, well, now they're all into Nirvana.

I slapped my knee:

– That's what I'm saying! Now those people are claiming to be one of us! Just yesterday they were saying that Cobain was only good at screaming, and now they're screaming along with him!

– And they said that it was just a bunch of teenagers being posers, wanting to look different, but now it's become like some kind of mass-market uniform or something.

– Who!? Who could take the truth and turn it upside down like that? The goddamned idiot asshats! Who?!

Pūpols pointed at me with a fierceness that was hard to ignore.

– What are you staring at? Answer me! Who's the enemy!

He brought his finger even closer to my face and actually poked me in the eye. It hurt like crazy, and my hands went up instinctively. One of them caught Pūpols in the nose.

Pūpols had a particular nose. It was forever waiting on some otherworldly impulse to just start spewing blood. Once, a long long time ago, he and I had come to blows in the orchard behind school, and I only saved myself from being trampled to death by hitting him in the nose. It bled freely this time, too.

– Gah, I'm sorry! I'm sorry! I didn't mean to!

He looked at me and saw tears streaming down my face. He'd practically gouged my eye out. Pūpols stood with his hand under his nose, the palm puddling with red, and watched my tears as they fell.

– Are you retarded? Why'd you punch me in the nose? And why are you blubbering like some girl? It was you, you were the one who not that long ago called Cobain a destructive moron, but Jackson a humanitarian dancer.

Strange. I didn't remember that. I mean, sure, at one point I had listened to Michael, and even tried to copy his moves in front of the mirror, working especially hard to perfect his famous crotch-grab. But that was so long ago. And I was one to quickly pick up the beauty of this new school of music. Wouldn't I remember saying that?

Just then Gatis burst into the hall. When he saw us standing there crying and bleeding, he said: – The fuck is up with you two?! And promptly vomited everywhere. As we later learned, he had been at a nearby park with some friends drinking *yorsh*, and after that, of course, he'd felt he was going to throw up. Kārlis' house was the closest, so he'd rushed in, and probably would have made it to the toilet had we not thrown him off with our strange scene.

Once we'd done our best to clean up the hallway and had calmed down, we told Gatis what was going on, and he said:

– Who doesn't listen to Cobain these days? I mean, what normal person these days listens to Nirvana?

Then Kārlis came home and kicked us out.

Gatis hurried off home to continue his vomiting. Pūpols, sulking and still holding his nose, ambled off across the courtyard.

And I, having pissed everyone off, wandered into the summer night.

I didn't have to go back home that night. The rest of my family had gone to our cottage in Ozolnieki, leaving me behind in Jelgava.

I walked along and thought about the times, about its particular characteristics. What more did we need? We were one step from breaking out and one step from falling behind, I could feel it. The feeling only intensified until it became visceral – freedom flooded down on the city. No, not flooded, but trickled down like a misty rain that soaks you to the bone.

It's unbelievable: you can clearly feel the freedom raining down, but the rest of the city is sleeping like the dead. It's like standing on the street and looking in through a window at someone you love, and you're pouring your love out against that window – the window can't stay closed for ever, can it?

I started to think about Milēdija, about how bad we were for each other, about how good it was that she didn't like me, and how good it was that she'd chosen Kārlis' brother.

If only I had a cigarette.

I'd walked all the way to the Jelgava Palace. Just for the hell of it, instead of turning in the direction of home I crossed the bridge to the Pārlielupe part of town.

I stopped along the bridge, and looked over the railing. Almost everyone leans to look over the railing when they're on a bridge, to feel that temptation to fall, that depth. When I got tired of that I looked towards downtown – there was nothing there. Then I turned to look the other way, towards Pārlielupe.

A large group of people was approaching. The dark shadows drew closer quietly and quickly, eventually turning into young and middle-aged men, their heads shaved. There were a lot of them. They were so unnaturally quiet; they didn't should, didn't curse. Their gait was just as unnatural – very quick, some of them even running. My heart wanted to leap into the Lielupe River – they were headed straight towards me, a silent and stone-faced army.

I pressed myself up against the railing, hoping to blend into them and escape their notice. What was going on, who had sent an entire army of thugs after me? They were close, so very close. Almost next to me. Watchful eyes, nervous mouths, row after row of them. As the last of them passed me, one of them glanced at me, hard, but didn't stop. I watched them go. Thugs who leave you alone. Who were they? Ghost-thugs?

I rubbed my hands over my face and decided that I was imagining things. I needed to go home. But first I had to stand for a minute to catch my bearings. I wanted to avoid a potential repeat-meeting with the ghosts, before the city swallowed them whole.

I don't know how long I'd been standing there in a daze, when a car pulled up next to me. It was the police, and a few officers stepped out of it.

– Don't move! Hands up!

One of the policemen rushed over to me and shoved me against the railing.

– Little bitch!

Two of the officers grabbed me by the arms, a third shone a torch into my face. After the rest of the night's events I didn't even care anymore; all I tried to do now was not shit myself. But something still made me shrink into myself. As they scrutinised me in silence, I heard something, two seconds of it. I could hear 'About a Girl' playing from the police car. Even our enemies were listening to our music.

– It's not him. Look at his hair!

And the officer tugged on my hair so hard it hurt.

– What're you doing out here? Are you stupid? Get lost!

An unintelligible voice crackled from the police radio to mix with Nirvana. The officers crammed back into their car and, wheels screeching, shot off toward downtown.

I didn't know it yet, but the next day the *Zemgale News* would print: "Citizens of Jelgava, beware. Don't open your doors to strangers, don't pick up hitchhikers!" This misanthropic outpouring was a result of that night's events. Eighty-nine inmates from the Pārlielupe Prison's Fourth Colony had escaped through a hole they'd carved out in the wall of the laundry room. It was a world record! Well done, Jelgava.

I still had no idea what the city was going to do with its newfound freedom. Police officers would be shot at from a stolen vehicle. Parents would forbid their kids from wandering around, finally giving the act of going for a walk meaning. To me, these criminals had really just been a symbol, a metaphor for our overall process of breaking out.

But that's not what I was thinking about there on the bridge. I felt like a traitor. No, I felt like Kurt had betrayed us so that I would now betray him and move on. I felt like someone had died again so that the rest of us could be free.

We were nearing autumn, and the cold moon shivered in the river.

II
THE MOON

1

The road from Jelgava to Riga isn't that interesting. No hills, no valleys. All you can do is imagine. It's like the entire region was carefully constructed to train the imagination. And once the train spits you out and you take in your surroundings, everything looks like something you can't wait to tell your friends about. But what do they need your sudden poeticism for? They're looking at it all right now, too, and are probably thinking about it themselves, which is why you're doing the same.

Behold, the Zemgale lowlands, flat, terrible. Nowhere to hide, no salvation. The sun lit up the sparse birch grove, drawing the eye to the cemeteries hidden there. There, in the distance, is Lithuania. And right before that wonderful country is the station for a town called Meitene – our word for 'girl'. How I'd love to be there. A little closer to us is the haunted Eleja Manor. Then comes Jelgava – no comment. And then Olaine, the end of it all, a living nightmare, the anarchy capital of Latvia, a rogue territory with its own set of rules.

That's where we found ourselves just then.

We were supposedly pro-anarchy, or at least we were for now – drawing jagged As with circles around them. But the anarchy in Olaine was the real deal, it consisted of dark and harsh laws. This is where all of Jelgava's junkies started out and got their drugs. MDMA was manufactured there by the conveyorful. The police supposedly confiscated them by the hundreds of kilograms and incinerated them. Once Kārlis went to Olaine with a group of his buddies for a friendly basketball game. Their bus was pelted with rocks. Sometimes they even threw rocks at the passing trains. I was on a train once when it happened. As soon as the train pulled away from Olaine the rocks started flying. One hit a widow on the other end of the train car, and another just barely missed my window. I was always lucky like that.

But now we were a better target for this city. We were smaller than a train, of course, but we weren't made of metal. Metal was only in our hearts.

And this was not the best place for young guys with hair longer than what was socially acceptable. Mine was down to my shoulders; almost. Gatis, whom no-one called that anymore except his mother and our teachers, was the only one with hair actually down to his shoulders. He'd been growing it out longer than I had, but it wasn't growing in length so much as in width. He took that in stride and always said: "Whatever, Tonijs looks way more like a poodle than me." It was hard to say exactly how long Edgars' hair was because it mostly stuck out in all directions, but it was definitely longer than the norm.

Our jeans are even skinnier than before and ripped at the knees. Everyone wears trainers with the tongues pulled out and black T-shirts. Gatis has an Obituary shirt. They're our new cult group. Well, the group was old – they'd been playing together since the eighties. They were from Miami and were one of the pioneers of death metal. And we are metalheads. Gatis is particularly into death metal, which is why we now call him Death.

It's hard to believe that he found the shirt at a rummage sale. It was a miracle, really. After that we all stormed the rummage sales to dig through the heaps of clothes. I even made my mom a list of what shirts to grab if she saw them: Death, Cannibal Corpse, Anal Cunt, Brutal Truth, Carcass, Hypocrisy. She never found any of them, but once brought back a Michael Learns to Rock shirt with three smiling guys à la Zack Morris on it. Despite my rebellious nihilism, my heart almost broke from how sweet it was. But I could never bring myself to wear the shirt.

But Death managed to find an Obituary shirt for fifty santims. Yet he still wasn't happy. He was a little superstitious and believed that he'd bought bad luck when he'd bought the shirt (though that didn't stop him from wearing it religiously). Even now he was saying:

– I told you! I told you! Something always go wrong when I'm wearing this shirt!

We'd just been kicked off the train from Jelgava to Riga. And for nothing – we just didn't have tickets. The brigade of conductors took one look at our hair and left us at the next station. The train moved on, but we stayed there, in Olaine.

– What now, boys?

Death looked after the train, but it had already disappeared into the distance. Edgars always had an answer:

– I think we should kill some dogs and sell their skins!

He was totally out of his mind. He lived next door to Death. Because he was a little crazy and because of his obsessive love for horror films, everyone called him Zombie.

– The townies'll skin us soon.

We scrutinized the city with eagle eyes, the city that spread out in front of us, overgrown with shrubs. We didn't see a single person, but the shrubs looked suspicious.

– Let's get out of here.

And we headed for the highway.

You could see the Zemgale lowlands better from here; the Jelgava end of the horizon seemed even more endearing, more so than Riga, which we were dying to get to. We weren't interested in Riga itself, but once you passed through it you could get to the Stocks. That was the centre of the world. Sometimes it was even called the Punk Stocks. My mom told me that hippies went to trade records there back in the seventies. This was out in the Biķernieks forest, where you could get by taking Trolley 18 or a tram. People would gather there – the rejects, those outside the law, those who didn't want to be anywhere else – gather in the woods and do their thing, which the city and the world knew nothing about.

So what *did* they do there? For now all we knew is that they traded cassette tapes. And that was enough for us. We needed tapes. Nirvana and Pearl Jam weren't enough anymore.

Sometimes I still secretly listened to Nirvana. But I listened to new tapes more often. I had Tiamat's *Wildhoney*. I'd heard it on the 'Rockade' radio programme. It was as good as a fairy tale – no, dark as a fairy tale, depressing as a fairy tale. The singer growled like a bear, and then he was joined by female voices, and I'd imagine the women were singing naked. Death got their tape for me through his usual channels. Kārlis, in turn, had Napalm Death's *Harmony Corruption*, which was something else entirely; they thrashed with superhuman strength and speed. Death had Entombed's *Wolverine Blues*, Cannibal Corpse's *Eaten Back to Life* and Morbid Angel's *Altars of Madness*, and some other stuff I can't remember. He definitely had Asphyx's *The*

Rack, which he loved more than anything, and he wanted their next album, *Last One on Earth*. Then he'd have all he needed in life.

I had never before heard music like this. I had never even been able to imagine that something like it existed. It was an entirely different world. It felt good to sit here on the asphalt, together with Death and Zombie, in the middle of the road to another world.

– Faggot! Whore! Cocksucker!

Zombie was unloading his frustration in true nineties fashion. Another car had just blown past us. As great as his wild gesticulating and theatrical poses were, Zombie's efforts to flag down a car weren't working. He'd been at it for fifteen minutes, judging by the sun (none of us had a watch). Death spoke up sullenly:

– We'll never make it to the Stocks. They start at ten.

– So maybe stop warming your junk on the asphalt and help! My arm's about to fall off.

I didn't believe that Zombie could ever be tired. Now he was plucking long reeds from the roadside and whipping them at invisible enemies.

I took over the hitchhiking. I saw a micro-bus coming up the road, and dropped my hand, tucking it behind my back before turning away from the road. We didn't have any money for fare. Then there was another Zhiguli; the man kept his hands on the wheel and his eyes on the road, while his wife smiled and shook her head 'no'. But their back seat was empty. They looked to be my parents' age, and my parents always stopped for hitchhikers. Then came a regular Audi or something similar (I'm not good with car makes, I only know my dad's Zhiguli). Then another foreign model, its driver a polite guy who gestured with his thumb to the right to indicate he was about to turn off the highway, otherwise he'd stop. It was brief, human contact. The next driver gave me a totally ambiguous gesture. What did it mean? Grow up, kid, don't go crawling out of your house until you have your own set of wheels?

And so I communicated with the drivers; my side of the conversation had longevity and growth, but theirs lasted only a moment. I communicated with the thousand-headed road parade all while standing in place – and then a car signalled to us and started to slow. Death turned to see where Zombie had gone off to, but the car was full of degenerates barely older than us, definitely coming from Olaine. They were just screwing with us and laughed as the car slowed – then they revved the engine and were gone. And even they, who had paid attention to us for a second, would probably forget us in two minutes, three kilometres.

– I'm done. It's not working. Your turn.

Death went to the shoulder, disappointed with the world; he sniffed and stuck his hand out in the space above the road. He came up with a mantra:

– Pull over, idiots!

The car was as long as a starship, its glinting body seeming to stretch on forever as it rolled to a stop. It was shiny, and must've been expensive. The monsieur leaned out the window and asked:

– Where're you boys off to?

For some reason the answer 'To Flatsville' came to mind, but Death replied matter-of-factly:

– To the Stocks.

– Ha ha. The stock market is in the other direction, boys. In Lithuania.

– To Riga, then.

– Where?

– Riga!

The man chuckled again.

– Well then let's go. We can take you.

Zombie ran up from the field, covered in bits of grass like a disoriented King Lear; before he got into the car the man turned to him and said:

– Brush off.

The car drove along quieter than a Zhiguli, and over the passenger-side headrest I could see a cascade of beautiful hair, so bright it was blinding when the sunlight touched it, and a romantic blood-red when in the shade. The passenger was a metalhead! But no, I looked in the rear-view mirror to see a girl's eyes starting back at me. Her father stepped on the gas and I pressed my nose to the window to resume my conversation with the road. We caught up to the carful of losers, all of them silently staring off in his own direction, and as we passed them up I gave them the finger. Then we passed up the guy with the ambiguous hand-gestures, and he looks just as serious as before. Then we passed the polite guy about to make his turn, but why hadn't he turned off yet? And there, even the Zhiguli with the couple my parents' age; the woman turns her head and sees me, and again smiles and shakes her head, no, no.

– What are you boys going to do in Riga?

The question came from our friendly chauffeur. None of us spoke up, waiting for the others to go first.

– What?

The man asked again. Death and Zombie answered simultaneously. Death:

– To the store.

And Zombie:

– To count old people.

No-one wanted to mention the Stocks again. For some reason it felt vulnerable in this car that smelled of leather and 'Wunderbaum'.

– Ha ha. You boys sure are funny.

It's some kind of unspoken rule that the hitchhikers have to make small talk with the driver. So the transaction is mutually beneficial. I was about to add that the weather was great, or something, when the man spoke up again:

– Who are you, exactly?

An existential question. Because, truly, who are we? Zombie answered slowly:

– B-o-y-s.

This in a voice that indicated he was trying hard to stifle a giggle.

– I mean, who are you, you all have long hair, are you from some kind of association or something?

We shrugged. We just were what we were.

– You boys aren't part of those crazy metalheads, are you?

Ding ding ding! But what should we say... Are we, or aren't we? Someone say something!

– What kind of music do you boys listen to?

Death couldn't take it anymore.

– Cannibal Corpse.

– Excuse me?

The driver turned his own music down – the most classic classical music ever, and a total potpourri of a playlist, too. He turned the music down even lower and half-turned to look at us.

– What?

– Cannibal Corpse.

– And what does that mean?

– It's English, it means 'the corpse of a cannibal'.

– Do you think I can't understand English?

And he turned up his Beethoven, ridiculously remastered with a thumping beat. A minute later he repeated:

– Do you think I can't understand English?

– I don't think that, no.

– Then why did you say I can't?

– I didn't.

– What do you mean you didn't? That's what you said!

– I'm sorry.

The man continued to steer along, not that you need to do a lot of steering along the Jelgava highway.

– I, for example, listen to good music. You know what this is? Do you have any idea who this is?

It was Beethoven's 5th, mixed to flow into Brahms' 'Hungarian Dances' in the most baffling way. But I said nothing.

– You don't!

I wondered if the girl next to him, probably his daughter, was still staring into the rear-view mirror with her girlish eyes. I didn't look.

– Why don't you boys listen to good music?

Death had clearly decided not to say any more; he had zoned out, his face blank. He was an expert at that. Zombie gave it a go:

– We like interesting stuff.

The man pressed his foot down on the gas pedal; I wanted to look at the speedometer to capture the moment so we could say later how fast this lunatic had been driving, but I didn't dare, because then I'd probably also look into the rear-view mirror and probably see the girl staring again. I kept my eyes on the road. There was a fox, run over.

– And why don't you boys look normal? You know why? I'll tell you! The man was worked up:

– You don't even want to be normal. It seems silly to you. You think you're smarter than everyone else.

He was getting out of control. And we were nowhere near Riga yet.

– And now you're in my car, and you can see, it's a nice car. But do I get any respect from you for it? No!

Now I was really freaked out. Because he was saying exactly what I was thinking at that moment.

– You don't care if a person has made something of himself. You just think, eh, so what if he's well off, he's probably a crook or a sell-out. No, but you don't think that at all. You don't care about anything.

Our monologue was making me feel incredibly uncomfortable.

– This world isn't good enough for you. You're the special ones. Living a normal life, trying to make something of it – that all seems stupid to you! Let those idiots drive their cars, let them buy us beer. Meanwhile, we have to focus on our cannibals.

He carefully maneuvered into the right-hand lane, then stopped the car along the shoulder.

– This is your stop.

We looked out. It definitely wasn't Riga. Just the roadside. The most notable thing was the bushes. Our reaction time was too slow for him.

– What part of that didn't you understand?

We got out. Did Death actually say thank you? It would have been so like him. The car pulled away. Zombie was chuckling to himself as if this was a good thing. But Death just repeated:

– I told you, it's the shirt! We're never going to make it to the Stocks.

I looked back at the road; what else was I supposed to do? Eventually the Zhiguli passed by, then the Audi, then the Ford, and its driver again gave us that curious gesture, maybe because he recognised us, but maybe he'd forgotten us because it was the same ambiguous gesture. But the polite guy who had said he was going to turn off didn't drive by again. He really had turned off. Back then some people were honest about what they'd said they'd do, and remembered. Even the car of degenerates, who should be coming up the road any minute, would likely remember getting the finger.

2

School had changed. Of course, it had changed before. Nirvana had arrived as the unifier and the pacifier. Songs about loneliness and pain brought us together and made us happy. Everyone was on the same side. Jurģis liked the acoustic version of 'All Apologies', it was peaceful and beautiful; Kārlis like the aggression of 'Negative Creep' from *Bleach*, and Milēdija liked 'Where Did You Sleep Last Night', the first half of which is so elegant you could almost listen to it with your mother, but at the end the screams rip you in two. I liked that song a lot, too.

Nirvana times had been good times for all. But the time had passed, and some people were restless. If everyone is your friend, are they true friends? Being number one in the top charts and the industry – is that how it was meant to be? That's why Kurt killed himself, he understood it all. He didn't want to be a start, we betrayed him by hailing him as one; we betrayed him by not betraying him.

That's why the world changed again. It was no longer uniformly bad or uniformly good. Carcass had a song, 'Polarized'. Society was being polarised. Or it was polarising itself. Either way, our group was again the minority. We had finally found a road not everyone wanted to go down.

We openly and purposefully did the wrong things. We had various reasons. There were even those who joined in because it was the only chance to join something, to be part of something. It wasn't a rule or anything; there were a few who stayed on our side whose prestige in school society was always significant. But most of them sided with the majority.

I observed with a quiet and monstrous glee that Milēdija didn't accept our other side either, she'd only bug out her eyes and purse her lips. She wasn't even that pretty.

Now I only liked metalhead girls. They walked through the school halls as if they'd always walked them. They wore their long hair loose down their backs, sweaters with long sleeves, ripped-up jeans or floor-length skirts. Heavy boots or trainers. They'd probably taken the boots from their fathers. But how were they able to grow their hair out that long? Tell me the secret! No, these were the girls who had only recently undone their braids, who hadn't yet thrown themselves into life – unlike the girls who had shortened their skirts as well as their hairstyles – these girls had left their long locks alone, their fathers' pride and joy, and now their hair flowed along with to the poetic sounds of metal. The legs they hid under their long skirts were gorgeous. They themselves were, too, and I couldn't understand; how were they so beautiful? I hadn't yet read Kafka, who wrote: 'The guilty are the most beautiful.'

I stepped up to the urinal in the bathroom, pulled out my dick and started to pee, like you do. I did all this with just my left hand; I had my house keys in my right hand and was carving the word 'Asphyx' into the chalky surface of the bathroom wall. They were a Swedish brutal death metal band, and had a distinct and easy-to-draw logo. I'd seen Death do it once. The bathroom wall in front of me was already covered in the history of the world: 'Nirvana, Sakne the Bitch, Nine Inch Nails' and now Asphyx. Kārlis was in the next stall over; we'd come in at the same time and now continued out conversation. I was working on the letter S and said:

– What're you doing?

– What d'you think?

– I mean I know. But what are you writing?

Because I could hear the satisfying sound of a key carving into the wall coming from his stall, too.

– Metallica.

– Why?

They were metal, but kind of commonplace, not very radical.

– What d'you mean, why? They're classic.

The stall divider made me feel invisible, and therefore bold:

– Does Milēdija like them?

– Yeah.

Something made me painfully squeeze what I was holding in my left hand. I asked:

– Did you hear Hypocrisy's *The Fourth Dimension*?

– Ages ago.

It was hard to fluster Kārlis. As in all things, he was even ahead of me in music. And yet, and yet – was he really all-in?

I finished carving 'Asphyx' and, with an artist's flourish, dropped my tool. The one in the right hand. And, naturally, my key ring fell right into the toilet.

– Shit! My key fell in the toilet!

– In shit?

– No, no. In clean water.

And I lowered my hand into the yellow pisswater. The keys were balancing on the edge of chaos, right on the lip of the hole. I swore that if only I could save my keys, I'd become a better person. I grabbed them and pulled the dripping mass back into this world. Now I had to fulfil my promise. I thought a moment and then said:

– I only really like the first track from *Fourth Dimension* anyway, the slow one, 'Apocalypse'.

Kārlis said nothing. I wiped my keys off with toilet paper and continued:

– It's normal to like the pretty songs. We have to deal with much. But we have to deal with it! Once we've started in, we can't stop. We have to listen to harder and harder music, and anyone who doesn't can just stay sitting on their goddamned pot!

I myself was right in front of my pot. And apparently I hadn't kept my promise. I had to take it all the way.

– Kārlis? Wanna bet that I'll throw my keys back in the toilet? I don't want to go home anyway! Wanna bet? I'll throw them in and flush them, and even take a dump on them!

His drawn-out silence was suspect.

– Hey, asshole?

Kārlis was sharp, he'd definitely answer me, maybe even throw a turd at me over the stall divider. But nothing happened. I put the keys in my pocket and stepped out of the stall. The neighbouring stall door was open and it was empty. It was an old trick – leave the bathroom in the middle of a conversation, so the other guy stays there talking to himself. *Dixi et animam levavi.*

3

When I was little I could never remember which river was the Driksa and which the Lielupe. They were both right next to one another, and actually were one and the same river, just split at this one point by an island. Around 1265 the Jelgava Palace was built on the island, then called the Mitau Palace. The *Livonian Rhyme Chronicle* told how the palace quickly came to fame: 'And all the Zemgalians / Cursed it loudly'. No-one really knows what it looked like. The palace was rebuilt several times and burned down even more – in 1376, 1625, 1659, 1737, 1918 and 1944.

Though there were times when the palace stood peacefully with its residents. And as soon as people started living in the palace they wanted to decorate it. Duke Jacob Kettler's bedroom had very fancy wallpaper made of woven wool. As time went on little fibres of wool separated from it, which the duke then inhaled and then coughed up along with pieces of his lung. This was seen as some kind of sorcery, and the steward of Vecmuiža was tried and burned at the stake for it right in the centre of the courtyard. When the palace wasn't on fire, its people were.

When Rastrelli was constructing the palace as it looks today, it took him forever to finish it; it was draining the duchy's powers like the pyramids had in Egypt. Some Count of Provence – the future king of France, Louis XVIII – once complained about the on-going construction and the lack of simple comforts when visiting the palace. At that time he wasn't yet king, just an exile, whose brother, Louis XVI, had laid his head down on the guillotine without so much as a peep only five years earlier. The proud exile had brought an entire entourage with him to Jelgava. There was the Jesuit L'Abbé Edgeworth de Firmont – the same one who had administered Louis XVI his final sacrament on the scaffold. Maybe he thought that the brother would also benefit from his services, but the Abbot died first, right here in Jelgava, and it was Louis XVIII who wrote the man's epitaph. Louis XVIII had also brought his trusted courtier the Marquis d'Oissel, who was supposedly a very tiny man who preferred to perch on the King's shoulder. He was also a hundred or two hundred years old. But the Jelgava climate got to him, and the miniature aristocrat got sick and died.

Marie-Thérèse of France, daughter of the King and martyr, also wound up in Jelgava. Louis XVIII didn't have children, and so he placed his concerns for the future of France on Marie-Thérèse's shoulders, and married her to her cousin Louis Antoine D'Artois. But the couple never had children.

I stood by the palace lost in these thoughts; the palace was huge and rosy-coloured. Kārlis had invited me here. He'd said there was going to be some kind of concert, and that his brother could get us in. The concert was supposed to take place next to the palace, on a smaller island that was part of the main palace archipelago. There was a bandstand there or something. Neither Kārlis nor his brother were there yet. So I was standing around by the corner of the huge, rosy palace and making up its history in my head.

Why hadn't they had any kids? They had been the last chance to continue the royal bloodline. Who knows, maybe they did have a kid, but Marie-Thérèse, changing its diaper one day, may have remembered her parents' – Louis XVI's and Marie Antoinette – decapitated heads, as well as the letter the poor King had written to her own little brother: 'If you one day have the misfortune of becoming King...' She could have panicked. She could have taken the child, a stack of clean diapers and a golden sword, and given the lot to a nanny, a kind Jelgava woman... Yes, that's exactly what happened!

The kind Jelgava woman taught the French wretch our beautiful Latvian language and appropriately modest manners. The boy was handsome, though a little odd (Marie-Thérèse and Louis Antoine were first cousins, after all). He never asked about his past, and his children after him didn't, either. And so we come to the seventh generation carrying Royal French blood in Jelgava. And no one knows about it. 'It will live but no eyes will see it', as My Dying Bride sang. Meanwhile the unwitting descendant of the King had a heart full of inexplicable desires. And he often feels out of place, he doesn't have a lot of friends, and he's basically dumbstruck when faced with any sort of practical issue. Yes, that's it! *Exactement!* Everything was falling into place...

So I stood there in my place, fitting right into the palace scenery, when Zombie came up to me, held out his hand and said:

– Pull my finger!

I pulled it, and there was a cracking rumble. Zombie had farted. The nearby ditch burst into peals of laughter; they were all there, Death, Kārlis, Kārlis' brother, Šolis and Šolis' buddy. I was happy to return to reality, to my friends in this rye-scented area of Zemgale. Kārlis' brother shouted for us to hurry up, we had to get inside; Zombie shot back that we'd have been inside a long time ago if Kārlis' brother hadn't been so busy scratching his balls. But we eventually made our way to the entrance. Kārlis and his brother really did manage to get us all inside by chatting with the guard at the door. I'm never comfortable in these situations asking just how we were able to get in. It's would be like stripping someone of their glory. And that's not cool. Even the guard knew it and glared at us, letting us know how lucky we were that night.

Though, Šolis and his buddy declined to come in with us. They said they'd be in later. I found that odd – it cost a lat to get in!

But who cares about them – I was inside and had forgotten all about my shadowy dream world. We could already hear these magnificently broken wails which meant someone was inexpertly adjusting the sound system and that the concert was about to start, live life itself, the life I was about to live! And my friends were right there with me. I looked around eagerly, trying to spot other metalheads, but didn't see any. There were quite a lot of girls and clean-cut guys, though. Death noticed this as well, and asked Kārlis' brother:

– Who's playing tonight?

– Otrā Puse.

– What?

I didn't know the band, but I liked the name – *otrā puse*, the other side. It was exactly what we were interested in. 'Break on through to the other side!' It might not be metal, but maybe a heavier alternative band, who knows. They were taking the stage. They looked like regular guys. But metalheads could also look like regular guys. They started their set. It was absolutely, positively nothing like metal.

– So what?

Kārlis' brother snapped at Death.

– We should support local bands. You got another option tonight? You can swim back home.

This is where the line between our tastes in music was drawn. The brothers were true music lovers and patriots, and event-goers. Death was more ideologically principled. But Zombie didn't seem to mind the music—he was sneaking up behind girls and pinching their butts. That's how he was. To get the most objective image of his behaviour, take everything I say about Zombie and multiply it by three. I just can't always talk about him and him alone. In turn, everything in this book that I do could, honestly, be halved. So, for example: we had just sat down in the grass and Kārlis inconspicuously handed me two beers, which I drank so inconspicuously that two girls passing by flashed me a single smile; Zombie, meanwhile, had pinched one butt and gotten one foot wet in the canal.

Kārlis and his brother went to stand closer to the stage, but Death stayed off to one side. I took three steps toward the brothers, but I stopped partway. Then Death called after me:

– Screw them. I have a Walkman.

We sat down in the bushes and listened to the Walkman. Death had a cassette with him; the cover was a Benediction logo he'd cut out of a Polish magazine. Death pushed the earbuds into my ears, and I listened. It was hard to understand, I could barely make any of it out. Death shouted into my face as loud as he could, thinking that he had to make himself heard over the music:

– Can you hear it?

His expression was earnest, as it always was when he spoke about music. Without waiting for my reply, Death took back the earbuds and put them in his ears:

– You can't hear shit, why didn't you say something?!

He sulked for a moment, pushed a couple of the Walkman's buttons, and gave me the next song to listen to:

– Try this!

Now I could hear it, even over Otrā Puse's songs. What I heard was really heavy and energetic, it was cutting, manic and thrashing. I couldn't stay quiet any longer and said:

– I had no idea Benediction was this good!

– It's not Benediction.

– What?

I looked at the coloured piece of paper under the cassette case's cover.

– Oh! I just put that there. I didn't have the real cassette around.

And that is how people who don't understand the importance of the relationship between objects and their names make the rest of us look like idiots.

– Then what is it?

Death took a pack of crisps out of his pocket and opened it.

– It's Latvian. Huskvarn.

– Latvian what?

– A band. Huskvarn.

Metal, in Latvia! How was that possible? Sure, there were punk and grundge bands, but metal was something so faraway and secret. It was like discovering Pluto, and then finding out that Pluto is right next door. And not half-bad, either. The real deal.

– They're from Jelgava.

Ah, they were from Jelgava. Now it made sense. My heart settled down.

Zombie ran up to us, panting and laughing at the same time, trying to tell us something. He put out his hand, doubled over and drew in a deep breath.

– Give me some crisps!

He took a handful and disappeared into the reeds. Death continued to shatter my worldview:

– We have all kinds of bands. Heaven Grey, Dzels Vilks, Dies Irae.

Am I the only one who feels like he was born yesterday?

– Are they all from Jelgava?

– No, not quite.

Then Kārlis and his brother joined us, both of them looking disappointed.

– What're you guys doing?

– Nothing.

– It's like Armageddon in there! The pop-kids are wailing on the metalheads. And you're out here with your hands down your pants! Hey, crisps!

They each grabbed a handful and ran off. Death sniffed and said:

– What is this garbage? Why are we here? We need our own place to go.

– Totally. We should absolutely make one. Somewhere far away.

– Why don't you come to the Junkyard?

I wasn't about to admit that my mom wouldn't let me.

– I like to be alone.

– Got it.

And I needed to throw in a little cool indifference:

– When was the last thing at the Junkyard?

– Do you think it's easy to set something up? We'll have another one soon. We already have all kinds of music.

– We should go to the Stocks.

– We should. Though there's no telling what it's like there. The kids in Riga aren't like us. I've met a lot of them. They're like – let's say you have five lats, they'll be like, let's all buy a bunch of drinks with it, and then they're gone.

If I were to ever have five lats, I wouldn't regret it. I said:

– But that's our scene. A forest of metalheads. And new music.

– Right, I mean, I'm all for that. We ended up going one Sunday.

– Which Sunday?

– Remember that time we all tried to go?

– Yeah.

– The Sunday after that.

They'd gone to the Stocks without me. Real nice.

– What's it like? Is it even worth going?

– I don't know.

Death passed me the crisps packet; he was in a sharing mood.

– I don't know. We never found it.

– What?

My voice betrayed two types of joy – that of a fool and that of envy.

– I don't know. We supposedly got out at the right stop. But there was just a hospital or something. We asked a few people – just normal people on the street – we asked, where are the metalheads? No-one knew anything. We never found it.

– Maybe it doesn't really exist?

– Supposedly it does.

I passed the crisps back to Death, and then we noticed the group. There were four figures standing in front of us, watching us with disdain. One of them was wearing a vest, the rest looked just as stupid. We stood up casually, as if we just wanted to stretch our legs.

– Death metal fans?

The guy with the vest spoke first. They were older guys, over twenty, with the calloused hands of hard labourers. I glanced around. There was no- one else, none of our friends.

He repeated his question and pointed at Death's shirt. It had 'Sepultura' written across it. It was actually a good question.

– Yeah. Sepultura play death metal.

I'd answered their question and the conversation was done, that's what I tried to tell myself. I looked over at Death. There was an unreadable look in his eyes. I asked him:

– Where d'you think the others went?

It was an attempt to shift the conversation. As if the four guys in front of us weren't there, as if we were having a more than normal conversation, but at the same time giving these guys an important piece of information.

– So, where do you think those maniacs went?

Death answered as if it really was a normal conversation:

– How should I know? Probably off exploring each other's sexuality.

One of the other guys, this one wearing a sports coat, stepped forward and swung. Death didn't fall down, but stumbled back a step, the crisps packet falling out of his hand. The guy in the sports coat immediately bent down and picked it up. That was their purpose in the world, to somehow wind up with a half-eaten packet of crisps.

The leader, the one with the vest turned to me. He shouted:

– You some kind of professor?

And he tore my glasses from my face. The world dissolved into a smooth jelly, but I understood that he was angry.

– Dress normal!

He tucked my glasses into the breast pocket of my unfashionable shirt. Why hadn't he thrown them into the reeds? Why hadn't he hit me? Had he sensed the Royal bloodline? Or maybe it was human fear of the unknown, of magic? Who knew what sorcery a kid in glasses was capable of.

But they didn't leave Death alone. One of the guys pointed to the Walkman:

– What's that?

Death didn't answer. He put the Walkman in his pocket.

– Hand it over!

I glanced around again, and still saw no-one. This couldn't happen, it couldn't. I looked at the guy wearing the vest, waiting for something to happen. He was looking at the canal, watching it tensely:

– Hold up, wait!

And then he pointed. The rest of them turned obediently to look at the canal. It was like they had spotted the Loch Ness Monster.

Remember, Šolis and his buddy hadn't gone into the show with us. It turns out they had brought a bottle of booze with them, but there were too many of us. We went in to see the concert, but they went off a little ways and lay down in the grass and drained the bottle. Then they'd remembered the concert and started counting their money. They each had two lats. It cost only one to get into the show. So they walked to the nearest store and bought one bottle of "Agdams" fortified wine each, which cost one lat fifty. When they got back to the Palace island, they went past the bridge and the guard standing there, and lay down in the grass a little further down. They each drank a bottle of wine. They were having a great time, and the setting sun made the palace and the water turn pretty, muted colours. When the wine was gone, they recounted their money. They had one lat left between them.

They thought about what to do. The buddy thought he could take the money, go inside and find someone he knew to borrow another lat from, then come back out and get Šolis. But Šolis wasn't convinced. He climbed down to the water and stuck his hand in it. Even though it was autumn, remember, the setting sun had warmed the water. Šolis said:

– Let's swim across.

They got undressed, folded their clothes into a tight bundle and swam. It was important for them to get to this concert.

And this is what the four proletarians saw – naked shoulders, wild eyes, long hair and a bundle of clothes held high above the water.

The one wearing the sports coat let out a frightened, superstitious whisper:

– It's a mob of Rambos!

He dropped the crisps packet and the four of them disappeared.

I said nothing. Death ran a hand over his cheek and asked me a very loaded question:

– Is Sepultura death metal?

– Aren't they?

– Well, I don't know. *Bestial Devastation* and *Morbid Vision* were, maybe. But now they play pure thrash.

– Well, I don't know either. I think, I'm sure, that *Chaos A. D.* is pure death.

I was in the mood for a discussion.

But at that moment Zombie and the brothers showed up out of nowhere. Kārlis' brother said:

– What's up, where did you guys disappear? This place is crawling with pop-kids, where were you?

– Everything's fine, we got ours, Death answered and spat. Šolis and his buddy crawled out of the canal, shook themselves off and asked:

– Did the show already start?

Kārlis' brother was totally annoyed:

– It's already over! None of you can keep his shit together.

Just then a group of totally normal-looking guys walked past us. Kārlis' brother spotted them and tried to rally us:

– See, there goes Otrā Puse! Should we ask for their autographs?

We all looked to see if we had something to write on, even me. But why? I wasn't even interested in them. But that was what you did back then. Music was important, and you had to take what you could get.

The band even stopped and stared at us. Maybe because Šolis and his buddy were stark naked and wet. While the rest of us were fumbling around as if we were looking for toilet paper in an empty bathroom, Death took the piece of manufacturer's card stock from the cassette case with "Lazer" emblazoned on it and went over to one of the musicians.

– Excuse me, but could I please have your autograph?

He even had a pen. The musician let out a sound of delighted disbelief, and bent over to balance the card on his knee and asked:

– What should I write?

Death thought, but not for long.

– Write 'Napalm Death'!

– What's that?

– An awesome band!

The musician paused, but not for long.

– Okay.

And he wrote.

– Like this?

– D-e-a-t-h.

– Got it. You're welcome!

– Thanks.

And so Death was the only one who got an autograph. The real deal. He put the card into his pocket and said:

– A perfect show!

I, little creep that I was, stared at my amazing friend in awe and total hatred. He had gotten everything – the punches, and the perfect show. And he had gone to the Stocks without me.

4

If that's how things were going to be, I'd go find the Stocks by myself. If the cool kids don't know how to find it, it'll be the lonely boy with a scientific approach who does. I liked being alone.

It all started out well. I didn't get kicked off the train, or the trolley. Back then I didn't know anything about Riga, not the Hotel Latvija, not the University. Yet I needed to find a place that not even the majority of Rigans knew about. It was a good thing you could catch Trolley 18 right in front of the central station – which, by the way, was far prettier back then. I'd been hoping that the trolley would be full of metalheads heading for the Stocks, and that all I'd have to do is stick close to them. But there wasn't a single metalhead in the trolley besides me. Behind the trolley windows, the city grew gradually wilder, like Jelgava. Panelboard houses surrounded in large shrubs. It supposedly indicated I was headed in the right direction; the Stocks was in the woods, after all.

I got out at the last stop. I didn't see any death-metalers, not even a heavy-metaler. I'd seen the hospital Death had mentioned at the second to last stop. All I saw here was a lake or a pond beyond the road, the trolley hut and behind that a forest. I headed for the woods.

It was sparse, and I could see the road all the way through on the other side. I looked at my watch (I'd thought of everything); it was a quarter after ten. Everyone knew the Stocks started at ten. But I saw nothing.

Maybe I was lost in the time-space continuum? Or maybe the Stocks really didn't exist? Had I ever been told first-hand that it would be here? It had only ever come through the friend of a friend or as legend. Seriously, why would people meet in the woods? Is a forest at all like a record shop?

I sat down on a bench. But I didn't get back on the trolley when it came around. Or on the next one. I wasn't in a hurry. The air here was good. It was a place of solitude.

Then, out of nowhere (there was no trolley in sight!), there appeared two longhaired guys a bit older than me, and they wandered past me. I ran after them.

– Are the Stocks happening today?

They looked back at me, neither surprised, nor unsurprised:

– Yeah, yeah. But later, man.

Everything I had heard was true. The Stocks really did exist. It took me only ten minutes to lose my faith, but I needed only a second to regain it.

I bummed around and walked circles at the trolley stop. I walked to the strange lake and saw swans. Soon the scene I had always imagined started to take shape – I was joined by death-metalers, and heavy-metalers and even girls. It was exactly as I'd imagined, only ten times smaller.

Which isn't a bad coefficient, really. Our minds are bigger than the world. When you take a kid to the zoo, and I mean a kid who has read a lot and thought a lot, and this kid sees an elephant, the kid doesn't say anything, but thinks – it's not all that big. The kid thinks this to himself because he doesn't want fantasy to begrudge reality. But the elephant seems small. Only later, when fantasy starts to fade and we look take a closer look at the elephant, which is snorting softly and scattering hay over its own head, when we're suddenly face to face with this elephant, we finally realise: God, is it huge!

The elephant was gathering in the woods, the woods that had just a minute ago been so empty. I joined the crowd that had stopped in a clearing among the trees. I'd finally made it.

The time has come to describe the phenomenon of the Stocks with a little more detail. It really did take place in a small clearing in the woods. Around twenty people had showed up; now and then one of them disappeared into the shrubs and a new person took their place, but not at any specific interval. For convenience, there were several paths that led to the clearing. The biggest came from the trolley stop. A group of men in their fifties were chatting to the left of the path. One of them had laid out some records on the ground, as if to sell them, but without making a big deal out of it. I wanted to go over to them and look at the records. I had a real appreciation for older music. Like the Beatles. Earlier because they'd been so popular; now because they seemed so strange.

But I wasn't here for the Beatles. So I joined the other group, the one to the right of the path. And the people in this group could be divided into three subgroups.

There were a couple of girls whose hair was almost as long as their skirts. But I got the impression that they weren't regulars here; no, they'd probably tagged along with someone.

I wanted to belong to the second subgroup. These were young guys with long hair and various other defining characteristics. Leather jackets, long hair, metal bracelets. They seemed more legit than the guys in Jelgava. Each of them was wearing a band T-shirt – Amorphis, Slayer, Cannibal Corpse, even Mayhem, Burzum among others. And their hair, the hair! One of them even had a beard, the longest I'd ever seen; it flowed into his hair in a downward stream, symbolizing a philosophical approach to the world and an internal rebellion. If you opened a dictionary to the word 'metalhead', this guy's picture would be next to the definition.

The third subgroup was odd. They were totally, completely normal people, older than the second subgroup, but younger than the hippies to the left of the path. They wore linen pants and patterned sweaters. Their hair was short. They were the most normal people in the world, but they stood around here like fish in water and seemed to embody some form of realness and belonging.

The circulation of music, opinions and everything else took place with everyone just standing around and talking. There were no long counters or cash registers. There wasn't even anything by the hippies with their records on the ground. I went and stood next to someone to join the conversation and get a better idea of things. I'd been warned about what the people in Riga could be like, so I felt confident in joining them. I needed to bring real music back to Jelgava. I was doing this for the good of my hometown.

Everyone was only talking about metal. One guy with even longer hair came up and announced authoritatively that Cannibal Corpse hadn't put out anything good since after *Tomb of the Mutilated*. He was wearing a *Bleeding* shirt, though, and *Bleeding* had come out after *Tomb of the Mutilated*. This guy with the curious shirt choice, the first guy I met there, was no regular guy. He turned to me suddenly:

– You got a cigarette?

His voice was languid, almost sleepy. His eyes, too, seemed to always be half-closed. After I gave him the cigarette he held out his hand:

– Tom. Sinister.

Yes, my friends, that's how I met Sinister. Just like that. It was the same Sinisters who today has 1,835 friends and is known by all. But he's not the only one I met that night! There was Cannibal, also known as Gints. He was so present at every metal-related event in Riga that I wonder whether he wasn't the one who organised them. What's more, Gints was always sober and photographing everything. He was also the singer for Latvia's heaviest group, Denervation. I don't know if the band ever played a real gig, it was that heavy. I also met Ēriks, also called Krabators, who was wearing an Amorphis shirt. He knew everything about music and responded to every world event with a sad smile, but at the same time was always telling funny stories from his own life. Then there was Venom, one of the grandfathers of Latvian black metal, who generously admitted that he had been put on this path by a man with the curious moniker Sonnenmensch – he was also always at the Stocks, a gloomy music connoisseur who listened to ten new albums a day. There was also a younger guy who went by Schnapps. What he was known for, though... I can't remember.

I stood with them in the clearing and had the sensation that I wasn't standing on the pine-needle covered ground, but on the world. Now and then my new friends would proclaim some manifesto:

– I'm so sick of Heaven Grey. It's time for that band to break up!

I couldn't believe my poor ears. At the time, Heaven Grey was Latvia's most notable death-doom group; they sounded almost like groups from abroad. They were our representatives on Olympus, proof that people could make it to the stars! I experienced a quiet horror at these words, but also a quiet giddiness thanks to my natural instinct to defy authority. These Rigans were unbelievable.

But wasn't it more unbelievable how friendly they were? They were none of the things Death had warned me of. No-one wanted to drink my money away for me, though of course I'd be happy to let them if I had an extra fiver, or any fiver at all. The two lats I had with me were going to serve a different purpose. One of the odd guys with short hair seemed to sense this and turned to me:

– What are you looking for, young man?

He spoke just like that, in that prissy manner of an old lord that normally pissed me off, but here in the woods felt legit, as if this form of address was being reinstated with a purpose – even though there was definitely a hint of irony in his voice.

I didn't know how to answer. Everything! At least – a lot. And then he came to my aid, handing me a blue binder filled with lists of bands and album titles, most of them new to me. Thankfully, I knew what I was looking for. There, Asphyx's *Last One on Earth*.

– And for the other side?

This may confuse the twenty-first-century reader, but I knew he was talking about the cassette. What did I want recorded on the other side? I hadn't thought about what else I'd want. I turned the pages slowly, looking through the list until my eyes fell on something unfamiliar, but that left an impression. This – My Dying Bride's *Turn Loose the Swans*.

That's how my collection wound up with this strange mash-up of a cassette, which had death metal on one side and doom metal on the other. It was an interesting genre. It wasn't a favourite of the Latvian radio programme 'Rockade', which called it the 'depressed rock of doomsday'. But the dictionary clearly labelled it 'destiny'. The metal of destiny. And it had been recorded on this cassette.

Fifteen years later I read a review of the My Dying Bride album, which said that no one who suffered from depression should listen to it. If only I'd known that back then! Then I would've worked extra hard to introduce this album to Jelgava, a city in which depression was everyone's ultimate goal. My dying bride, what a name. The night they formed the band (beer, there had supposedly been lots of beer), the guys had considered My Dying Child. Why hadn't they gone with that? A name like that may have deterred me. But to kill off your unwed bride... I couldn't say no to that.

Death got a hold of *Last One on Earth* (which he didn't end up liking that much; he thought *The Rack* was better), but destiny made its way into Jelgava, as if there weren't enough of it already, and I fell even deeper into this iron depression. I'd end up spending hours listening to this music, contemplating the world.

But then, in the woods, I hadn't yet listened to it. I didn't even have the tape yet. This polite man took my empty tape and my money and put both in his bag without another word. I didn't say anything either. The local order of things was clear: give them an empty tape and money (one santim per minute recorded), then come back a week later for your tape, now excitingly full. After that night, I went to the Stocks every Sunday, arriving with an empty tape and leaving with a full one, but also leaving with a new desire for what I had to wait a week to get. It's an endless cycle, because I always showed up to claim my prize with yet another empty vessel in my pocket. It was like a cigarette, which Oscar Wilde described as 'the perfect type of a perfect pleasure', since it made you feel good by leaving you wanting more.

Ēriks looked at me with a sad, teasing smile and asked:

– Aren't you that guy who's collecting information about bands to write about Latvia's metal history?

It was a mysterious question, and I answered just as mysteriously:

– This place has such a strange beauty to it! The leaves have some sort of bumps on them. Are the trees sick?

The leaves of the maple trees really were covered with black bumps, like teenage acne. But then I was distracted by hair. Amazingly long hair; I'd never seen a guy with hair like this! It would make any girl jealous. And not just girls – any metalhead would be jealous, too. All the red in Ireland was there, washed with the blood of Cuhullin. That hair reminded me of something. Maybe something in my metalhead genes? None of my friends had hair like that. But wait, it's the girl from the car that stopped for us, the one that then kicked us out on the side of the road on our first attempt to get to the Stocks. The same colour and style, the same intelligent shape of the skull. Look, she's turning around, those are the same eyes that I'd seen in the rear-view mirror! What a coincidence. Now the girl was glaring at me, and I finally saw her entire face.

What? It was chubby Nellija from the other class! I'd never looked close at her hair or eyes. In the best case you looked the chubby girls in the chest. She was dressed differently, in boots and a long skirt. She looked at me. Glared at me, aggressively. She could ruin everything. She could come up to me and say:

– Did you finish your homework? And why aren't you at Sunday school? Will you lend me your Imants Kalniņš albums? I know you like good, old-fashioned folk music like that.

We'd never actually spoken to one another, but I felt like she could unmask me, reveal to everyone and to me that I was who I was, and that I wanted to be something else.

– You're that four-eyed nerd everyone makes fun of. Hey, everyone, let's laugh at him! Go ahead, he's afraid of everything!

But she said nothing. She turned away and continued her conversation. She had things to talk about. The guy she was with looked full of himself. And was dressed very nicely, but enviably metalheadish – a long coat, lots of chains and other metal accessories. His expression was one of total awareness of his superiority, but his posture was one of an anxious fear that one of the nearby animals may touch him. He was even cautious while talking to Nellija. But how did she even get here? How did she get in? How can this be the real deal if even chubby Nellija is one of them? No, there must be some mistake.

I'd finished my transaction. The clean-cut guy had my money – his name was Didzis, imagine that, just Didzis – and the following Sunday I had to come back to pick up my tape. Another of the clean-cut guys, who went by Oķec, said that I should look at what he had on offer, too. I already fit in. At the end of the night, when everyone parted after unspoken good-byes and headed home, I wasn't alone. I walked out with Sinister, and we talked about everything in the world. That is to say, we only talked about music, but we hit it off.

– If you're into death-metal, you should really check out this band, Torture. It's two brothers. One of them died in a car accident.

Sinister knew how to talk about music.

– Another good one is this band from Australia, Deströyer 666. The frontman was convinced he was a vampire. But his girlfriend didn't believe him, so he bit her.

In turn, I could only repeat what I'd heard from Death. I could, of course, always make something up. Like Gilkins used to make up movies. "Guys, guys, I saw *Predator II*. At my cousin's in Riga. It was awesome. Schwarzenegger stands there smoking a cigarette, a grenade launcher in the other hand. Then he looks out the window and..." And so we listened to a detailed description of the entire movie, without realising that it hadn't even been filmed yet.

But Sinister's knowledge seemed encyclopaedic and iron-clad, so I tried to tread carefully:

– I also like this band called Paradox...

I'd never heard of a band like that, but it seemed like an appropriate name for one. Sinister was unflappable:

– Which Paradox? The one with one 'x' or the one with two?

– With two.

– They're pretty good.

I checked later and, paradoxically, there really were both a Paradox and a Paradoxx.

We were smoking my cigarettes, and had already made it out of the woods. There turned out to be a little window in the hut at the trolley endpoint from which they sold beer. A group of women was milling about the window. One of them was visibly pregnant; in one hand she held a beer in a jar labelled 'Green Peas', and a cigarette in the other. But she looked at us as if we were the most unnatural aspect of this scene, and even elbowed her neighbour, a woman holding a jar of beer with a 'Mayonnaise' label on it. They both had flowers on their dresses.

The trolley pulled up like a limo and we got in, obviously ignoring the issue of tickets. I glanced around to see whether that lunatic Nellija wasn't in it, too, but she wasn't; maybe her dad had come to get her. But the pretentious guy in the long coat and chains was here; he was sitting up front by the window, his body language broadcasting that he wanted to be left alone to despise the world. Sinister kept talking in that relaxed way of his, already making plans.

– The best would be if we could have a radio station, a station for metalheads. We'd talk about new and old groups, about the philosophy of metal. Then we wouldn't have this complicated process of getting music, then they'd be sending us their music themselves. From all over the world.

For a moment, the pretentious guy tore his attention away from despising the world and looked at us. He looked sceptical of this plan.

Sinister thought for a moment. He started to rummage through his bag; it was full of tapes and a carton of Quattro cigarettes. He pulled out a tape:

– Mortiis. Man, do I like this guy. He had plastic surgery done to elongate his nose and ears, so he'd look like a troll.

Then Tom looked at me, remembered who I was, and asked:

– You got any cash?

– One lat. You want to get a drink?

He tugged on a lock of his hair and closed his bag.

– No, I don't drink. But we need a lot more than that. Like a hundred lats.

– I know where we can get it.

– Yeah?

He looked me directly in the eyes, deep into my head, which at the moment was totally empty, and said in a quiet voice:

– Then we need to form a band.

Back then a lot of people wanted to form bands. Whoever suggested it usually offered the first person the lead guitar role and also knew someone who could play the drums, but they'd find a bass-guitarist along the way. And if you asked the guy who suggested it in the first place what he'd do, the answer was logical:

– Me? I'll sing.

Sinister was far more serious about it. He always seemed to be half-asleep, but in a constant state of excitement, almost like van Gogh. He talked about the necessity to say what no-one else would say, what no one else thought of; he said the exact things I was thinking in my mind. And there and then, he said that we'd need an electric guitar – someone would have to find the money to get an electric guitar. A guitar like that will translate everything you want to say.

But Tom, what will you do?

He wasn't that interested in what everyone else was doing to try and set himself apart.

– I'll sing.

And he turned back to the window, knowing that, for the time being, I didn't have to say anything, that I was already enchanted, that

I already knew it all anyway. I sat facing forwards, determined, not to watch for my stop – I was imagining an unexpected destiny, the one we'd been waiting for and the one we thought we deserved, the one we tend to be afraid of when we finally come face to face with it. But not me – I faced forwards, determined.

5

It was incredibly snowy and cold. My housemates and I were outside in the snow looking for the neighbour's dog. It was an ancient spaniel; the dog had always been nice to me, and I liked to watch as he cautiously climbed the stairs back up to its flat each day. But now he was lost, out in the freezing night, and we went to help our neighbours look for him. I found him. He was trudging about in a snowdrift, his chin was white – I couldn't tell if it was from the snow or from age. The dog raised its head and spoke to me in a low growl:

– Don't worry. Stop tremble. It's bugging me. Like you're some kind of terrier bitch.

Then I woke up. Alone and freezing. Like I hadn't slept well. Once I'd rubbed the sleep out of my eyes I remembered that I wasn't at home. Right, I'd crashed at Zombie's place last night. There's the drawing of a man licking blood off a razor, and there's the contorted face of a devil, posters for Deicide, Cannibal Corpse, Napalm Death. Very homey. I stood up.

In the morning I wake up and reach for my shoes.
But I look down and see I'm already wearing them.

My mom taught me that poem when I was little, and today it was true. Mom. Right. I was supposed to go with my mom to visit friends. That's why I was here. I mean, no, my mom didn't ship me off to watch horror films with metalheads, no. But that's why I didn't go with the rest of my friends to the Smilga dacha today. I was still bummed about it; it would have been a real metal-filled Saturday. Death had asked:

– Maybe you can still come?

While Zombie had snapped:

– What's with you? Man up! I have other places I should be, too!

But I didn't have the guts to ditch my mom. Which is why I was here now. What time was it? I walked through the apartment. It was empty. Not even Zombie's mom was here. I called home. I won't go into the details of the conversation, but when I hung up it was clear that I had to get home as soon as possible. I went back into the bedroom. I drank some water from a ceramic mug that had been set next to the bed, and looked for something to cheer me up. I spotted a collection of tapes, though pretty small compared to the mass amounts of VHS. There were a few good things here: Sepultura, Slayer, Pantera, but I'd already heard it all. Tristitia's *One in Darkness*. That was exactly what I needed right now. Tin, tin, tin, tintirintin. I had to listen to the acoustic intro. One song can't make you late for anything.

Why am I sitting here when I should be racing home? I went to the front door, but it was locked. Zombie's door didn't have one of those latchkeys, and you couldn't open it from the inside. I remember him saying last night that I should just leave at the same time as his mom, if I was going to be a traitor. She usually left later in the day. But left she had, and without noticing me. The intro was over, and the song I'd been waiting for came on – metal always expressed whatever I was feeling at the moment. 'Pray for forgiveness!' Who was I going to pray to for forgiveness? I needed to get out of here, but I just sat and waited for the next song. I was ready to wait for 'Hymn of Lunacy', which is exactly halfway through the album, but I had to get back to Ozolnieki.

I was able to open the balcony door. Why was the world so bright? It was the first snow. I'd seen it in my dream, but my forgetfulness denied me that prophetic pride.

I looked down into the abyss. I was on the second storey. Two metres per storey, so four metres up. Or maybe it was three metres per storey? Then it was six, total. That was nothing. The ground was padded with soft snow and dog shit. If this were the fourth storey, like our apartment, then fine, it would be obvious that I couldn't jump. But this was on the fence, and it was exactly the kind of fence I needed to get over. Would Zombie jump? He would, even if he had the key. They'd all jump, and then they'd ask me – why didn't you jump, too?

This balcony was full of memories, of life. Pūpols had puked here, and the neighbour's cat had eaten all the croquettes. Zombie's fridge had stopped working, and the croquettes had been set out on the balcony. Zombie had blamed Death for the theft, his friends were always hungry when they came over, and Death went outside for a smoke more often than the rest of us. Death had been really offended, but we'd had a good laugh about it.

I stepped over the railing, clung onto it and slid down as far as I could. It couldn't be that much farther to the ground. The music playing was still very appropriate for the moment. I jumped.

It happened fast. Once on the ground I tried to figure out if my plan had worked. Now I was lying facedown in snow or dog shit. I stood up, but fell back over, and my leg really hurt. And it didn't just hurt; it wouldn't listen to me. I rolled myself over carefully and lay on my back in the snow. And here we are.

I could hear 'Hymn of Lunacy' playing from inside the apartment. Finally. This here was true metal. Lying broken in the snow. I rolled onto my side – god, it hurt – I wanted to get a cigarette out of my pocket. Even though my lips were trembling, I wanted to put a cigarette between them, to keep up appearances in this monumental life-event. But I'd left my cigarettes upstairs. I'm not going to make it, mom, forgive me, I'm here all alone, my friends are gone, and I'm gone, forgive me, mom, come save me and I won't hurt anymore.

Footsteps. Someone was coming. I tried to look inconspicuous, casual. It worked; the footsteps went past and faded away without indicating any real interest, though maybe picking up speed as they passed.

Upstairs, 'Dance of the Selenites' started. The last song:

Etheral, natural
Leave me your wings
Of dust, of muck, of moon and dirt!

Etheral, natural, I've never really understood what that really means, leave me your wings, now that's what I'm talking about! It would be amazing to come back home with dirty moon-wings. But nothing happened, and it was only years later that I understood why. I'd misheard the lyrics a bit. What they were actually singing was:

Etherial noctua
Leening your wings
Of dust, of much, of mundane!

I heard more people coming. This time I sat up halfway. A group of thirty-somethings walked by, looking at me with forced smiles.

Then the last song ended. But I stayed where I was. I wished someone I knew would walk by. I wouldn't want my friends to see me in a moment of weakness, but I wished they were here. Even Kārlis' dad. Or Pūpols' brother. They lived nearby. But the only people walking by was an unfamiliar, middle-aged couple. They looked nice, and I said:

– Excuse me...

I was going to say something else, to explain somehow – but I didn't get the chance because they walked right by me.

I forgot to add it was cold. The first snow was making a point of it. My poor body had melted it quickly, but it just froze again, and was covering me in a new layer. I didn't want to lie there any more. When the next people came by, I spoke more directly:

– Excuse me, could you please...

And again, I didn't need to finish my sentence because they walked on by, too. Students, old women, intellectuals. I had no shame left, and I announced:

– Help me, please... I broke my leg.

Those more sensitive turned their heads away, and I understood that I'd become an invisible and mute ghost. Even my leg felt more corporeal and real than ever before, rooted to the ground, reverberating with every footstep of every person who walked by.

– Please, can someone call my house, the number is...

Oh, girls! They weren't bad-looking, either... It was an old fantasy of mine – to be injured in the company of girls. They'd think it was manly, they'd fawn over me like a wounded soldier. And offer themselves up to me, or whatever it is they do. They were almost close, lifting their feet like the Clydesdales.

– Hello, ladies! Could you please give me a hand, I broke my leg...

– Gah!

One of them screeched and took an elegant leap away from me. Her knees had an interesting shape to them. I promised myself that I'd remember those knees forever.

– Don't be scared, it's just me, I broke my leg, could you please...

They laughed, either about their friend's reaction, or about me, I don't know. I watched their backs as they walked away, and, almost like in my previous life, the one up there on Zombie's balcony, it seemed I was seeing a bottomless pit taking shape, and though her bottom was still right there, and it was still interesting, it drew further and further away, swaying gently, and now I really was in a pit, bottom-less.

My lips were still trembling from the cold. My entire body was shaking, as were my thoughts. What was I going to do with just one leg? If I ever made it out of here. I remembered the first time I'd ever gone to the Square[1]. One of the first of the thousands of amazing things I saw there was a guy in a wheelchair. He had long hair and a leather jacket, and a beer in one hand. People were racing him around, taking sharp turns, some of them jumping on the back to ride along with him, and he looked happy. I watched him and remembered this kid, Andrītis, from back in kindergarten. I'd found him once in the playground behind the cypress trees, pressed up against the wall and crying. Andrītis had a lame leg, it hurt, and he couldn't run around with the rest of us. Nothing on me hurt back then, but I didn't want to run around, either. So he and I sat behind the trees and smashed rocks together. We were trying to make fire. I can clearly remember that Andrītis smashed his rocks, and they sparked.

But here and now, a car suddenly pulled up, very close, where cars weren't supposed to pull up. The door opened and the music of Mikhail Krug filled the air. Two men got out of the car and approached me. They were both wearing patent leather shoes. This spoke volumes.

– What're you doing down there?

I turned my head to them and tried to talk, but my teeth wouldn't stop chattering.

– Why're you on the ground, Rapunzel?

I managed to explain something to them. A hand grabbed me by the collar and pulled me to my feet. I tried to stand, but couldn't. The hand, convinced I couldn't stand on my own, let go, and I fell back into the snow. They men talked something over. A cigarette butt landed by my nose.

---

1   Līvu Square in Riga, then colloquially known as 'Veldze'. Before it became a popular pasture for herds of brutish British tourists, it used to be a forum for the alternative lifestyle.

Someone grabbed me by the collar again, I lost contact with the horizontal surface and rose into the air. The ground-level viewpoint I'd become accustomed to disappeared and was replaced by a face. Ho-ho, the face said. It was the kind of face I'd usually avert my eyes and cross the street to get away from. I'd never been this close to one of them, but I was literally in his hands.

I had no idea where he was taking me, dangling above the whole world like that. I managed to think – if only my friends came back just now, I'd say hello to them from the clutches of this massive, random thug. He brought me over to the car – it was a black BMW – and put me in the back seat. The other guy, short and stout, pulled me by the collar from the other door and sat me upright. Then they both got in up front, and we drove off. A few lucky charms dangled from the rear-view mirror: an icon, a rosary, a miniature skull and a naked doll. I could also see both of their leather-clad shoulders and their shaved heads. They both seemed to be older than me.

Mikhail Krug stopped singing. The tape had died. The short, stout one cried out in dismay:

– Hey, it stopped! It stopped!

And he started to pound the entire radio panel with his fist. The tall guy told him he'd tear his guts out, explained that the stereo wasn't the problem, and told him to put in a different tape. Then he braked suddenly, stuck his head out the window and shouted:

– Oho, yeah, shake that ass!

I didn't even try to look, though it would have probably been worth it. It was enough to observe the two of them, and now and then I just wanted to close my eyes and my ears. They both smoked non-stop and were always in motion. The short one was swearing about the four-tape collection, unable to pick one. The tall one was talking about some mysterious character who was a 'little cunt, shit, getting in-fucking-volved with the cops, fuck'. It was all so fascinating, that I didn't even want to ask where we were going. I stared at the ceiling of the car and listened to the music they had finally decided on:

An enemy is an enemy forever,
Don't break bread with him, don't invite him into your home,
Even if the air smells of peace,

Even if he is meek, he is still the enemy.
If he, like you, has not squandered his honour,
Once an enemy, always an enemy.
Be true in your aim, and stay your hand,
You will be the one to die if you spare your enemy.

The song wasn't terrible, though there was no double-bass drum kit, no electric guitar. But it had bit of an ache to it. Sometimes I'd secretly listen to something totally un-metal. But even Grishnackh admitted to sometimes listening to whatever else was on, especially in the car. We made a turn and seemed to slow down. Someone shouted into the window:

– You can't pull in here!

A few turns later we came to a stop. They opened the door and pulled me out. We were at the New Hospital. But why? It was a good joke – now they were going to beat me up. It would've been even better had they taken me to the morgue first.

The thugs held me up under the arms and carried me into the hospital – to registration, to the X-ray room (nothing was broken, just a few torn ligaments), and to get bandaged up. While my leg was being wrapped in a cast, they stood in the hallway under a palm tree and smoked, and convinced the orderly on-duty to be their third in a game of *zole*. Once the cast was finished, they carried me back to the car, drove me home, and helped me up to the fourth storey. My mother's fury, which was why I'd been in such a rush, quickly turned into worry, relief, kindness. She profusely thanked my rescuers and asked them to stay for coffee, wanted to give them a bite to eat, money, but they just waved her off:

– Aw, no, stop! God bless.

They drove away across the flowerbeds. But I could finally lie back on our old couch, my leg propped up, and think – I wonder what my friends were up to?

6

There's a building on the outskirts of Jelgava that many tourists find interesting. It's on the edge of a park, surrounded by shrubbery, as if defying the reality of the rest of the city. There were other buildings like it, such as the Courland Knighthood manor or Hotel Linde, but those have been razed to the ground three times over. But this one is still standing, tangible like a ghost with a body. It has a classical facade with four columns, though maybe they're a little on the narrow side to qualify as true classicism. It's like the new city just sat down on top of it, getting it all dirty; but the building still proudly carries its name: Villa Medem.

The Medems were an important family. Wasn't it Konrad von Mandern, or Medem, who had founded Mitau? Yes, the same. But that's not all – do you remember the Medem sisters, the lovely Dorothea and Elise? Was there anyone in Kurzeme who had called them anything but 'beautiful Dorothea and clever Elise'? The beautiful Dorothea became the Duchess of Courland and lover to Talleyrand. The clever Elise became a poet. She didn't even crack a smile when Casanova arrived in Jelgava. She must have been five at the time. And even when Cagliostro stayed at Villa Medem fifteen years later, Elise didn't fall in love with him. The count taught her how to communicate with the dead, promised her travels to distant planets and the power to create new worlds herself. All that probably didn't happen at the Villa, though. Cagliostro did stay in Jelgava in 1779, but I think the Villa was built by Johann Adam Berlitz in 1818, or even as late as 1836. But what I *do* know is that 1994 is when the Junkyard moved in. A metal club that was open Friday nights.

I had spent a lot of time trying on clothes in front of the mirror. I still didn't have a single, real article of metalhead-appropriate clothing. My jeans were unripped, but at least my shirt was untucked and the tongues of my shoes pulled out. When I showed up at Kārlis' place to get them, Pūpols looked me over:

– Not bad. I was worried you were going to wear that lame blue shirt you have.

By the way, none of them had noticed I was limping.

We had a strict ritual for going to the Junkyard. Once we – Kārlis, his brother, Death, Tonijs, Pūpols, Zombie and me – were all at Kārlis', we'd go next door to Zombie's place. Probably because it was easier to drink there and he had a bigger TV. Which was important because our ritual included watching the RBS Tops. I had always watched the show, but here and now it was different. The music scene had radicalised, gone were the days when we rejoiced at Nirvana coming in at number one. Now, Death was going around school with a petition to get Obituary's 'Don't Care' at the top. He sent the RBS studios a large sheet of paper with a drawing of Obituary's logo and around seventy signatures. The studio got the letter, but for some reason the song never made it to the charts. But it was just as well that neither Nirvana nor Obituary were included, because now anything on the tops was subject to ridicule. All the Soundgardens and Offsprings – half-assed garbage. Bon Jovi – a joke, girl rock. For some unknown reason, though, Sinead O'Connor was spared. But the closer we got to the top of the charts, the more fun we had. The social majority's attempts to go alternative had decreased, the masks had fallen away, and the top positions in the charts were dominated by pure pop: East 17, Boyz II Men and, at number one, Take That. We watched closely and kept up a running commentary. Zombie seemed to know all the lyrics by heart and sang along in a singularly parodied operatic vibrato. The others made remark after clever remark, and made fun of every move the pop stars made. The new generation of rock was traitors, neither hot nor cold, and we spat them out in silence. But pop was the proper world order, one in which we needed to be the minority laughing at the majority. We watched the guys from Take That as they danced in the rain, and knew exactly what should never be.

When the show was over it was finally time to head out. Down to the street, a few turns, shrubs, shouting at the other groups of people heading to the same place, the sound of music already playing, possibly Bolt Thrower, and then we were there. In front of a classical building with four columns maybe a little on the narrow side. A noble and tender feeling came over me. This was *the* time and *the* place. I was surrounded by my peers, a sea of ripped jeans and flannel shirts, trainers and army boots.

And in this place of total security, Nellija was suddenly coming straight towards me. Nellija and a friend of hers, who was a lot prettier than she was. Headed straight towards us, as if they were leaving the Junkyard. I tried to look in the other direction; I didn't want to talk to her. But she didn't say hi, just called over:

– You limping?

She didn't wait for an answer; she had said what she'd wanted to say and they moved on. My friends looked at me, and Kārlis' brother said:

– You really are limping. Why's that?

I finally told them the whole story. Their reactions split them into two groups. Death and one of the others said:

– Are you insane? Why'd you do that? What's wrong with you? You could've hung out and watched a horror film or a porno, found something to eat in the kitchen, a perfect day. Why did you jump? Are you out of your fucking mind? Idiot. Moron.

Zombie and someone else said:

– Bullshit!

They weren't surprised that I'd somehow managed to get out of the apartment – they just didn't believe me. But it was all forgotten pretty quickly as we reached the front of the Villa, and everyone went to say hello to people they knew. Everyone except me because I didn't know anyone else.

Well, it wasn't that bad. DJ and his entourage were coming down the front steps. So it wasn't only the lost children of the world who had become metalheads, but also some of its darker authorities. My heart skipped a beat – remember, DJ was the one who used to get on my case now and again. But would he leave me be here? He spotted me immediately. He came over to me, very close to me, and said:

– You're here too? What's up, weezy!

Then something really stupid happened. See, I was as fragile as a flower petal, a nerd, who had spent his entire life getting made fun of and pushed around. I just couldn't take anymore. And that's why, that's why. DJ's greeting had been extremely friendly, but "weezy" made something in me snap.

I shook his outstretched hand and replied:

– Go fuck yourself.

I think he honestly didn't believe what he'd heard:

– Say what?

My response to his greeting was an unusual one. DJ was a cult personality in this scene, and had always been a central figure to any scene, so he wasn't used to hearing things like that. He hadn't considered that this kind of response was more likely to come from a coward than someone with guts. I repeated myself:

– Go fucking fuck yourself.

– What?

He looked like he was going to faint. He jerked his hand out of mine and grabbed me by the neck. I tried to twist away to one side, Kārlis' brother stepped in, and it must've looked like a fight had broken out because suddenly there more people involved, maybe everyone in the immediate area. The world turned upside down. But there was no blood spilled yet. The number-one tactic applied to any metalhead fight was for someone to put his entire body between two potential enemies and shove them away from one another, keeping them at arm's length. With enough people doing this, the scuffle was finally broken up and the mob calmed down, scattered across the perimeter of the Villa courtyard. There were still two guys, completely unrelated to our initial exchange, who were dangerously close to one another, fists raised, shouting, No YOU shut up and listen to me – but they, too, were quickly separated. DJ was on the other side of the courtyard; he looked around until he spotted me and shouted with existential despair:

– Fuck, but why, but he said!

But he was already being carried into the Junkyard – let's go, time for some music. I was brought to stand by the railing of the front steps – stay here, have a cigarette. I had just taken a seat on the railing, safe between Kārlis and his brother, when some unseen force grabbed all three of us and we fell backwards into the darkness. Zombie had snuck up behind us and yanked us down; he just couldn't leave well enough alone. For a second I had honestly thought that I was going to crack my head in two, that after escaping one enemy I was going to die because of my friend's practical joke. We got back to our feet, and Kārlis' brother asked:

– So what happened back there?

I had to say something, but I didn't have a good answer. There was a lot to explain. About my internal exile, my childhood decision to read about forts instead of building them for real outside, etcetera. I mumbled something in response. Kārlis' brother said:

– You're one to talk. It's your first time here and you're already fucking things up.

And he was absolutely right. Luckily Zombie didn't care about any of it. He said:

– The music tonight really blows, huh?

It was typical Zombie, coming to this castle of dreams and criticising it. But he was right, the music playing was something industrial, Psychopomps, maybe. Ugo must've been the one deejaying. Back then he was more into the punk and industrial stuff.

I had made my way to the front door and could see the darkness spilling out of it and onto the city, but I still wanted to be inside. Then DJ came out with his entourage, Ugo among them – so who was deejaying? – and my friends casually pushed me inside, out of their line of sight.

It was amazing! A large, dark room, filled with shadows of dukes. A row of theatre seating along one wall. Someone was sleeping on the ground by the chairs. Further along the wall were some girls. Wasn't one of them Kristīne? There was a raised platform at the front of the room, a makeshift stage. On it was a table, and on the table were some stereos and some speakers; and climbing up behind them was Death, who had just replaced Ugo. He grabbed onto the edge of the table; the table wobbled and the tapes fell to the floor, but he finally managed, and soon we were listening to Napalm Death's 'Suffer the Children':

Your unflappable conceptions
Moralistic views
Never open to criticism
Your overpowering ruse

Promises of sanctuary
In eternal bliss
With starry eyes and cash in hand
Pledge all to the master plan

Everyone there either sang along out loud or at least mouthed the words. Death was the only one headbanging; he'd somehow gotten off the stage and was whipping his head around in front of the speakers. The idea behind headbanging is to achieve a trance-like state by attacking the fortress of your consciousness – the brain. Your brain gets slapped around when you violently shake your head like that, and our inner worlds are able to momentarily free themselves of thought and coming into direct contact with existence... In brief, it's a form of meditation. Of course, it's also a way to remind the world how long your hair is, kind of like a pissing contest, only more refined. My inner world really needed some calming down and I could get it by headbanging, but my hair wasn't long enough. So I just stood there. But then a guy with hair even shorter than mine bounded over to join Death, and started to whip his non-existent mop of hair around. He even shouted up to the empty deejay chair:

– Decide! Play Decide next!

Decide was a fairly popular band at the time because they were loud and sang about numerous Satans. All the nutrients and vitamins you could ever need. I had seen this shorthaired, lawless guy somewhere before... But Napalm Death songs are short, and Death was already scrambling up on the stage to line up the next song. He had a good heart and a good sense of hearing, and Decide's 'Sacrificial Suicide' blasted through the speakers – and the demo version, at that. It's a really great song. The vocals were so energetic and hissing and you could only make out one word that was repeatrā, ed throughout the entire song: 'Satan'. The shorthaired guy went crazy and started to scream, repeating at regular intervals:

– Death to all that is sacred!

I wondered where he'd gotten that from. No Latvian band had lyrics like that. How had he come up with the phrase? Then I remembered where I'd seen him before. In church – of course. He may even have been an altar boy. Everything fell back into place, everything was right in the world again. You have to be a priest to take part in a Black Mass. Well, or a pretty girl. There were a few over there by the wall – and wasn't one of them Kristīne?

Obviously, there was a lot to see and contemplate at the Junkyard. And I did just that, but something kept niggling at the back of my brain, making me look over my shoulder now and again. I'd made an enemy here, after all. And then DJ came into the room and headed for the stage. Kārlis' brother gestured to me – let's go outside for a smoke! Although clearly you could smoke inside, too.

I'd come here to be with friends. How had I wound up with an enemy? I looked back towards the stage – he was talking to Death, but watching me. I looked away, slowly, bored, and headed outside with my friends.

As we smoked, a face balanced on top of a thick stump toddled over to where we were. It was Čiriks, a chubby kid who always showed up wherever a potential fight was brewing. No-one had ever seen him take part in a fight. He was only an instigator, a motivator, a goader; a little sadist who'd wriggle out of the mud and threaten others with his strong friends, people he'd hang around in an strangely perverse way. And now here he was, his little face screwed up, asking:

– Which one of you came at DJ?

I hadn't really even come at him; Čiriks must be talking about something else, right? Kārlis' brother answered for me.

– Nothing happened, it's all good.

He was a little older than the rest of us and wasn't afraid of the Čiriks of the world. He just knew it was best not to get involved with them. Čiriks looked first to him, then me with disdain, and then slithered off down the stairs.

We resumed our conversations. I laughed along with everyone else, but I didn't feel right. And didn't want anyone to know. Like when a person comes home drunk and the rest of the house is still awake, even though it's midnight, and the person smiles in an attempt to show them he hasn't had anything to drink; he says something funny, a joke, but knows that it came out wrong and off the mark. Then the person quickly says something else to fix it, weaves an intricate contextual web into which the stupid things he's said can settle like pearls on a thread – but he can feel he's only digging his hole deeper, that it would be better to break off mid-sentence, but no, he has to say something, and his family exchanges silent looks with one another. For example, Zombie had just casually announced that he had our physics teacher stashed away in his closet at home, and I, wanting to be like my friend, repeated his earlier sentiment:

– The music tonight really blows, huh?

Tonijs looked at me, and the curls of his hair tightened:

– But it's Ministry!

Pūpols giggled. He knew how much I liked Ministry, and I did. And then there was DJ, coming outside with his arm around Death. But Death immediately dropped his arm from DJ's shoulders and put it around mine. Without any build-up, he whispered into my ear:

– DJ is going to come over here and say something to you, and you just go along with it. Don't make a scene. He's batshit, don't take it personally.

Then he stepped away and wrapped his arm around one of the four classical columns holding up the Villa's gable. DJ sat down next to me and asked to bum a cigarette. He inhaled deeply and asked:

– You know the band Unleashed?

That was the big question. Music could right all wrongs. Why didn't he ask about At the Gates, Brutality or Carcass. Fine, I get it, it would be dumb to ask about Carcass; it would be like asking if I knew what Europe was. But he could've asked about Demilich. Then I could talk and talk, and he'd understand. I'd never even heard of Unleashed. I said:

– Sure.

Kārlis chimed in:

– That bugger Pūpols has two of their albums.

But DJ was talking to me.

– And what about Hypocristy?

What the hell was that?

– It's *Hypocrisy*!

My friends chimed in again to help:

– Right, right, Hypocrisy, Hypocrisy.

DJ thought for a moment. Then he leaned close to me and asked, without rhetoric, quietly, as if he'd missed the punch line:

– Why did you come at me?

Man, I hadn't been able to answer the question the first time someone asked me.

– I'd just gotten here... and all of a sudden you...

– What?

– 'Weezy'...

DJ leaned back and looked around. A generic metalhead was walking past. DJ called to him:

– What's up, weezy! Gimme five!

The metalhead reached out his palm:

– What's up, here's ten!

So that's all it was. 'Weezy' really didn't mean anything bad. And so DJ wasn't my enemy; he had accepted me, just as Ugo had, but I'd pushed him away. The misunderstanding had been due to a kind of language barrier. What I should have said was, sorry, I don't have my metalhead—dipshit translation dictionary, forgive me. But I said nothing.

DJ got up and walked down the steps, as if he were offended. He headed for the street. Čiriks sidled up to him and spoke quietly to him. DJ nodded decisively, walked into the street with his head held high, stopped, turned around and called:

– C'mere! C'mon!

He was talking to me. I looked to Death, but he was gone. He'd disappeared from his spot by the column. I didn't look at the others, but I knew they were there, so I got up and walked down the steps. I was limping a little more than I had ten minutes ago, but a little less than I really wanted to; I couldn't let my friends see me faking it. DJ didn't seem to notice my limp at all, and kept gesturing – come on, come on. He was handsome, famous, strong, terrifying.

I had almost reached him when there was the sound of screeching brakes, a black car stopped right next to DJ. Two guys, their heads shaved, got out – one tall, one short and stout. The tall one punched DJ in the face, and he fell to the ground. Then the tall one bent down and picked DJ up by the jacket, then tossed him aside onto the sidewalk.

He'd been standing in the middle of the street, after all, and the car had almost run him down. The short, stout one looked around with a sneer, to see if anyone else needed to be taught a lesson, and then his eyes fell on me.

– Oh, hey! How's your leg?

He reached out his hand to me. I shook it and answered politely, thank you, it's fine. The tall one recognised me, too:

– Good to hear! Haven't busted anything new, have you?

– Everything's more or less in place, thanks.

– Let's get a drink sometime. *Davai!*

– Bye!

They hopped back into their BMW and took off. DJ got up and headed back to the Junkyard, cupping his face in his hand. I didn't go back just yet. I was thinking. Do two run-ins with them make them my new friends? Will I still have any real friends left after tonight? After all, I'd renounced one of my own and accepted the hand of a stranger.

7

And so we reached the start of 1995. It was a major and terrifying year. Do you remember the film *Terminator 2: Judgement Day*, starring Arnold Schwarzenegger? The movie was made in 1991, but takes place in 1995. Its creators had predicted the future. That's what 1995 ended up being, a never-ending judgement day. And I'm not convinced that it's over yet.

The best music in the world was released in 1995, with the exception of what had already come out in 1994, and maybe even a little earlier than that. As soon as I had been turned on to metal, we were given the best representatives of the genre, the classics, the golden standards:

Genre	Genre classic (band, album)	Year
Death Metal	Cynic; *Focus*	1993
	At the Gates; *Terminal Spirit Disease*	1994
	Death; *Symbolic*	1995
Black Metal	Mayhem; *De Mysteriis Dom Sathanas*	1994
	Impaled Nazarene; *Suomi Finland Perkele*	1994
	Immortal; *Battles in the North*	1995
Doom Metal	Anathema; *The Silent Enigma*	1995
	My Dying Bride; *Angel and the Dark River*	1995
	Celestial Season; *Solar Lovers*	1995

By the way, Death's *Symbolic* was released exactly on my birthday. Talk about symbolism.

But at the beginning of 1995 I didn't yet understand that I'd created this world, that everything was happening because of me. I stood at the window and thought: 'God, I'm such an asshole. I ruined everything. I betrayed my friends. Shook hands with the enemy, and they all saw me do it. Now what do I do?' And I stared out the window. It was a rough winter. One of the first winters in the new era during which our parents could no longer say: 'That's nothing! In my day it was much worse than this.' The snow fell and tumbled and didn't melt. The old– crystalised sand and shit – mixed with the new, and it covered the ground in an endless layer, which is how I, trudging through the snowdrifts in downtown Jelgava, was connected to Milēdija, who was shovelling show near the Glūda train station; to DJ, who was sitting on a snow bank on the side of the Dobele Highway; to my metalhead friends, who were building a snowman just a few blocks away from me, and to the world at large with freezing, shimmering strings.

8

The Junkyard, by the way, was kicked out of Villa Medem. It was probably for the best. Metalheads have to be chased off with a stick, you can't let them gather in groups. But when I heard the news, I shivered. What if it was all my fault?

It was Nellija – the one and only – who stopped me in the hallway and asked:

– You going to the Junkyard this Friday?

Like I was some kind of ignoramus. I plastered a smile across my face and said:

– Of course I'm going, Wouldn't miss it!

– Me too.

I liked it when people mocked me. I replied:

– Good thing you reminded me. I'll even curl my hair.

– How come?

An eighth-grade girl skittered past us like a spider, trampling my heart with her little boots. I decided to make my answer pretentious:

– Because one must be dressed appropriately when one visits Villa Medem. Did you know, that the Medem family...

– But it's not at the Villa anymore.

– What, really?

– It's at the Bunker now. You didn't know?

– I knew!

The Bunker was a partially dilapidated, post-industrial building next to Death's apartment building. Since when had the Junkyard moved there?

– It's in the basement. This is the first week there.

– I know, I know. In the basement. Of course I'll go.

– With your friends?

– Who else?

Nellija gave a sniff, turned around and left.

How come no-one told me anything? I walked to class dumbstruck. But I knew why. Once I sat down Kārlis asked:

– You going to the Junkyard on Friday?

Result!

– But of course. At the Bunker, in the basement, down the stairs, it's a great venue.

Milēdija was standing right there, leaning with her butt against my desk.

– What do you mean? Aren't you guys coming over to my place?

'You guys' and 'my place'? I have absolutely no idea what's going on in my life right now. I didn't even try to respond, but I got the urge to turn down the offer. Kārlis hurried to say:

– We'll see...

That psychopath Edmunds yelled across the room:

– Did you hairy animals find a new barn?

Kārlis shot some comeback at him, nothing particularly funny, but Edmunds respected Kārlis and shut up afterwards. I could've had the wittiest comeback in the world and it wouldn't have made a difference. But there are more important things going on. The Junkyard had returned.

The Bunker was a long building next to the pet shop. It was Jelgava's first-ever pet shop. One summer, some smart alec had convinced the deadbeats from the Other School that the pet shop would pay for wild newts. There happened to be a massive amount of yellow newts in the pond next to the Other School, and they were all eventually brought to the petshop downtown in bags filled with water. But the pet shop wouldn't take the newts; they said they'd never bought newts off people. So the newts were let go right outside the store; maybe there's still a small colony of them there to this day.

Death, Kārlis, Kārlis' brother, Zombie, and Pūpols all lived on the same block – which is probably why there was never any setup required for our pre-parties at Zombie's place. At least not that I knew of. When Friday night rolled around, I let my mother know that I was going out to listen to music, and I went. I had a few tapes with me that I'd picked up at the Stocks: Winter's *Into Darkness* and a few other things. I even had my own cigarettes, or a couple, to start.

There really was something happening at the Bunker tonight. There was a group of people waiting by the door. They waved to me; it was the crazy bunch of newt-catchers from the Other School. Kačoks, Robčiks, Eižēns, Salt, and more.

– C'mon over, you maniac!

That's what they called me. We huddled into a friendly circle, and a few seconds passed as we all shook hands. This had recently become the style of greeting, everyone suddenly acting like grown gentlemen. It got on my nerves a little. And all of their hair was on the short side. What if my real friends showed up and saw me with them? I mean, they were great guys, and they had a litre of 'Magic Crystal' vodka with them – which was colloquially called 'The Blue Hills' or 'The Lizard's Grin'. The best was when Eižens turned to me and asked:

– Any of you ever go to the old Junkyard site?

I was the only one. I told them about it with an air of dignity, without embellishments, without superfluous information. I could feel myself growing taller. They listened raptly. I was of an older, more real world. Someone passed me the bottle out of turn, and I took a swig worthy of my status – but a little too big of one. Some of the vodka went down the wrong pipe. And up my nose. My entire body convulsed. This was neither the time nor the place to throw up on myself. I willed myself to keep it together and decided that I could get by with a macho loogie-hacking. I started to gather the mess in my mouth into a gob.

Then a guy I didn't know, who was standing next to Salt, said:

– Why hasn't someone started a sort of newspaper for metalheads?

It was a good question, but at that moment I was leaning forward, preparing to spit. The guy I didn't know continued enthusiastically:

– And hell, why shouldn't we...

He moved as he spoke, swinging his arm out into the centre of our huddle in a classic gesture of someone making an announcement. He did this at the same time I had leaned forward far enough to release the contents of my mouth. Gravity did its thing, and the massive gob of saliva, et al, puddled right into the middle of the guy's hand.

It was an accident. I froze in shame, in fear of what would happen next on this night that had started out so well. I looked up at the guy's face, ready to take what I had coming. But what I saw wasn't anger, just surprise and humiliation. He had only wanted to say something constructive, for the good of the cause, but instead this authoritative character had spit right into his hand (the guys from the Other School didn't know my nerdy past; to them I was just an old metalhead). I closed my empty mouth and said:

– I didn't mean to.

I may have also said 'Sorry!', but it wouldn't have been heard because the entire group burst out laughing. Eižēns was howling and wheezing, and Salt was doubled over. They all thought it was the funniest thing. Only the guy and I stood quietly. He wiped his hand off on his pants.

If you think about it, though, it was a little funny.

We could've stood there for another year at least, but a group of people passed by on the other side of the street and called out discreetly:

– Stay brutal!

They were here – Kārlis, Kārlis' brother, Death, Zombie, Pūpols and Sammie. I childishly ditched my friends from the Other School, maybe said a 'See you inside!' and ran across the street without really understanding where I stood – was I a member of their great brotherhood or a puppy that came obediently when called, a cocky punk or an emotional wuss. Once across I jumped and crawled up the snow bank only for Zombie and Pūpols to grab me and wrestle me to the ground. I thought – maybe it doesn't matter; maybe this path of constantly doing stupid things is my destiny, and see, my friends love me no matter what. Eventually, they helped me to my feet and handed me a more than half-empty 0.7-litre bottle of Merkurs brandy, and Sammie offered me half a sausage sandwich (that's how he got his nickname – he almost always had a part of a sandwich on him).

– Let's go in! Go!

And we went inside.

At the entrance we found the first bit of proof that the old Junkyard had been better: there was a one-lat cover charge here.

But it was amazing. A set of steep iron stairs led us deep underground, where we came to a bunker door with a large circular doorknob like on a submarine. There was even a TV inside, in case someone wanted to experience a little bourgeois hominess. The TV caught my attention; it was showing an endless collection of sex scenes with detailed close-ups. Movies like this weren't that easy to get to back then. The people organising the Junkyard wanted their guests to have the best of everything. You couldn't hear the apparently German dialogue and moans, though, because of the two giant speakers filling the underground room with flowing metal. This was an old bomb-shelter, one that had never been used for its intended purpose. Now it was a shelter for us from the silence of the outside world. The narrow cement space felt even more packed than the duke's ballroom had, and the clouds of cigarette smoke made it seem like a paradise beneath the surface of the earth. I think they were even selling beer here, in the event someone was dumb enough to forget to bring something along. Like me, for example. But I had friends. And there they were. The two brothers were slamming their foreheads against a metal wall. They were only pretending, of course, and were making the sound by kicking the wall, but their technique was so refined that it looked real. Pūpols took Sammie's last sandwich. Zombie and Sammie had turned their attention to the TV screen. Death was storming the deejay's table. I surveyed the room – who else was here? And there was Nellija, with that offended expression she always had. I looked at her as if to say:

– Do you see? These are my friends. We are *forever eternally stay heavy stay brutal*, but you're just a bookbag.

Her eyes said:

– I don't believe you.

I got flustered and looked away. Standing next to her was that other girl, a curious being with bright yellow hair and brown eyes. Ser wasn't saying anything to me with her eyes; she wasn't even looking at me. Nellija leaned over to her and shouted something into her ear. It really was loud in here.

Once in a while Ugo got a hold of the stereo and put on one of his punk songs, but the majority of what we heard was pure metal: a little thrash, a little doom, but mostly death metal. The biggest hit back then was Cannibal Corpse's 'Zero the Hero'.[2] As soon as it came on, everyone rushed to the stage (there wasn't really a stage) to stand shoulder-to-shoulder and headbang. Some people even did so with

---

2 I know, and knew back then, that this is a Black Sabbath cover.

an arm around each of their neighbours' shoulders. It was a brotherly gesture, but also made it easier to stay upright. I joined in with the headbanging, though I've never been one to hug, or half-hug others. This time, the guy to my left with his arm around me had an open drink in his hand, which kept sloshing in my face in rhythm with his movements. I said nothing out of tact, instead whipping my head along with him, clearly feeling my poor little brain ricochet around my skull and the world become a jumble of strange thoughts – I'm here, I feel good, I don't need anything more than this, I love how compacted our world is. I thought about Milēdija and thought out to her – see, you're not here and that's great. I'm not thinking about you. See, even Kārlis is here, and not with you. I thought about composing a sonnet or a miniature right here and now. But what do we need tender words for when metal is thundering all around us? Each time the next song started up, Death and I would identify it loudly:

– Carcass!

– Entombed!

– Bolt Thrower! (I'll admit that I didn't recognize every third song or so and let Death shout out the answer alone; he wouldn't hear me in this noise anyway.)

– Konkhra!

– Brutal Truth, I mean, Brutality!

– Sepultura!

– You nuts? It's Brujeria! (He could hear me after all.)

Nellija and her friend were standing right near us, and I hoped that they could hear at least part of our discussion. I watched them and shouted into Death's ear about the new music I'd picked up at the Stocks, and he yelled back for me to lend him the tapes sometime. No problem, I have them with me, in my pocket! But where did I leave my jacket... Somewhere here, right, in a safe spot on the floor by the bathrooms.

As I walked to the bathrooms, I suddenly stumbled forward as the floor pitched under my feet. But it wasn't the floor, and not even the considerable amounts of Merkurs and Lizard's Grin that I'd had. The crazy brothers had kicked the wall sectioning off the bathroom so many times that it finally just collapsed – just toppled and fell over.

It was a pretty shoddy partition for a bomb shelter. The wall fell with a loud crash, revealing several surprised-looking metalheads lined up at the urinals. They all hastily pulled their pants back up – except for Zombie, of course, who rushed out in wild enthusiasm to jump around with everyone else just as he was, with his pants around his ankles, and no-one, male and female alike, averted their eyes, instead throwing their arms around him and joining in. It stung me a little that people could only be moved by things like that.

I took a deep pull on my cigarette and tried to see where Death had gone, but he was lost in the crowd; I spotted Edmunds and that fat-ass Čiriks, who were hanging out right by the door. I looked away haughtily, smoked my cigarette down to the filter and went to find an ashtray. I didn't need to find one, but I felt like being fancy, and someone had just introduced the concept of a 'Latvian ashtray': a plastic cup with a finger's-width of liquid in it. Someone around here must have one. I found Nellija's friend holding it, standing calmly in the eye of the storm. I went over to her, smiled, and dropped my cigarette butt in the ashtray. I didn't hear what she said because it was so loud, so I just smiled; what could someone so pretty say that was bad? Her brandy-coloured eyes went wide like when explaining something to a small child, and she lifted her cup – it wasn't an ashtray, but a regular plastic cup, almost full with some kind of fancy drink in it. I'd walked up to a girl I didn't know and had thrown a cigarette in her cocktail.

I wasn't well versed in etiquette, but I understood that I'd made a mistake. I said the same words I'd spoken only a few hours earlier that night, but again no-one heard me. I staggered backwards away from them, hoping that I looked more drunk than I really was. My feet got tangled up in some sort of rag. It was my jacket. I probably should buy the girl another drink, but I'd spent my last lat getting into the Junkyard. I put on my jacket. Maybe I could give her one of my tapes? Not Winter, it was the anthem for the season. Not Tristitia, either. I had only recently started to really understand this epically strange album. This music was the real deal, and would be played only for me, me who is destined to only do harm unto others, to be nothing but an evil clown. I'll hole up in my house by myself and listen to my tapes.

Suddenly the music stopped. It had been shut off. Someone was shouting:

– But listen, why aren't you listening to me, I'm serious...

This was probably intended to be spoken privately to someone into his or her ear, whispered at a volume relative to the surrounding noise. But now everyone heard it. I was afraid to look up, afraid to lock eyes with the guy from the Other School whose hand I'd spit into, or with the girl with the bitter-coloured eyes. Then the lights came on, leaving me like a puppy in a spotlight. Then some policemen stepped into the middle of the room. Real policemen, around ten of them, in black uniforms and carrying batons and guns.

I'm afraid of dogs, and of people in uniform. I wanted to clutch the beautiful elbow of the brown-eyed girl, but I resisted. Maybe I shouldn't have.

One of the policemen shouted:

– Everyone line up with your hands against the wall!

But no one listened to him because our ears were still ringing from the music, and what's more, police officers here are treated like devils or imps that everyone can see, but no-one believes in. I heard the policeman clearly, and I really wanted to obey his order. But I couldn't do it. At least, not until everyone else had. Or at least someone.

The policeman kindly repeated what he'd said, and then started to re-explain through actions. No-one pushed me; I turned around on my own. They also made us stand with our feet spread apart; I didn't like that at all and my legs were shaking, but I could feel that something amazing was happening. They frisked all of us, looking for who knows what. Later I got used to these kinds of searching, tentative pat-downs, but back then at least one person was already used to them and shouted loudly:

– Hey, I've got an Uzi down my pants! Check my pants, you'll find an Uzi!

The police didn't find any Uzi. After conferring with one another quietly, they left. Now we felt exactly the way we needed to feel. Everyone looked at everyone else, and burst out laughing as if they'd been holding it in for too long, and shouted: 'No fucking way!' Something had finally happened, just like in the old days. Death hurried back to the empty deejay chair. But the hosts said that the party was over. They unhooked the equipment and started winding up the cords.

It was freezing cold outside, but it wasn't snowing. I looked around; the city stood secretive, it knew everything. I noticed some dark stains in the snowdrifts by the door. Droplets, splatters, chunks. I asked like an idiot:

– What is that?

And Kārlis answered:

– Blood.

Sammie said:

– Someone always gets theirs.

Death thought for a moment:

– Who got theirs last time?

– When was the last time?

– At the Villa...

– Did someone get theirs then?

– Maybe not...

– I don't remember.

They had absolutely no memory of the thing that I'd been obsessing over this whole time.

I didn't know who'd gotten theirs that night. By Monday rumour had it that Čiriks' gang had been pulling metalheads out of the Junkyard just to beat on them. Others said that when the police had shown up and then left, they'd struck anyone who had been standing by the door. But why were the police even there?

There's an old Irish legend about a princess named Deirdre, who one day sees a raven pecking at a bloodstain in the snow – and she falls in love with the scene. Black, white, red. Something hot, something cold, something that can fly. The same happened to me. It wasn't my blood, or Deirdre's. We just wanted to see it. That's what we royal descendants are like.

I don't know if it was the fresh air or the relief after all that tension, but the full affect of the various alcohols I'd consumed over the course of the night finally kicked in. My legs and tongue stopped working right, but I felt great. My friends were walking with me, their mouths staggering and legs slurring too, we trudged over the snow, we were on an arctic expedition that had found shelter from solitude. Being together with everyone is the same as being nowhere; you have to find a solitary road to share with a few others, and we had found it. They had forgiven me my terrible sins, they had accepted me, it meant I really was a prince, and even the girl with the yellow hair and brown eyes had spoken to me, and I wasn't thinking of Milēdija at all. I was free. I was content in that bloodied snow.

Zombie added:

– But maybe it was just some girl shaking out a tampon.

9

There was a door on the third floor with the number 23 on it, the universal number for disaster. 2 + 3 = 5. Even all the doors in *Master and Margarita* had numbers that added up to five. This particular door led to the algebra classroom. Its shelves were filled with the types of books no-one wants to read, not even when you're bored out of your mind and desperate. Back then there were far more interesting things written elsewhere: like on the green desks. We'd painted the desks ourselves that summer. The paint under the desks never dried completely, so at first you'd see girls walking around with green smudges on their knees, but now they were more careful about it.

There we were, all thirty-six of us. Our homeroom teacher was also our algebra teacher. She loved the subject and, when she'd come into the classroom, would always say something like:

– We'll work on three planes: we'll solve 'standard' problems, and parallel to which we'll work on new materials. I've also found some interesting assignments from the Math Olympiads.

There was a lot to calculate, and in three different directions – sometimes we even tried. But once one of the kids from the back of the class, Jānis Labrencis, pushed his notebook away and said: 'I bow my head in the face of this problem'. I thought it was pretty clever if him, so I gave up too. The rest of our group had given up a while ago without any witticisms. Algebra was a different, abstract world. The smart kids in the front row believed that it existed objectively and had even made successful contact with it. To those of us farther back, it remained an unknown and invisible thing that could punish you at the end of the semester for your ignorance. But for now the end of the semester was a ways off and we felt good. We sat in a cultured manner and played sequence – a bastardised version of poker, without lies or pretence.

I was having zero luck with cards that day. Nothing but Charles (the King of Hearts) and David (the King of Spades). I couldn't do anything with them in sequence. I folded, and sat watching my classmates. What personalities, what destinies! What legs! Diāna, Linda, Guntiņa.

I recognised all of them without having to look up any higher. And there, right up front with the smart kids, Milēdija. I couldn't see her legs. She turned around and looked at me, and smiled. I did nothing. It was possible she was smiling at someone sitting behind me. I stared at the green surface of my desk. It was scribbled with the same stuff as in the bathroom stalls. Death, Entombed – carved by an unknown hand. Maybe it was Death. I'd responded with Anathema, and had even added a considerably detailed drawing of their complicated logo. The unknown metalhead should appreciate it, but he'd do it silently. In turn, I'd responded to the words 'Hairy morons' with 'Pimple-head', and had gotten a 'Come and get it, retard!' I could sense that a note was headed my way. It was close. Guntiņa tossed it onto my desk. My neighbour was sitting hunched over his cards.

I took the note. The words 'To Kārlis' were written on the front. I glanced up at Milēdija, who looked back at me and pointed – pass it on! I knew full well that Kārlis sat right behind me. I tossed the note to him and returned to my thoughts.

Someone had also carved a pentagram into the desktop. The one with two points of the star at the top. Just like the one you can see in the northern stain-glass window of Amiens Cathedral. Who knows why it was now associated with Satanism. Next to the pentagram was an upside-down Latin cross drawn in pen, also now associated with the same ideology. It's actually called the Cross of Saint Peter. You can see it on the papal throne.

Kārlis tossed the note back onto my desk. It didn't have 'Stay Brutal!' written on it, just Milēdija's name. I tossed it onto the desk in front of mine, and then drew an equilateral triangle on my desktop, and another smaller triangle inside that. In the spaces between the edges of the two triangles I wrote 'SATIRNE GAN SANTALINI'. You were supposed to draw this symbol with the blood of a bat on parchment paper and then place it on a sacred stone. Then you were supposed to place the paper under the threshold of a door. The first girl to cross over the threshold will immediately take off all her clothes and dance around naked until she drops dead, unless someone removes the parchment. That's what the *Grimorium Verum* says. Man, how I'd make someone dance if I had parchment paper and a bat!

Of course, you need the draw the symbol in the right material. The metalheads from the Other School told me that once a teacher had noticed one of the students had a bloody hand. She'd made the student open his hand – he had some sort of symbol carved into the skin of his palm. The scar was seeping blood. The teacher asked:

– And what do we have here, hmm?

The student had replied:

– Faith.

What symbol was it? No one knows. Some cult that secretly had shown up in Jelgava.

Another note was dropped onto my desk. This one had my surname on it, in the dative case. I noticed almost immediately that the handwriting was different, so I didn't experience even a theoretical wave of emotion. The message inside read: 'What are you doing?' I scanned the classroom. No-one looked suspicious, except for the one girl who always looked suspicious and usually that meant nothing.

I drew a circle inside another circle, and two crosses positioned inside the inner circle. This symbol is for when you want to become invisible. And who doesn't want that? The only other things you need are black beans, the head of a corpse and, or course, alcohol. You put one bean in each orifice of the corpse's head, draw the aforementioned symbol on its forehead and bury the head at a crossroads. Then, naturally, you take the alcohol and pour it over where you buried the head. You do this seven nights in a row. On the seventh night one of the beans will have sprouted, and the spirit of the corpse will be sitting next to it. The spirit will ask, 'What are you doing?' And it will reach out to take the bottle. But you don't let it have it right away.

– Jānis, what are you doing?

Ms Siliņa was standing by my desk.

– Nothing.

I answered confidently, as someone who knows he's innocent, but this time it didn't land quite right.

– So it seems. Let me see your notebook!

Siliņa had this policy – she demanded that her students always follow along with the class work and take notes on everything. But this time I hadn't written anything down. All I'd done is draw a gravesite.

Pūpols taught me how. He spent hours drawing the graves of everyone around him. Usually they were for the teachers. 'Sure, sure, Līcis,' Pūpols would say, and draw Līcis' grave. He didn't always do it because of a specific reason or reprimand. Today I'd drawn our teacher's grave just because. A tasteful cross and headstone with her name and surname. Pūpols usually added cause of death, but I didn't do that, and wanted to draw our teacher's attention to this one positive aspect. But I said nothing. Siliņa placed a finger on the drawing of her grave.

– What is this?

She asked the question with genuine interest, like the scientist she was. Now she was trying to make out the name on the headstone. I felt extremely uncomfortable and wished that she wouldn't.

Suddenly the classroom door flew open and an unfamiliar, red-curled head looked in to announce that I was to report to the principal. The principal was a lazy woman and usually sent some diligent student out to run these errands.

I slammed my notebook shut and stood up. Some people said I went pale. But that's not true. Whether you're a natural-born rebel or one of the little guys, there's always something catastrophic about getting called in by the authorities. But this time, first and foremost, I felt relieved to be out of the gravesite episode, and second, that I maybe didn't really have to go to the principal's office, but that the unfamiliar girl was here to kidnap me.

No such luck. The principal's office was full of people. Of course, the principal was there, as was another woman whose title I've forgotten. But there was also Cips and Anrijs, my metalhead friends from the Fifth Line! And Death, too.

– What's going on?

But the principal asked me:

– Well?

But I said:

– Yes, ma'am?

And she said:

– What can you tell us?

And I asked:

– About what?

And she added:

– What do you all do together?

I paused. We do a lot of different things, and I wasn't sure that they were things these women could either understand, or that could even be explained. The principal must have read my mind and elaborated:

– What cult are you part of?

The principal caught me up to speed. The four of us go around proclaiming the end of the world, shouting out satanic mottos, worshipping death and disseminating our beliefs. And we drink in cemeteries. I was surprised at how accurately she had described our activities, but I didn't know where she'd got the information. But part of what she described was all new to me. What's more, according to her intel, our home base was the attic of one of the apartment buildings near the school, and our leader is some older man with a huge beard. It was these last details that let me deny everything in total disbelief. I was so convincing that the principal said:

– That's what I thought, too, that it's all just a bunch of nonsense. After all, you're all such normal boys!

And all four of us nodded in agreement. Right now we were ready to be totally normal. The principal added:

– And the part about the man with the beard?

By Jupiter, I honestly had no idea what that was about, and the other three were equally and earnestly dumbstruck.

The woman whose title I can't remember offered her hypothesis:

– Maybe you boys just listen to your music a little too loudly at times... Maybe you sing along... maybe some older person hears the lyrics and gets scared...

Then Anrijs spoke up, laughing lightly:

– We can't even keep up with those raps to sing along!

He obviously said it to show how removed we were from anything dangerous. But we didn't listen to rap.

– We don't listen to rap!

Death had spoken. He was sulking.

– I mean, what I mean to say is that we're normal, but we don't listen to rap, either.

The principal suddenly looked tired.

– We don't have to go into the specifics. Go back to class.

Cips had a final, direct question:

– Who told you all those things?

– Go back to class.

And once in the hall she shooed us all off our separate ways, so we wouldn't have the chance to discuss things. I was the last one to go, standing for a moment longer trying to wrap my head around it.

Then that crazy Nellija from the other class came out of nowhere and asked:

– What was that about?

– What?

– In there.

– Nothing.

– Some deep shit?

– Where?

– What's with you?

– Why?

– Is there something wrong with you?

– Are you daft?

And that's how I finally got to know Nellija. She said that everyone called her Lija, and that we could call her that too. But that's not what we called her. And I'd never heard anyone else call her that, either. Everyone called her Liar.

10

What was better – the Junkyard, or being by myself at home, in front of my stereo? Wasn't the Junkyard only fun because you could take what had happened there and think about it by yourself back at home, in front of your stereo? And wasn't the number one fantasy when sitting in front of your stereo, sometimes even standing, along with the thundering lightning and flashing thunder, being at the Junkyard?

What was the right way to listen to a song? Are you supposed to imagine yourself as the song's protagonist, or try to relate the song to your own life? Is the song about me or am I about the song?

I had less time for maths and family drama. These trivial things were being pushed out by metal. My tape collection was so big that I couldn't gather them all up in my arms at once. I could do the kind of structuring and classification that young minds most loved to do. I had a lot of doom, a solid amount of death, a smattering of thrash and also that other genre that many of us were into now, maybe even obsessed. I can explain exactly why I got into it.

It didn't start at the Junkyard or at home. One day during physical education, or maybe in ethics, I was rewinding a tape. Normally you'd do this with a pen-cap or scissors, but I was too lazy for some reason. The Walkman was whining and thumping like a chainsaw cutting through a nail-riddled board. Kārlis turned around and asked:

– What's that black you're listening to?

I hadn't heard of this genre yet, but I was immediately interested in music that would sound like that. Black metal is considered the most extreme expression of metal music. But for our giddy brains it was one more bucket of dynamite on an open flame. It was the ultimate – totally black, it had to be the end of the line, we'd reached our goal. Until recently I'd thought that doom metal was the be-all end-all, but now Death and I were sitting in front of the stereo, and he said:

– The best doom is black.

I automatically repeated the sentence in pure Latvian:

– The best fate is black.

Do you remember Immortal's *Pure Holocaust*? Of course you do. And Mayhem? Stupid question, I know. And yes, yes, I mean the old-school Mayhem, not the surviving members. But I can't help it, I have to explain what you all already know.

Mayhem was founded in 1984 by a Norwegian guy named Øystein Aarseth. He played the guitar and went by the name Euronymous. We never understood how to pronounce it, namely, on which syllable to place the emphasis.

Euronymous believed that his mission in life was absolute evil. When the band became famous a journalist asked, ahem, I've heard that you, the artist, have a good relationship with your parents. That you're a good son. How does that fit in with absolute evil? Euronymous self-critically referenced human nature:

– Not even Christians can be good all the time.

Such a good answer!

And note that Euronymous, the group's founder, didn't sing, but played guitar. Mayhem's first singer was Maniac. He was soon replaced with a melancholy young guy who went by the name Dead. He really knew how to set the mood. He was the first person in black metal to show up on stage in what was called corpsepaint. This style of face painting was reminiscent of mimes. They were basically the same thing – depressed jokers.

See, Dead wanted to look dead. He'd bury his clothes for a week or a month, then dig them up an hour before a show and wear them. Sometimes fans could see crickets crawling around on him. Dead would also cut himself during shows.

One night, when they didn't have a show, Dead slit his wrists, then wrote a note: 'Excuse the blood'. Then he shot himself in the head.

Haven't we heard that before? A note and a gun. History repeated. That is, if you ignore the fact that Kurt died in 1994, and Dead died in 1991. Our time shifted back and forth, and rarely stayed in one place.

Euronymous was the one to find his friend's body, and he immediately photographed the scene and later used the image as the cover art for their bootleg album *Dawn of the Black Hearts*. For everything to fall into place, for scripture to come true, there were those who doubted the truth of the story. In this case, detectives

Venom and Slayer. After looking at the picture, they said it looked like murder, that 'everything looked too perfect'. It really was perfect. Legend has it that Euronymous cooked up and ate a piece of Dead's brain, and that he made necklaces with fragments from his skull – whereas the band's drummer, Hellhammer, took his femurs to use as drumsticks. And so Mayhem had lost its vocalist. Necrobutcher left the band, too; maybe he started to think the rest of them had more than a few screws loose.

But legends never die. Things were up in the air for a little while, and then the band was joined by the intelligent young Kristian Vikernes, who had just traded in his ill-suited name and now went by Varg Vikerness, aka Count Grishnackh. What a name! Grishnackh was the Orc captain from the Catholic novel *Lord of the Rings*. The young Norwegian Orc also had a solo-project, Burzum (another Tolkeinism). He played bass guitar for Mayhem. They recruited guitarist Blackthorn from Thorns, and Attila, from the Hungarian band Tormentor, as the new vocalist. These five men recorded Mayhem's last real album, *De Mysteriis Dom Sathanas*, the *non plus ultra* of black metal. There's nothing more to be said.

Later on, Euronymous' mother asked that they re-record the bassline, so Grishnackh's playing wouldn't be heard alongside that of her kind, sweet son... Grishnackh still maintains that the album contains his original bassline.

One night after *De Mysteriis Dom Sathanas* had been recorded, but before it was released, Vikernes and Blackthorn went to visit Euronymous. What did they talk about on that icy-cold night? No record of that exists, but I think it went like this, with Blackthorn asking:

– Can I smoke?

And Varg answered:

– No. I already told you. You can't smoke in my car.

– Why not? Smoking is evil!

– The ancient Norse gods didn't smoke.

– What's with all of you? Euronymous won't let us smoke in his flat, either, because it'll ruin the tapestries.

– I don't care what Euronymous says.

– So I can smoke?

– No.

– What's with you guys? It's not good for you, this not-smoking. Trust me.

– Smoking forced on us by the Jews.

– God, I could kill for a cigarette. Now I'm going to have to smoke like a madman once I get outside.

– But you can't kill a legend.

– Huh? What?

– Calm down, we're almost there.

When they got there, Blackthorn stayed outside to smoke. Which is how he didn't become the only witness to what went down between the other two. Venom said it happened like this: after Grishnackh's gloomy phone call, a gloomy Euronymous answered the door, dressed in nothing but particularly gloomy underwear... While I thought the exchange went more like this:

– Hi, Kristian!

– Hi, Øystein!

– Is Snorre downstairs?

– Most likely.

– Want a smoke?

– Can't, don't have time.

– Right. Rock, paper, scissors?

– Rock, paper, scissors.

I obviously don't know the details, but Euronymous was stabbed to death. There was a lot of speculation regarding motive – dominance, conflict, love, deception – what garbage. He was stabbed over twenty times. 'Eternally Euronymous, murdered by traitor's hands'. Vikernes had laughed in the court room, and the prosecutor tacked on counts of arson of several churches, possession of weapons, and breaking the speed limit. You drove too fast, boys. He was given the maximum sentence, which in Norway is 21 years.[3]

I listened to *De Mysteriis Dom Sathanas* every day. I liked listening

---

3   The last man standing, Hellhammer joined the Christian unblack metal band Antestor, proving that, in the end, metal is the most important factor. Grishnachk was released in 2009.

to it every night even more, when it was dark out. When I could, I'd turn off all the lights and listen to it in the dark, staring at the wall, which I couldn't make out anyway, or out the window, where I could see a tall chimney, a black or invisible silhouetted against the night sky. When I couldn't understand the words – as was a natural occurrence with metal – I made up my own, thereby developing my spiritual side. My family no longer objected to my music, but it didn't mean they became metalheads.

As was bound to happen, I soon understood that Mayhem had become a cliché. The brilliant Finish black metal band Unholy would burn Mayhem and Burzum albums at their concerts. A true subculture guarantees you not only friends, but also enemies. I listened to the victim, to the murderer, and to those who condemned both of them. It turned out even black metal had its underground, full of bands like Abigail, Blasphemy... For the first time I saw that Hašek's good soldier Schweik had been right – beneath the world we see there is another, even bigger, world.

When there's an earthquake, even a butterfly moves its wings. What Latvia needed was its own legendary black metal band, that much was clear as day. For the time being we didn't have any black metal bands, but we needed a legendary one, immediately. It was standard; Venom was the first black metal group in the world, and certainly legendary enough. We needed one just like it. Although... Huskvarn supposedly had played something a little in the style of old-school black. But Huskvarn had always considered themselves thrash metal, so that's what we'll call them. Venom, who took his name from that same inaugural black metal band, stepped forward to become the next legend. Venom was the same guy I'd met my first time at the Stocks, the aristocratic metalhead with the long hair and sour expression.

He was sharp and wistful. He liked anything that unsettled all that was good and constant in the world. He turned the adjective "bad" into something unsteady because for Venom, everything that was bad was good. He was a staunch atheist and nationalist. In addition to Pol Pot, he also liked Machiavelli, Satan, and Greek mythology. He'd even written his own versions of myths: 'Arachne crawled out of the hollow of the tree, spitting out her own teeth'. He also liked Celtic Frost and, if you can imagine it, even Venom. He spoke so highly of the old blackmetal band that I sometimes wondered if he wasn't a secret heavymetal fan. He was always sceptical about anything legendary. And yet he wanted to be a legend himself.

In 1994, Venom and Slayer formed a band called Dark Reign. This happened about two months before the first iteration of Alfheim was put together. These two groups were destined to battle for the honorary title of First True Evil Latvian Black Metal Band.

But the battle for first place was nowhere near being over. Venom had done almost everything. He'd legally changed his surname and spilled his own blood. Yes, exactly, all according to script. Once Venom was sitting in Kaļinin's basement (a place where only the most absolute chosen ones could be [I never was]) and bitching about the water dripping on his head from a leaky pipe. His best friend and band mate Slayer was sitting next to him. One thing led to another, and Slayer took a knife and stabbed Venom in the leg. Venom took offense and left. Half of the crowd at Veldze was talking about it. What more could they do to win?

I understood that, in order to form and maintain a band, there had to be a victim. Or a stabbing. What could I do? I got the idea to stab my eyes out, because blind people tend to have a great sense of hearing, and it could come in handy with music. But for the time being I held off and waited for another idea to come to me.

But once again I was a little too late. Another small step behind the rest. What was the point in starting a band if it wasn't going to be the first one?

But neither Dark Reign nor Alfheim had put out a single record yet. And the way I saw it, a band was only truly born once it released an album. But that was probably because my relationship to metal had developed with me alone in my room, my arms around my stereo. For others it may have all started with a concert, a sacrificial cat, or a hectolitre of beer. But Latvia's metal history was taking place right before our eyes, and I needed to be part of it. I was about the same age Euronymous had been when he had first started. I also had Sinister, who was older than me, and just as crazy about black metal. He was already drawing possible band logos (we didn't have a name yet). He'd found a third band mate, a guy who was always talking about axes. The world was ours for the taking.

I should also mention the main factor in all of it: the Moon. The indisputable anthem for black metal was Mayhem's 'The Freezing Moon'. Before they played the song at a concert in Leipzig, Dead had said:

– When it's dark and when it's cold, the freezing moon can obsess you.

These words became our personal mantra and the explanation for our destinies. That's what happened. The cold, the moon, insanity.

Almost every blackmetal band, and metal bands overall, invoked the Moon: Carpathian Full Moon, 'Moon over Kara-Shehr', *Diabolical Fullmoon Mysticism*, 'Call of the Wintermoon', Moonspell, 'Behold, the Rising of the Scarlet Moon' and more and more and more. The Moon, that mad skinhead, the sun of criminals and lovers, the lantern of vampires, to which people's minds flit like moths to a flame – there is nothing more beautiful than the Moon. The young girl who started out at the Jelgava Dorothea Girls Primary School and then the Jelgava Trinity High School for Girls, and who later become the demonic poetess Aspazija, had been telling it how it was for ages:

> Let others have their nuts, their pies,
> We have the moon, there, in the sky
> A sweet, white, round moon,
> It only shines like that me and you.
>
> Don't cry, my child, be still,
> I'll tell you something wonderful:
> We'll hitch the tomcat to the cart,
> And to the moon we'll both depart.

For hundreds of years, people had been thinking about nothing but the Moon. But I had my own reason.

It happened a long time ago, and of course, on a winter morning. I was navigating the Jelgava snowdrifts, though on my way to kindergarten, not high school. I hadn't yet gotten lost in the wonders of my internal world, wasn't yet hobbling through life like a blind man, but was fully aware of my surroundings. Up above me I saw the moon. At that age I already knew that things were only perfect in stories, and that you shouldn't take reality so seriously. But there it suddenly was, completely, entirely innocent. Like a bullet hole to a better world. I could see the spots on it; there was the Indian who'd been dragged up there, or the Latvian girl with the nice bum – the were numerous stories with numerous theories. The Moon excited me.

Everyone had seen it. All the kids were crowded around our teacher, shouting over each other:

– There's a pretty Moon out today! I saw it!

I wasn't at all jealous; still excited, I joined the group and said:

– I saw it too!

But one girl, stupid Sanita, turned to me and said:

– No, you didn't!

I don't know why she said that. I came up with a few reasons later, and thought about it a lot. But one thing was certain, that that winter morning was the day black metal came to Jelgava.

11

On one of the first sunny evenings of early spring, Death asked me:
— Your parents aren't home now, right?
And then added:
— From what I heard.
I nodded. My parents had gone to our cottage. Death had understood everything perfectly. Now he was rubbing his face and was apparently scheming something. I waited silently. Were we going to throw a party? Have our first band practice? Seduce some girls?
— I know this guy who just broke out. Needs a place to crash for a few days.
Even better!
— He can stay here!
Death looked up:
— Really? That's great!
And he held out his hand:
— Give me your keys. I'll give them to him when I see him tonight.
— I can meet him here.
— I don't know he gets in. You might not be here.
It occurred to me that I definitely wouldn't be here because I wouldn't have my keys. But then I remembered that my mom had left her set, and I had them in my pocket. I gave them to Death.
He sniffed in farewell, said 'Stay brutal!' and left. And I had to leave to meet Pūpols at Rainis Park.
We met on time, like people did before the days of the mobile phone. We sat around for a good while, but we didn't have anything to drink. I had thought he'd bring something, and he in turn thought I would.
No matter. We spent our time undressing with our eyes the girls who wandered past. We ended up following the prettiest one. We came to some kind of communal garden area. The girl opened a small gate and let out a dog. We turned and ran. As I raced down the gravel road, I remembered that my house guest might be waiting for me.

Where did he break out of? What do people break out of? Psych wards, for one. Jelgava has a psychoneurological hospital, doesn't it? It does. A misunderstood genius, perhaps. Or wait, no, an overly sensitive soul who will look deep within me and recognise my genius. Maybe it's even a girl? I mean, Death didn't said it was a 'he'. A girl, then. I'll play My Dying Bride for her, serve her croquettes. No, My Dying Bride is so overplayed they probably even listen to it in the psych ward. I should play something more... Celestial Season? Ceremonium? In the Woods? They're neither here nor there, but as a girl she should like it.

Though now that I think about it, Death did say it was a guy.

And the psych ward isn't the only place you can break out of. People break out of prison, too. But no, that's insane. You can't break out of prison, they've got guards there.

And then I stopped abruptly. The unequivocal and ironclad logic of every movie ever dictated that the person waiting for me back at my house was none other than Juris' brother – the guy I refused to lend my stereo to.

And then I remembered that I was being chased by tonight's prettiest girl's dog. And I was just standing there – and there came the dog, its ears flapping threateningly.

In case I haven't mentioned it before, I'm terrified of dogs. Cynophobia. And of people in uniform. Just like August Strindberg had been. There wasn't a single person in uniform in sight, even though they would have come in handy tonight; and the dog, its ears flapping threateningly, drew even closer.

The dog raced right past me, its left ear slapping against my ankle, and continued to chase after the still-running Pūpols. I hoped he'd get away. There was nothing left for me to do but go home.

Dusk had fallen by the time I made it back to my building. I saw the kitchen light was on. The cocky, cold-blooded criminal was probably eating all my croquettes. I slowly climbed the stairs. Then I stood in front of our door, trying to think of a game plan.

The world came to my aid. I heard someone unlocking the door from inside, and I sprinted quietly up to the fifth floor.

From there I heard the person carefully lock the door and walk down the stairs. When I heard the downstairs door slam shut, I pressed my face to the stairwell window, but he must have been walking right along the edge of the building, out of sight. Clearly a professional. Probably off to kidnap some kid for dinner.

I unlocked the door and went inside. I didn't see any guns or knives. I went into the kitchen and opened the refrigerator. The croquettes were untouched. I went into the family room. There, in the corner by my desk, was a new collection of things. It was pretty modest and compact. There was a carefully folded shirt, a few balled-up pairs of socks (it all looked like men's clothes) and a fat book.

I picked up the book. It was heavy, and felt good to hold. It had been read intensively. Maybe a little carelessly. A corner of the cover was bent, as if it had been used to hit someone over the head. The cover itself was black. Like a Bible. The title page read: *Encyclopedia of Metal*. I paged through it to make sure it wasn't a book about metallurgy or craftsmanship. But it was about real metal. I flipped through to the Ms: Mayhem, Morbid Angel, Morgoth, etcetera, etcetera, My Dying Bride. It also had pictures. I flipped to the back: Winter; I flipped to the front: Anathema. But did it have Brutal Truth? It did.

It even included bands I'd never heard of. Blasphemy. Black metal, judging by the name. The album cover looked legit, too. And the album title, *The Fallen Angel of Doom*, god, how great! It was produced by Osmose, one of the most sullen black metal record labels. Members: Nocturnal Grave Desecrator and Black Winds – Vocals, Deathlord of Abomination and War Apocalypse – Guitar, The Traditional Sodomizer of the Goddess of Perversity – Guitar, Three Black Hearts of Damnation and Impurity – Drums'. What romantics. Now I had knowledge. It was easier to get things once you had knowledge. But for now I had to calm down, sit down and study up.

Then someone unlocked the door. And then nothing. They didn't come in, didn't take off their shoes, which is what someone from my family would have done. The front hall was silent. He must've noticed the light on in the room and were standing there wondering what to do. Wondering what was waiting for them in the other room – a trap or a victim?

What do you do in this kind of situation? What had to happen for one of us to make a move? I was at least sitting and was holding a book. What was he doing? The phone rang. It was out in the hall. The only person who could be calling is my mom to ask if I'd eaten the croquettes. Or Death, who'd figured out what was going on and was trying to warn me. Or the police. In any case, I could probably manage to pick up the receiver and get out a quick cry for help. I ran into the hall, where I found a young guy my age. He didn't look scary at all. He had longish hair and was wearing a Sepultura shirt.

– Hey.

– Hey.

– Death said... I mean, Death...

– Right, yes, it's fine.

I rubbed my forehead.

– Where did you bust out of?

– Home. School.

– Oh.

I lingered for a second and then did as my dad had taught me:

– Come on in. Welcome.

– Isn't that the phone?

I picked up the receiver. It was Milēdija.

– Hey.

– Hey.

– What are you up to?

– Nothing.

– Me to.

The runaway stood nervously next to me. The phone was quiet, on both ends.

– Okay, well, never mind. Bye.

And she hung up.

We went into the family room. I gestured to the armchair with the book, and then realized I still had it.

– Sorry, I took your book. Just to look.

– That's fine.

– Do you have any other stuff with you?

– Yeah, some socks and a shirt.

– Want some croquettes?

– Sure.

I went to the kitchen, put some croquettes on two plates, went back into the family room, put on Beherit's *Drawing Down the Moon*, and we ate.

12

After the Junkyard was kicked out of the Bunker, it moved into the kindergarten. The one behind Tonijs' house, before you take the turn to get to my mom's work. During the day it was an actual kindergarten, but on Friday nights, when all the kids were home for the weekend, we took over. That was the path of the Jelgava Junkyard: from a villa to a bomb shelter, from a bomb shelter to a kindergarten.

Winter had just suddenly turned to spring when we moved into the kindergarten. The snow was melting and we could green and brown patches of grass peeking through. I was still wearing my winter jacket, but instead of wrapping my scarf around my neck I let it hang elegantly down to my legs; in turn, girls were rushing to shed as many layers as possible. All these elements of spring were leaving people with an aching sense of excitement. As if we were remembering something big and beautiful that once passed us by, and which we'd probably let pass by again, but without knowing what to do about it. We can't even remember what that thing was, just the smell, something in the air reminds us of it.

I was the first to arrive that night. Death had said he'd be a little late, and he was right. He'd also said: 'Bring a bottle of something with you!' And I'd done so; the bottle was in my pocket and I was standing outside. From inside the kindergarten I could hear:

– Battles! Battles in the North!

Evening was settling down on Jelgava, and the spring air was warm. People came in small groups; I was the only one by myself, but it didn't bother me anymore. I was our so-called cult's leader and holder of the encyclopaedia of metal. I stood by myself, accepting greetings with dignity. I didn't want to go inside and talk with anyone. It was nice to stand outside, in the darkening world, on the brink of something amazing. I felt more a part of this scene than the majority of these kids showing up tonight. But everyone said hi to me, and I mean *everyone*. Even a few girls. I imagined that if someone were to ask me what I was doing outside by myself, I'd say:

– I'm hoping for the Moon.

And then I'd look up at the heavens. Two people walked up; it was dark enough that a near-sighted person wouldn't recognize them, but one of them called out:

– Hey!

And I answered:

– Hey!

It was Ģirtiņš, the one with the beard, and his girlfriend. This Ģirtiņš was a great guitar player, which was another reason to be jealous of him. His girlfriend was one of my sister's students. She was wearing an intensely low-cut shirt that night. Ģirtiņš threw down his cigarette and asked:

– Why're you out here?

Without taking my eyes off her cleavage, I gave my prepared answer:

– Groping for the Moon.

A Freudian slip. His girlfriend looked at me in surprise:

– Do what now?

I could tell her exactly what I wanted to grope, but I tried again:

– The Moon, I'm waiting for it.

– Is that a new band or something?

I threw up a hand.

– Let's go in.

Once inside I slipped into a corner and took a drink from my bottle of Merkurs. This stupid life and monogamous philistines, and the silly moon maidens, who needs it. Life should bite you in the throat, like Merkurs does. Of course, that's the traditional approach. To accept the path you are already on as the one and only. 'Walk the path of sorrow', as Satyricon sang. One more swig of Merkurs. It went down smooth as life. Now I could take a look around.

The space here wasn't as fancy as at the Bunker or the Villa. No iron doors, no columns, just a smallish, windowless room. There was supposed to be a show tonight. I never would have believed that a room this small could accommodate a concert, much less without any sign of a stage. But a lot of other people did believe, and the room was packed. Or maybe they were just here to be here. Mele's pretty friend walked by, her hand protectively over the opening of her cup. Sammie watched her go. Ziedonis was carrying a big box. And then the guys from the Other School tumbled in. The kindergarten was in their neighbourhood, after all. Crab, Sīnis, Bundle, Eižēns, the whole gang. Their hair was now a lot longer than what was considered normal, but still shorter than mine – the perfect combination. We threw our arms around each other in greeting, and I was genuinely happy to see them; I just didn't show it.

Sīnis pulled a bottle of 'Kristofors' – locally-made gin that we colloquially called 'the ship' – out of his pocket. I paled a little at the memory of its taste, but I drank, and drank heartily; the smell of juniper made every cell in my body cringe, but the Crab passed me an open bottle of tonic. Turns out they were quite refined, my friends. I poured the tonic in to mix a fancy cocktail right in my mouth. The world became even better, I could feel it. I even wanted to say something about it, but I didn't know what. It was just like with the smell of spring.

Twang – the sound of a guitar. Twang, twang, twang, twang! What was that? We all turned toward the sound. There was a group of young guys setting up; Ziedonis was pulling out wires around them and looked very business-like. I didn't want to admit it, but I didn't know who they were. Dull Doll, someone said, seeing the confusion in my eyes.

Well, sure. I'd heard people talking about them; they were a newly-formed band. The first twangs of the guitar were indicative that they weren't starting their creative path in the right venue. Of course, all the alternative factions are kind of like us... But then again not really... What did I care, I just felt bad for all the people who had come here to find metal. I felt a little bad for the band, too.

Then some kid I didn't really know came up and shouted into my ear:

– Death is waiting outside for you.

And there he was, and I saw that I had been saving the rest of the Merkurs for nothing. Death was whipping his torso up and down as if he'd decided to slam his head into the ground as hard as he could, but then changed his mind at the last second. It was maniacal, uncontrollable headbanging, complete with some strange dance steps forward and back.

– Hey! he called out in one of the moments he managed to lift his head – I can't get in!

And again he lurched forward, then back upright.

– I don't have a lat.

Standing upright now, he didn't say anything else, and just stared at me. But I didn't have a lat, either. I went inside to talk to Ziedonis. He sometimes let his friends in for half-price. I doubted that Death even had fifty santims on him (I didn't). Maybe this time Ziedonis could get him in for free? I didn't want to be begging him. Where was he? Over there with the guys of Dull Doll, looking all official as he turned a knob on the amp. They'd just finished their set, the audience had listened to them politely, and the singer was saying:

– Thank you!

Someone in the audience, probably Ģirtiņš, shouted back:

– Thank *you* for stopping!

As happens between sets, the audience started to mill around – some went outside to smoke, others moved closer to the stage, because Heaven Grey was about to go on. And poor Death was standing outside, braving the storm; now where was Ziedonis? I bumped into Mele ('Hi!'), Sammie, Ģirtiņš, his girlfriend, Crab ('Can I borrow a lat?') and Death. He was standing right inside and was headbanging like before, except now he had a just-opened bottle of beer in his hand.

– How did you get in?

– I don't know!

And he let out an odd giggle. He clearly wasn't lying.

– I don't know.

Do you remember the task Nasreddin Afandhi was given by the travelling philosopher? To answer the forty most-complex questions with a single answer. Afandhi listened to all forty questions and said:

– I don't know.

More than seven hundred years have passed since then, but no one has been able to come up with a better answer. Death cackled like a mad philosopher and took a swig of his beer, which oddly enough seemed to sober him up a little. It didn't matter how he'd got in. We were here now, and Heaven Grey was starting their set.

There's nothing new or negative to be said about legends. And I truly have nothing negative to say about Heaven Grey. They poured their hearts into playing some old-school death metal songs, sometimes adding a few new doom elements, all of which made me nostalgic, and like on every night like this one, I reminded myself that we lived in an amazing time, that music was big and that we should take that whole guitar and band thing and actually do something with it. I resolved to talk to Death about it right after the concert. For now I pushed my way to the front row. Cramped, wet from the other bodies surrounding me, I felt like part of a single organism, at least that's what I liked to imagine, a single cell in a powerful organism. Couldn't I embrace the other cells, and not just wait for them to do the same? But then Heaven Grey played their greatest hit, and I had to stop thinking about life and start thinking about music.

Time flows, flows just like a river.

The river flows swiftly, inconceivably.

And these words seemed like deep, philosophical questions, even though time wasn't flowing at all then and the meaning of the lyrics was even inconceivable to the guy who had written them. But all of that is trivial compared to the vast grey heavens I walked out under right after the concert. The rosy ends of cigarettes glowed all around, and I was one of them. I wasn't alone. There was Death, his jacket all askew and – what was he holding!? He had his arms around a girl, and they were kissing like they were possessed. It was Milēdija. No, it wasn't and it couldn't be here, why would she be here. It was Mele's pretty friend; no, it wasn't her either. All cats look alike in the dark. It was a totally unfamiliar girl with very dark hair. When they broke away from one another for a moment to come up for air, Death noticed me and said:

– Hey!

He seemed stone cold sober, even though the only reason he was upright was because the girl was holding onto him.

She looked at me, too, then back to Death, then to me again and said:

– Hi!

Just ask me what I'm doing out here. I threw out all sorts of clever remarks about the concert and the meaning of metal. Death managed to respond coherently, but the girl just kept ruffling his hair and laughing. It was a pleasant laugh, clear and crackling, but it gave me chills. My teeth even chattered. But why? It felt familiar. I took out my bottle of Merkurs and offered it to them. The girl drank, her head tipped back to show the world her endless neck and the pulsing hollow at her collarbone. For some reason it got on my nerves, and I started to criticize Heaven Grey.

– They were great. Banging away, cutting, sawing. But... is that what metal is for? Isn't it somehow a little too perfect?

The girl listened to this:

– How come? I liked it!

– But where's the pain? Isn't metal supposed to be the antithesis to the world? Why do they want people to like them?

A few of the guys from the Other School had joined us and were listening intently.

– We're supposed to be about rejection. They've kind of given in to the Satan of acceptance.

Heaven Grey was not at all guilty of these things, but I was on a roll.

– It's time the band broke up.

That was crossing the line. No-one said anything.

I was embarrassed. I took a swig of Merkurs and gave the bottle to the people standing around before heading back inside, to use the bathroom, or so I told myself. I ran into the guys from Heaven Grey on my way down the stairs; they looked tired and were carrying their instrument cases. I wanted to hug them and ask for their forgiveness, but I didn't. It wasn't until I'd reached the doors that I turned to look back up at them. A few of the people standing outside cheered when they came out; they hadn't taken me seriously. Death's new girlfriend was standing right by the stairs. My insides went cold again. Standing at half-basement level I was face-to-face with her knees. Her knees had an interesting shape to them. I'd seen them once before. Those interesting knees and those very same boots. And that same screech of laughter, clear and cracking; I'd heard that before, too. Another shiver ran through me and I went inside.

It was a lot emptier now. Someone had put on Anathema's

'Sleepless'. It was exactly what I needed right now. As soon as the drums came crashing back in after a lull in the song, I was completely convinced that the judgements I'd passed on myself and others were stupid and unnecessary, that it was all in my head and, in the end, the snow had melted and the ice had shifted. But then a group of clowns rushed in and stumbled up to the podium and put on Pantera. Children, is this really the time for you to play the music from my first tender foray into metal, music that I've long since turned away from with a wry mile? But they just jumped around and danced like they'd found the source of true joy. My friends from the Other School came in and stood next to me, observing these kids with the same sadness. But where I had just muttered 'Goddamn jumpers' under my breath, they had crossed the line and were laughing loudly, mimicking their dance moves and shouting ironic slogans at them. It was like an echo of my controversial speech earlier. They wanted to take a stand against something, too. Maybe it was their way of backing me up. Either way, it made me uncomfortable. And I felt sorry for the younger kids.

I went outside to smoke. To find Death. But he wasn't out there. There wasn't really anyone outside anymore. The ideal moment for a lonely or at least relaxed smoke. But as soon as I took a drag, an unfamiliar voice addressed me:

– Give me the new Therion!

It was a good way to start a conversation, cut right to music. My new acquaintance turned out to be pretty knowledgeable for such a runt (he was a grade younger than me). He knew stuff, there was no denying it. I, of course, glanced around, bored, but I had to admit that some of what he said was spot-on.

– That's how it should be. The majority of music is shit. Good things don't come along often.

– True, true. Hm.

He looked at me. Then he looked away, across the street, and said:

– Want to start a band?

I looked away too. So he wouldn't see my smile. But I didn't know what I was smiling about. I felt incredibly happy, but didn't want to show it. I also didn't believe that we'd actually start a band, but this situation in which two complete strangers bond over the same dream

– it was something else.

I was trying to decide whether to ask him his name or what he'd play in the band, when Crab burst out of the Junkyard and raced by without looking back. Not far behind him was Sīnis. They both ran out onto the street and disappeared from view. I thought – strange, if they were going to be rude and just leave like that, why didn't they grab their coats? Because they'd both had on black coats when they'd arrived. They'd both taken off as if they'd lost their minds, or else as if someone was chasing after them.

And that was the case. Almost immediately after them came a mob of those same young Pantera fans. To clarify, the reason I referred to them as young is because they were new to this scene. Physically speaking they were almost at level with us, and a few of them were pretty fit. It became clear why they had run off, and that my friends' chances weren't great. As a good friend, I immediately took off after their pursuers to try and help minimize the damage. When I reached the street I saw the backs of the Pantera mob; they ran as hard as they could, but I eventually slowed down. There was no way I was going to catch up to them. And Crab and Sīnis had such a good head start, that they were likely far ahead of them and already to safety. But I didn't stop running, either, and continued at a light jog. A small, chubby Pantera fan ran up from behind to join me. He must have thought that I was on his side, and said, panting:

– Why'd they have to go and do that? Why'd they have to poke fun at our music? I don't get it, we're all friends here, how come Pantera is worse than the rest, can't we all just like what we like?

I picked up my pace and pulled away from him. I didn't want to listen anymore.

I'd lost sight of the others. I turned down one street, then another; nothing but darkness. I headed back to the Junkyard.

The pack of Pantera fans had returned as well, but there was no sign of Sīnis or Crab. From what I could gather they had managed to escape. The Pantera fans turned to me, exasperated:

– Why'd they have to do that? We're all friends here, why do they have to go calling people posers?

There was genuine hurt in their voices, and they turned to me like some expert on metal ideology. But I said nothing, just took drag after drag of my cigarette. Eventually they stopped asking. Then the party was over. Ziedonis was rolling up the cords. I didn't see my new bandmate or Death anywhere. The stragglers were putting on their coats and heading home. After the Pantera fans had left – they even waved goodbye, as if we'd forged some sort of strange friendship – I went down to the coatroom. It was empty except for two black jackets – Crab's and Sīnis'. I took them and went outside; I'd bring them their jackets the following day. I doubt they were going to come back here tonight looking for them, and you could only get into the basement on Fridays. The guard locked the basement door behind me.

The snow was completely gone, and the streets looked empty. I felt exhausted, almost drunk. So much had happened tonight. It wasn't comfortable carrying the two coats. I dropped them on the ground and sat on them. I found a pack of cigarettes in Sīnis' coat pocket. I sat there, smoking, trying to make sense of the night's events. And couldn't. All I could think was that I had to do something, something big and extraordinary had to happen. But the street, the buildings, the fence and even the trees seemed indifferent to what I was feeling – it seemed impossible that the trees branches weren't transmitting some kind of code to make the fence open up to another dimension. I tilted my head back to look at the sky, to blow smoke into it, and saw the Moon. I'd hoped for it, and there it was. The Moon was a sign of security, it was so round and bright, it couldn't just be Earth's four-hundred-thousand-kilometres-away satellite; it was clearly a sign for lonely metalheads. And what this sign say? I didn't ask, but just stared right up at the Moon.

13

One weekend I went on a picturesque trip with my two thug friends. Hanging out with the metalheads always required mental effort, stress and attention. It was easier with the thugs. I'd already accepted that they weren't going to beat me up. I could unwind around them.

The thugs often went out into the countryside to relax. The air was better there, that's what the tall one said. His name was Kandžejs. The short stout one, Kroģis, didn't really care either way; it hadn't occurred to him, either, that you could go somewhere else for fun. Unfortunately, the fresh air wasn't enough for Kandžejs – he wanted to fish, too. This time he was incredibly serious:

– You can sell pikes at five lats a kilogram. You catch fifty kilograms worth – that's two hundred fifty big ones!

Were we going to catch fifty kilograms of pike? Kandžejs brushed off my concerns:

– Don't piss on my parade, I've got this.

And so we piled into the black BMW and drove off. We had a car. I didn't get to drive a lot. Well, my dad had his Zhiguli, but that was different. The BMW was like freedom on wheels, where we could talk about anything, smoke and drink. We each had a bottle of Tērvetes beer in hand, everything was great, but when we reached the road to Eleja the devil started to loosen up my tongue.

– A girl named Diāna from my class lives in that house.

And I pointed to a small house. How did I know she lived there? And why had I said that? Whatever came into mind came rushing out of my mouth – that's how it was around these guys. I kept going:

– She's pretty.

And she was. But Kandžejs braked so hard that Kroģis cried out as he spilled some beer on his pants.

– What're you doing, asshole?

– We should go say hi.

And he turned the car into Diāna's driveway. I grew pensive:

– Do you know her?

– No, she's your classmate.

I only knew her well enough to know her initials – D. M. Like Dark Millennium, a great band, old-school. There's this one song on *Ashore the Celestial Burden*, I think it was 'Beyond the Dragon's Eye', man that was a great song! Gentle and lulling at the beginning and then – boom! There wasn't a lot of heavy drumming or bassline, but that voice could tear the roof off, and it was in that old style of singing where you could actually understand the words. Not like now, when songs are performed like they're going to be hits. It was like being in a chamber theatre, where you were shown dark and curious scenes that appeared to be realistic.

Kandžejs had already rung the doorbell and, great, D. M. herself answered the door. She must've been expecting someone else, or no one at all, because all she was wearing was a T-shirt and pants, red pants. It was probably meant to be very sexy, and I was mortified. But Kandžejs said:

– Hi, Diāna!

– Hi!

Then she looked at me, but I said nothing. Kandžejs continued:

– Jānis said that a pretty girl from his school lived here, and we couldn't drive by without stopping to say hello.

She laughed; Diāna liked what she heard. I was the only one here who felt stupid and was excelling at achieving a tomato-red appearance. The gallant gentleman continued:

– The weather's good today, and it's supposed to be a lovely evening. We'd like to invite you to join us by the bonfire. We'll have red wine and pike fillet with celery root. We'll also recite poetry.

Two more girls came to the door, whom I didn't know and who weren't as pretty as Diāna, but the *charmeur* didn't miss a beat:

– And your friends, of course, are invited as well!

Diāna turned to them, well, what about a picnic? They wrinkled their noses. Diāna turned back to us:

– Okay. But not right now, we're doing laundry. Where will you be?

– In Ruļļi. At the bend in the river.

– Great. We'll see you there.

And she scratched her thigh, and I couldn't look away. Then there was a goodbye overflowing with compliments and offering the girls some beer, then we were finally back in the car.

– Now we've got something to work with.

Kroģis voiced his opinion:

– Her friends were pretty awful.

– No worries, just put a paper bag over their heads before you bone.

This was batshit. I was all ready to relax without any stress, but now we were planning orgies. I mean, that had always been a fantasy of mine, but it was a cause for anxiety. Because you only have peace when you don't have anyone, at least when you don't have any prospects.

Kandžejs dropped us off at the romantic bend in the river and drove off; he was supposed to bring the car back to someone. Thug business. We were left with orders to pitch the tent, a stack of firewood (parquet boards) and an unlabelled, one-litre plastic bottle filled with clear liquid.

Kroģis and I each took a swig of what was the best moonshine in Jelgava, and then did a passable job pitching the tent before we lay back to doze. It really was a lovely evening. If only those girls wouldn't show up. No, but I did want some kind of adventure. But how would it go down? And what if I wound up with the one with the bag over her head? Kroģis was thinking more practically:

– I don't know how but our tent is full of mosquitos. The girls aren't going to like that.

We crawled into the tent and lit cigarettes, hoping to smoke out the insects. We smoked so much that we had to evacuate ourselves. The smoke hung in the tent in horizontal layers, just like girls like it. Then Kandžejs reappeared carrying a large rucksack.

– Igarjoks dropped me off. I think I have everything.

And he started to unpack it. The first thing he took out was binoculars.

– To get a close-up of the ladies?

– No, to keep an eye out for inspectors. All this here is strictly *verboten*.

Then he took out another bottle of moonshine and two short sticks. Kandžejs brought the binoculars to his face, had a look around, and then the lit the tip of the cord at one end of the rod:

– *Davai*, bitches, let's catch some fishes!

And he threw the rod into the lake. I watched to see what would happen, but Kandžejs shouted:

– Hit the deck!

This really was some stress-free night. I flattened myself against the ground and for the second time that day wished I could just crawl right into it. The first time had been when Diāna had looked at my tomato-red face.

– Cover your ears!

I did so without question.

A small *splash!* came from the river. It hadn't been so bad. My friends got to their feet, as did I. Kroǵis said:

– It didn't work!

I didn't understand.

– But there was some sort of splash!

– The detonator worked, but the dynamite didn't catch. *Davai*, let's try again. Kandžejs lit the second rod and launched it into the river:

– For the motherland!

I dropped to the ground and landed face-first in a molehill. Staring down into the earth, I heard it again – *splash!* And then a silence so pronounced that I could almost hear the fish laughing.

– What hole did you pull that dynamite from?

Kroǵis didn't like it when things didn't work the way they were supposed to.

– Not one I'm gonna stick it back into.

We got to our feet and looked at the river. Both sticks were right there, floating among the reeds.

– Who's going to go get them?

That was a good question. None of us could walk on water. I asked a question worthy of Francis Macomber:

– Can't we just leave it?

Kroǵis snorted with professional disdain:

– You can't just shit up a river with dynamite! How would that look?

And Kandžejs added:

– A pike could swallow it, someone will catch it, take it home to fry it, and the whole pan will explode.

Right. I looked at the river.

– And it won't explode now?

– Who knows with shit like that. If it won't go off when you need it, then god only knows what'll happen when you don't need it.

Very well said.

– You're a metalhead, right?

– Yeah.

– Isn't that, like, your style? To fish an explosive out of a river with your bare hands?

It was. It was about as metal as it gets. If I were here with Kārlis or Death, or even Diāna's group, I'd be happy to dive in after the dynamite. Because of that I asked:

– Wonder where the girls are at?

At that moment we heard a splash twice as loud as both sticks of dynamite combined. Kroģis had fallen into the river. He'd stepped on a piece of driftwood to try and reach out and hook the dynamite with a stick he'd found, and had fallen in. Now he was calling everything a motherfucker and threw the dud sticks up onto the riverbank. One of them hit Kandžejs in the back.

– What the hell?

And he picked it up to throw it right back. I begged them:

– Guys, okay, let's take five!

They obeyed me and calmed down a little. We started a fire from the parquetted boards, and Kroģis stripped off his clothes.

– Where're the girls at? I don't want to have to get dressed again if I don't have to.

He was scraping mud off of his pants with that the same stick. Kandžejs looked on in surprise:

– That's what you were using to poke around the lake? I've got fishing poles.

– You have something inside that skull of yours, too?

– I have everything we need to fish.

He started to dig through his rucksack and his excitement was renewed.

– Gentlemen, the girls will be here soon, but we still don't have any fish. Let's go, let's go, get to work, everyone up!

He took two telescoping fishing poles out of his rucksack and pulled them out to their full length. Phew, I thought, only two, I can sit back. But then he tossed them to the side next to the tent and started to pull out something odd and shapeless.

– The *putanka*, he explained.

I didn't bother to ask. They'd already overpowered me today. The shapeless object turned out to be a net. Kandžejs looked at it like it was a naked woman.

– Any pike that gets into this is there to stay. *Davai*, into the river, let's go, Kroģis, you're already wet!

Both of these madmen moved quickly to toss the net into the river, and then stepped back to look at it.

– I don't think we did it right.

– Well you're the fisherman.

– This isn't the best spot. Let's move it over there, past the bend.

The iron weights knocked against our ankles as we carried the dripping mess past the bend.

– This is the spot. We just need to stretch it across the river and then we can just sit back and scratch our balls.

– How are we supposed to do that?

– With your hand!

– No, get the net across the river?

– I have a boat!

And he really did have a boat. A rolled-up plastic one. He just didn't have a pump. But no matter, we'd blow it up while having a smoke. We'd exhale the smoke into the boat, it would be great, smoke rises.

We blew up the boat.

– The valve doesn't have a cap. We'll have to hold it shut by hand.

We got into the boat, Kandžejs up front, holding his left hand over the valve and paddling with the right (because we didn't have oars); Kroģis was in the middle with the net on his lap, paddling with both of his giant hands; I was in the back, covering the other valve opening with my right hand and paddling with my left. The water was fairly cold.

Once across, we secured the net among the reeds, blew the boat back up, and headed back to the other side. After the net was secured on both ends, the voice of reason finally spoke through Kroģis:

– I think it's time for a drink.

We needed it. Kandžejs took out a carton of grape juice, poured half of it onto the ground and topped the carton off with moonshine:

– We have our red wine, we practically have our fish – everything is just as I said it would be. The girls are probably already somewhere nearby.

The sun was setting, and it looked really romantic through the wild undergrowth. Like the Anathema album cover for *The Silent Enigma*. The bonfire was blazing, the wind was good and even the girls didn't seem so terrifying anymore.

– We should talk about something, Kandžejs suggested.

– You think?

Kroģis wasn't convinced. He wasn't one for small talk.

– What should we talk about?

– Jānis, you're the genius. Tell us something.

– Like what?

– How're things with metal?

Now that I could talk about. I took a drink for good measure and said:

– Grishnackh is supposedly writing a new album while he's in prison.

Kandžejs even seemed a little interested:

– Where is he?

– Bergen, Norway.

– Ah, how nice. That's basically a hotel. Have him write a new album out here. He'd probably only write *СЛОН* on the wall, nothing more.

The idea that an imprisoned metalhead would be dreaming about *слон* – elephants – suddenly seemed very logical to me:

– But why *СЛОН*?

– *Смерты Легавым От Ножа*, or Kill Narcs with Knives. He could also write *ПОСТ. Прости, отец, судьба такая*, or Forgive me, father, such is fate. Usually you get it tattooed across your knuckles the first time you're locked up.

– Unholy burned a bunch of Burzum and Mayhem CDs at one of their concerts once. You see, Unholy were so underground that the latter two seemed mainstream to them.

– What do they even sing about? I can't understand them.

I condensed my thoughts:

– It depends, really. Black metal bands sing about the Moon.

– The moon?

– Yup, the one shining brightly in the sky.

– It would shine even more if, say, we had Diāna to pass around.

– Yeah, yeah, yeah. They also sing about Satan, demons. Queen Inanna. About raging through red clouds and holocaust winds. But mostly about the moon, and ice. Sometimes about steel vaginas. Maze of Cako Torment even sing entirely in a language they invented.

– Very interesting.

– Death bands sing about philosophical things. A lot about death. About eating corpse. Doom bands sing about broken hearts. Suicide is a common topic, too.

– Glo-glo-glo-glo-glorrr!

Kroģis gargled his red wine, unknowingly singing what was a pretty decent guttural growl. Then he said:

– I don't get it, though. You're a good guy. Don't even want to kill fish.

A good guy. What would Euronymous say about that?

– You like all kinds of pretty things and birds. Why do you listen to songs about a bunch of cannibalistic twats?

– I mean... They're also really beautiful. Like Impaled Nazarene, it's about those iron... It's really nice.

– Don't know. I didn't like it.

I had made them listen to my music whenever I could pull Kandžejs away from his thug songs. And it was strange; they'd obviously heard the same thing I did. Their ears couldn't be constructed that differently from mine. And their hearts were the same ones that liked to relax by a bonfire. What facts, events, mental experiences collect in one's perception to turn a single phenomenon into several? When the impressionists started to paint their colourful scenes, critics laughed – did the artist's model spend a week rotting away in a bog, why is her neck blue? Their eyes were all eyes, and even now people's eyes are eyes, but now the impressionists are liked by moms and wallpaper manufacturers. Was the same thing going to happen to metal? No, it couldn't. Remember Kurt; we have to protect our sorrow with wry faces and choked voices.

Kandžejs joined our conversation about aesthetics:

– Speaking of cannibals, there was one guy in prison who ate himself. None of this corpse eating, he was totally alive.

And then he elbowed me.

– Cut out a piece of your thigh, fry it up and – *davai*! Or else slice open your hand, trickle a half-litre of blood into a bowl, dip some bread into it and eat it like soup.

That was really something. Something Carcass or Visceral Evisceration might sing about.

– Why did he do it?

– A lot of reasons. Because there's nothing else to do. And to prove he had balls. Could you do that?

– We don't have bread.

But Kandžejs called out:

– Where are the chicks? I'm filled with poetry!

He started to recite:

> *On the mountain there is a hut*
> *by the name of 'Boozer'.*
> *Alcoholic beasts*
> *around its tables in their seats.*

It was a long poem, animalistic through and through, full of various unexpected turns. All I remember is that at the end one of its protagonists 'took out his cock and shot himself'.

I recited a poem as well:

> Beyond the window a blue autumn eve,
> and wind stifling against the pane.
> Every matter of the heart,
> Drinks eternity like milk.

Kroģis got up and went into the bushes to piss. Then he suddenly tripped over the night air and went tumbling into the bushes. Kandžejs hooted with joy:

– Kroģis is already dancing! Let's go, alright, party!

And we got up too and started to jump around with Kroģis in the middle, who'd forgotten why he was up in the first place and why he'd fallen; he'd forgotten enough for him to dance like people had danced at the beginning of time, waving his gigantic hands overhead. Kandžejs did the tango, his entire body filling our dance floor, which for some reason felt more vertical than horizontal. We no longer took turns speaking, but spoke all at once, losing our train of thought. Kandžejs opened the second jug of moonshine and another bottle of juice; a lot of it spilled onto the ground, and we drank and danced until the grass all around us was trampled flat, and Kroģis kept getting up and falling down and then he shouted:

– Get your hunger sticks out of here!

He was tangled up in the fishing poles. Kandžejs hurried to save an important lure or something and stepped right onto the tent, and blue cigarette smoke poured out of it. It all looked very picturesque, except that I didn't really see it because it was already dark.

– I just hope nothing bad happened to the girls. Maybe they got lost.

With these words Kandžejs slumped back to the dying fire. Kroģis took a deep breath and hollered with all his might. His had a strong set of lungs:

– Ladies! We're over here! With drinks!

– What're you yelling for? You'll just get the cops to come out. Put some wood on the fire!

Kroģis added some wood to the fire, without even telling Kandžejs off.

– Blow on it, too, otherwise it'll go out.

That he didn't do. Instead he asked:

– Where're we going to find cops out here?

– Shh. These days they're all over the place. They get five hundred lats for every fugitive they bring back.

He spat, thus expressing his disdain for this information. I suddenly felt very sober, suddenly it all made sense. Where exactly did Kandžejs come from? Why had he only just recently shown up? Had anyone seen him before the events in April? He was one of the guys who had broken out of prison. Maybe he'd even been one of the guys who had passed me on the bridge that night. How strange fate is, how unexpected and, at the same time, logical the way things fall into place is. I'd been waiting for a fugitive to come to my apartment, but instead, I had come to him, and it wasn't Juris' brother, but in a way, my own.

He asked:

– Have you lost it? Why are you laughing like crazy?

I really had been overcome with a maniacal laughter, the kind you get in moments of divine revelation. I fell silent and lit a cigarette; the wind blew the ash into my face, caressing my like fate, like a warm greeting from hell. Kroģis was talking about a mailbox that had made some guy in India rich.

– I don't get why, but everyone wants these mailboxes. And this guy's a legit millionaire.

I'd never imagined that having more than fifty lats. But five hundred – that's exactly how much a Gibson Les Paul cost at the AT Trade store. An original. A guitar-cum-golem that embodied not only the solution to every problem and the fulfilment of every dreams, but also the beginning of a new war. And it became clear to me where I'd get the money: take my friend, who was rolling around on the ground, and turn him in!

– From shit mailboxes! He got rich from a bunch of shit mailboxes that don't even make any sense! That's how it's done – make money from shit!

– We do a lot of shit, so, so far so good.

Suddenly I heard growling next to me. A proper, quality, thick growl from the depths of the throat. Even if we had taken a stereo with us, no one could have a tape with a sound like that. It was a vision, a sign, a signal for sacrifice.

Kroģis had thrown up on himself. While still laughing. He wasn't bothered by little things like that. I wanted to laugh and puke too. I wanted to be accepted as a human being who was not only envied, but hated, and feared. But they just kept laughing and making me laugh, they broke me, but I didn't break, even though the breaking point was near.

The next thing I knew I was cold and it was morning. My first thought was that I'd slept through the girls showing up. I looked next to me – nope, no girls. Just blades of grass in clayey soil. I looked around. No signs of an orgy. The tent was empty; no one had slept in it. Kroģis was snoring nearby. Both sticks of dynamite were lying in the fire pit – the last logs Kroģis had drunkenly thrown in, but hadn't blown on the embers.

I looked to the river to see the one final picturesque scene – Kandžejs pulling the net out of the water. A classical motif, and its protagonist reflected that beauty characteristic of the condemned and the betrayed. There was a single fish in the net.

14

As soon as you get to Jelgava, as soon as you've crossed both bridges, you see a church tower. It's not particularly tall and isn't architecturally interesting. Our tower is in ruins. An empty shell that was engulfed by flames fifty years ago. If you snuck into it and looked up you could see a square patch of sky. The church itself had been razed to the ground in the 1944 battles, but the tower survived, though half its original height, empty and contemplative.

In case you're wondering, it had been the Holy Trinity Church – the first church in the world build specifically for Lutherans.

Now the tower served a different purpose. See, the local government (read: the local underground government) wanted to covertly support metalheads. It was announced that the city wanted to rebuild the Holy Trinity Church tower and, to raise funds, they'd organise a music festival called 'For the Tower'.

On your way out of Jelgava, past the second bridge but before Store No. 6, is a kind of wasteland. There, to the right of the highway if you're headed towards Ozolnieki, is a goat. It was a fairly large goat, about three metres tall. It had been built out of metal pipes by artist Mārtiņš Vilkārsis. The reason for the sculpture was, as were many things in my life, writer Aleksandrs Čaks. He had written a poem titled 'Jelgava':

> A city small as a dust mote,
> It's local symbol – a white goat

Some literary scholars argued that the poem wasn't about Jelgava at all. Jelgava wasn't "small as a dust mote" in Čaks' time. The poet was most likely talking about New Jelgava. Do they think Čaks was a moron? The poem was titled 'Jelgava', what more proof did you need?! And the goat stood there with iron resolve.

The open-air stage where the 'For the Tower' festival took place was approximately half-way between the tower and goat, but on the opposite side of the highway. The Palace was on the other side of the Lielupe River, and you had to cross a bridge to get to the open-air stage. Two bridges, actually, across the Lielupe and Driksa rivers. That's how it all started.

The whole city was saying that this was going to be a fateful trek across the bridge for the metalheads. A bunch of short-haired cretins were supposedly planning on taking the opportunity to surround us in that narrow, confined space. They'd steal our leather jackets, kick the shit out of us and throw us in the river. Supposedly one guy had already been thrown into the river. You could think these were only rumours, but this time they said it was for real.

That night I approached the bridge alone. As always at fateful moments. My real friends said that they still had to meet up with someone and take care of something, so they'd meet me inside. And so I went alone, totally, totally alone. Just Eva and Robčiks were with me.

We spent the whole way talking only about the awful things waiting for us at the bridges.

When we got to the first bridge, our conversation stopped. I glanced at them; Robčiks looked terrified. Dusk had started to settle. Eva said cheekily:

– You two sure know how to make a girl feel safe!

She and I had made out before. And now she's acting like this. No matter, I'd brought it on myself. I'd had the world at my feet (or under them, or something), but I'd chosen rejection, I'd chosen to soldier on alone through a gauntlet of our adversaries, the only way out in the waters below me. I tried not to look up, not at Eva, not at the dangerous road ahead. Gently, as gently as I'd slid my hand over her stomach, I now slid my hand across the railing and stared down into the water. Like the time I'd seen the inmates. That was so long ago.

Then, suddenly, the water was gone. We'd already made it across the second bridge! And nothing, absolutely nothing had happened! It had been so stupid to believe those rumours and to keep quiet on the bridge, as if we'd been afraid!

The open-air stage was just up ahead. Rows of chairs in the middle of a field and a stage at the far end, on which something was already flashing and thumping. Someone was doing a sound check. We still had to get by security, big muscly types, who were collecting admission fees. But then we wouldn't have any money for beer.

– Should we try to get in without paying?

– How, though?

– Sneak in somehow.

Robčiks tried to think:

– Maybe from the river, through the reeds?

– You insane?

I didn't want to go wading through the reeds.

Someone called my name. I turned around casually; it was a metalhead I'd met before, one of the respectable ones. I didn't know his name, but he knew mine, and Eva and Robčiks saw this. I went over to him and held out my hand. But he said:

– Death said for you to wait for him here.

– Okay.

And then he very pointedly added:

– There's another way to get in!

That made me feel like one of them. I looked back at Eva and Robčiks. The guy hurried to say:

– No, no! Not all of you. One.

– But of course! Of course! Thanks.

– Wait here.

He left, and I went back to my friends. I lit a cigarette and said:

– Hey, okay! I've got to wait here for a buddy, you guys go on in.

Eva turned and headed for the entrance. Robčiks didn't know what to do. I helped him with a look that said: 'Go, go! I'll see you inside'.

I looked across the river to the palace. It was so big that it didn't seem to be so much rising up as it seemed to be lunging. It looked like there was something shining in one of the windows. Ms Anna, the palace custodian and long-term resident, had once told me in confidence that the place was full of ghosts. Especially the second storey, where the chemistry department was. One night a security guard had been making his rounds and had heard someone playing the piano. He went to check it out. The door was locked. The guard open it – there was no-one there, no-one playing. He close the door, ha, and the music started up again. He went through this a few more times. Sometimes the playing continued even when the guard was in the room, but he still saw no one. By then the guard was really worked up and shouted: 'Who are you?' But there was no reply. Only music.

Maybe the invisible pianist was playing even now, but you couldn't hear it because Frontlines was already doing their sound check on stage. I wanted to see them up-close. When were they going to get me inside?

Just then my friends wandered over, also having made it across the bridges without incident. Pūpols, Death, Zombie, Tonijs. We exchanged greetings, and Zombie asked a logical question:

– How do we get in?

I answered his question with another question:

– Wasn't Death supposed to get us in somehow?

Zombie turned to face our friend:

– Oh really?

Death bristled:

– I don't know.

– Know what?

– If it'll work.

– Well c'mon, get us in, what's the deal?

– I was supposed to meet up with Mareks, that was the first part of the plan.

– Where is he?

– Inside, I guess.

– Then go inside!

With that, Pūpols brought the discussion to an end. We all looked over at the entrance. The security guards, it seemed, had been eyeing us for some time.

Tonijs usually came up with a plan:

– Let's leave, pretend like we don't want to be here. Then we'll sneak in from the side.

We turned and left. I wondered if it looked at all believable, like we didn't want to go to the concert and had just come out here to have a look. I expressed my concerns. Tonijs had thought of everything:

– Well, then let them think that we have to go meet someone. Yeah, that we're going to go meet up with some girls!

Zombies called out for good measure:

– Madara! Madara, sweetie, where are you?

Pūpols started to sputter with laughter, but Death, who was glancing over his shoulder, hissed:

– Shut up, they're still watching us!

We'd just reached the main road, but he kept hissing:

– They're still watching!

Then we crossed the highway and stopped. Maybe we were out of their line of sight here. Tonijs laid out the plan – we'd climb down to the river on this side, along the bridge supports back to the other side and sneak back to the stage through the reeds. The riverbank on this side of the bridge looked fairly overgrown. I couldn't quite make out the type of plant in the twilight, but I was pretty sure they were nettles.

Two girls crossed the bridge and came toward us. It was Mele and her pretty friend. They came out of the night like ghosts. Surprisingly, her friend opened her mouth this time to talk:

– You called?

– Us?

I didn't even know her name. None of us did. But Mele was convinced:

– It was you! What do you want?

For whatever reasons she seemed even grumpier than usual, while her pretty friend was uncharacteristically happy. Grinning like an idiot. But Mele took the lead:

– We have an extra ticket. You guys need one?

We all started to grin like idiots. We didn't know what to say. The friend spoke first:

– Take it! It's a gift!

Everyone's hands shot out to take it; someone did, but it wasn't me. The friend continued:

– It's my birthday today!

Now we really didn't know what to say. Someone said 'Mmm', someone else said 'Ooh', until I gathered my senses and said:

– So, drinks on you!

And oh, how my friends laughed. The birthday girl closed her mouth, confused. Mele took her by the elbow, let's go. Tonijs waved the ticket and said:

– I'm going to go, okay, and I'll find Mareks so he can get you in, okay? *Davai*, see you inside!

And he ran off across the road to join the girls.

We stayed where we were. Zombie said:

– Alright then!

And he disappeared in to the roadside thicket. And we followed, we followed.

A few steps in the thicket was already well above our heads. The ground sunk beneath our feet.

– I stepped in water! Zombie called out.

We were standing on a narrow, nettle-ridden strip of sand right by the water. I suddenly realized that Tonijs was a traitor. He abandoned us. This had been his plan. Mele was a traitor, too.

Meanwhile, Death had taken charge:

– Time for a drink!

Pūpols reached into his jacket pocket. He brought out an already-opened bottle, which by the taste of it was black-currant flavoured Riga vodka. Death also passed around a small bottle of some unidentifiable liquor. We all lit cigarettes, and the smoke rose above the darkened Jelgava skyline, where there had once been a synagogue, but now were just regular buildings and the tower, the tower we were all here for tonight. After the bottle had been passed around three times and then tossed in the river, carrying away with it a message of emptiness and the final chords of Frontlines' set, we all turned to the right and headed under the bridge.

I walked carefully along the narrow strip of sand. Something splashed next to me. It was Zombie; he hadn't gotten back out of the water and was now trudging along in it up to his knees.

– Why are you in the water?

– Because.

And there was the bridge. We walked under it as if it were a roof. The strip of sand ended; we stepped onto the hard, but very steep embankment under the bridge. Death patted one of the concrete columns:

– Solid bridge! Should we drink to it?

And how his words echoed! The acoustics scared us, and we drank in silence (this time I didn't notice who took out what). I chugged the sweet beverage, it went down like the river with a painful glugging that echoed against the railings. Something huge drove over the bridge, probably the last bus to Ozolnieki. Death pissed into the river and it sounded like a waterfall.

But even more imposing was the voice that said:

– You guys are idiots!

I poured some vodka down the wrong pipe, but my heart spat it back out. It was a female voice, and a tearful one at that. Could it be the White Lady? Ms Anna had seen her once with her own eyes, crying out in the palace courtyard next to the giant bell. How far were we from the palace?

But it wasn't the White Lady. It was Mele and her friend. Pūpols' anger flared:

– What're you doing here?

– Nothing. We just wanted to sit for a bit.

– You have any more extra tickets?

– No.

– Where's Tonijs?

– Who?

– That guy.

– He's inside.

I took another drink to calm my racing heart. It was all so, so stupid! Shouldn't we be inside to?

– So are we *not* going in?

– We're going. Give me a drink!

– What are you pissing in the river for? Are you stupid or something?

It was Mele talking. She added:

– It's so uncultured!

I wondered if she wasn't actually a ghost. Then , quietly, before Zombie was able to guffaw, I head a piano.

– D'you hear that? A piano!

– Where?

– From the palace!

– It's not from the palace. It's an acoustic trick. And it's not even a piano.

Death was always the rational one.

– It's Skumju akmeņi, their set just started. Let's just go, guys.

And we set off again. It really was Skumju akmeņi playing, I could just make out the words:

> In the moonlight my stones of sorrow,
> My flower of sorrow blooms like crimson,
> When it opens, it scatters stone seeds.
> And I'm like a child ignorant to life.

By now we were right alongside the open-air stage. One of the security guards yanked me out and held me tightly, even though I didn't try to run. There were a few other guards standing all around us. The one holding me asked:

– What should we do? Bring them to the cops?

His question wasn't directed at me. But I knew one-hundred per cent that I absolutely could not wind up in jail because then my parents would get caught up in all this, but they had nothing to do with it. But then Mele spoke up:

– They were coming to visit me! I live right over there!

– Where over there?

The guards looked at the reeds, at the river. Three more dark figures joined our group. The guard turned to them:

– We caught them trying to sneak in through the reeds!

– Those are my guys! My band, and we're about to go on!

It was Mareks. And next to him – Tonijs.

The guards all turned to look at Mareks, who said:

– For real.

And he pointed to us one by one:

– Guitar, vocals, bass, second guitar and manager.

Why god, why was I the manager! Anything but that!

The guard had a follow-up question:

– What about drums?

Mareks answered, sounded the slightest bit offended:

– I'm the drummer!

Then the guards all turned to look at the third guy, who had come with Mareks and Tonijs, and looked to be more in charge than anyone. He asked Mareks:

– But, but, but, but didn't your band already play?

– No, man! We're next!

The guy in charge looked embarrassed over not knowing the difference. He had the same long hair, but looked a little older. He gestured to the guards, fine, let them go. We all went inside. One of the guards asked:

– But what were you doing...

Another said:

– And the girls! The girls? Who are they?

Everyone looked to them, but the girls squealed:

– It's okay! It's okay! We have tickets!

And that's how we all got in. Tonijs was furious:

– What took you so long? We were waiting around like a bunch of idiots.

Death asked Mareks:

– Are you really on after Skumju akmeņi?

– We played our set ages ago, Mareks answered and left, also furious.

We sat down on a bench near the stage. Finally, after all the excitement we'd earned a bit of music.

It was beautiful. The band's vocalist was a woman – something that, for this genre, was rare in and of itself. At least back then it was. And she was even growling!

The mute Earth smoulders silently!

But the rest of the audience wasn't that into it. There was only one fan jumping around in front of the stage, a rather pretty blonde girl.

Zombie brought us each a beer in wobbly plastic cups. I took a sip and realized how good this music was. Helēna sang the ballad with even more tenderness, and the blonde girl jumped even higher. I was overcome with emotion, and I tried to get Zombie excited too:

– It's nice, isn't it?

– Sure; pigs squeal just as well.

Such were his compliments.

Skumju akmeņi finished up their set, and there was a long pause, as if we hadn't just shown up thirsting for music. We had just taken our seats, Pūpols had only spilled beer on himself once and the question of 'What now?' lingered in the air, when an long-haired guy we'd never seen before raced over to us and whispered:

– They broke Nose's nose! Come on!

We got up and followed him. He led us right up to the stage and around the corner, where a small group of people had gathered. Nose was standing with his back against the stage, wiping blood off his face. His nose really was broken, and properly at that – there was a dark cut across the bridge that was bleeding profusely. Nose touched the blood with his fingers and drew stripes with it across his cheeks.

There were two younger guys standing next to him. But not my thugs. It was my childhood friend Anrijs, and Beast's brother – who I was with the first time I'd gotten drunk. These three were surrounded by a group of metalheads. Beat's brother seemed to be answering a question someone just asked:

– But he pushed me! I mean, maybe it was an accident, I don't know. But am I just supposed to let everyone push me around?

I stepped forward and asked Anrijs:

– Anrijs?

He shook his head – no, I didn't do anything. Some curly-haired guy, who seemed to be running things, gestured for me to get lost. It came off a little offensive, and I wanted to shout at my old friends: 'You're going to burn in Hell anyway, so kick this poodle's ass!' But I didn't say anything, and I didn't leave, either. Anrijs kept his eyes down and was slowly moving his hand towards his inside jacket-pocket.

Just when it felt like something was about to happen, the security guards showed up. They we already angry for some reason. They snapped:

– What's going on here?

Death motioned in Nose's direction, see for yourselves. The guards looked at him. He just kept wiping blood off his nose and streaking it across his face. One of the guards asked:

– Who broke your nose?

But Nose said nothing. The guard lost it and yelled:

– Who broke your nose?

Nose really wasn't having a good night – first his nose is broken and now he's being yelled at. But why isn't he saying anything? Death and the curly-haired guy were silent, too; everyone was silent, even Anrijs, who was looking off into the distance and swallowing nervously. Nose just shook his head and waved his hand – both gestures were ambiguous – and then he left.

The rest of us wandered off in separate directions, quietly and without looking back. A guitar wailed, it was very familiar, a shiver went through me – could it be? Death and I looked at one another and raced back to the stage.

It was Huskvarn! Back then, when everything was new and unknown, they were already ancient and famous (I had their newest tape, *Bomb Brain Melodies*). Everyone was headed to the stage, yes, Huskvarn! The drums sounded like a cannon that shot down everything that had happened so far tonight. The guitars wailed again, louder this time. The entire world truly, truly shook. We made it to the front row easily. A lot of better- and lesser-known celebrities had gathered here. Asleep on the bench closest to the stage, his genius' eyes closed, glasses snug on his face, was the famous Joṇevs, totally off in dreamland. Even closer to the stage, of course, Gustavs, a kid who followed Huskvarn around to all their concerts like a prodigal son. At that time he didn't yet know that he would later become a rapper and go by the name Gustavo.

Urbix grabbed the microphone and shouted:

– Good evening, Jelgava!

He didn't know it, but these were the exact words the riflemen used as their password during the Christmas Battles in 1916. It should wake the spirits of the Latvian Riflemen (and it did). The drummer barrelled down with all his might: takatakataka! With a double bass drums, of course.

The palace pianist, over in the chemistry department, slammed shut the piano cover, held up a translucent middle-finger in the direction of the open-air stage, and disappeared.

Urbix roared into the microphone again, louder:

– Good evening, Jelgava!

This time his words travelled. A forgotten corpse at the edge of a marsh struggled to sit up. He was still half-buried, a bullet-hole in his forehead, but he listened. He heard what sounded like cannon fire coming from Jelgava. 'They've already made it to Jelgava!' the corpse-rifleman said and wriggled its way out of the ground. He even stuck his hands back into the marsh for a moment, and then pulled out a Mosin rifle. He swung the rifle over his shoulder, buttoned up his coat and began a brisk march in the direction of the sound.

Meanwhile, we were already making heads roll. Ours. My hair was long enough now for me to participate in full-on headbanging, that wonderful metalhead dance where you didn't have to ask a girl to join you and be subject to her pity; you could just whip their bums with your hair, but carefully so you didn't accidentally smash your face into them. But girls were irrelevant here. I was a unique spirit in a thousand-headed body. Their bums were also my bums. But I didn't need any of that, just the music that washed over us, and we ourselves were the music, and we washed over everything.

And then I fell over. I slammed into the side of the stage, crashing into someone along the way. I knew this wasn't a safe place to bump into people, so I glanced over at my victim. The legs were a girl's. A millisecond of a scenario flashed through my brilliant mind that this was the kind of meet-cute that would make a beautiful and tragic novel. I got to my feet, straightened my collar and looked at the girl. But she wasn't alone, it was a couple, ugh, in a tight embrace. After I crashed into them they had momentarily unlatched their faces from one another to stare at me blankly. It was the girl Death had made out with at the kindergarten Junkyard, she turned and there were those oddly-shaped knees. She spotted Death and called to him, her lips glistening:

– Hey, I know you!

Then Huskvarn let loose another explosive passage in the greatest traditions of Jelgava thrash metal, and Death's answer was swallowed by the sound. The girl watched him with a curious interest and tried to say something more. The guy she was holding onto looked at her in confusion. And I stood there like the biggest fool of all and didn't know where to look.

Then Huskvarn took a break, and the girl said to Death:

– You have a new jacket!

I looked at my friend. He was wearing a leather jacket. Was it really new? Hadn't it been the same black one this whole time? But maybe she was right, the old one had had a rip in the sleeve.

But Death gestured to me, come on, and we left.

I felt bad for Death. I thought, what bad luck. I at least could wander through the metal world knowing full well that I'd never run into my crush, she was someplace safe, in the arms of a friend. But Death, he couldn't have that. I wanted to comfort him somehow, but back then I didn't know how. What was I supposed to do? Give him a cigarette? Does that counteract love? And I didn't have any cigarettes, I'd been bumming them off Death all night. Although, in the name of historical accuracy, I have to admit that as well as empathising with him I did also feel a twinge of joy and relief.

The corpse-rifleman was creeping towards the stage. He was almost there, just behind the port-a-potties. Any closer and he'd be right out in the open. He wasn't afraid, just observed the situation at hand. It wasn't a simple one. He saw people aimlessly milling about. The rifleman strained to remember the mission plan; but the plan had literally fallen out of his head. All that was left was a feeling, tamped down with native soil.

Suddenly two figures came right towards his hiding place. The figures were me and Death. We each had a beer in hand, and a cigarette in our lips. I asked:

– Wrw gng?

I didn't know how to talk with a cigarette in my mouth. Smoke was getting in my eyes. Death answered me.

– T ps.

The rifleman didn't understand our language, but, when we put down our beers, he was right to suspect that we were about to pull out our weapons. He lifted his rifle, but didn't know which one of us to take out first. For whatever reason, he picked me.

– Pēteris, hey! Death called to another metalhead who was standing a few bushes over. He replied:

– Hey!

The rifleman opened his magazine and looked in. Empty. He must've shot off his last round before he was taken out himself. But he couldn't really remember that far back. He tightened his grip on his rifle. He still had the bayonet.

Death exchanged a few words with this Pēteris guy. I stepped over to introduce myself, but didn't get the chance. Pēteris said:

– Damn, I'm about to go on stage.

– Who do you play with?

– Y'know. Grindmaster Dead.

And Death turned to me:

– Grindmaster Dead is about to go on!

But Pēteris cried out:

– Oy!

The rifleman had stabbed him right in the heart. Because he was a ghost, he was faded and invisible, and so was the bayonet, but it was still sharp, and Pēteris pressed his hands to his chest.

– What is it? Death asked.

– Nothing.

But it was something.

– We're going, we're going.

And he hurried off to the stage. I didn't understand what had happened – was he drunk or something? But what was there for me to understand. That was Pēteris' story, not mine.

Grindmaster Dead played a killer set. I couldn't believe my ears, which was always the case when I witnessed something amazing. Real doom metal, like overseas. I pretended I was at a concert in another country, seeing a group from Sweden, or maybe even the Netherlands perform. They really sounded one of the legit bands from overseas. What I didn't know was that this was one of the band's last concerts – that Grindmaster Dead as my unseeing eyes knew it would be finished as of tonight.

I glanced at Death to see if he'd forgotten his stupid heartache. He looked just as melancholy as usual. I nudged him:

– Pretty awesome, right?

– Totally.

– What's up, jerks!

It was Arturiņš, the kid who had wanted to form a band with me in kindergarten, and his buddy Čurka. I was surprised I hadn't run into them earlier. We shook hands, and they stared telling us:

– We went to Store No. 6 to pick up some things.

We could clearly see one side of Čurka's jean jacket was heavily weighted down.

– Everything was fine on the way there. Then on the way back – oho, man. There were, like, six of them. We hit the deck immediately. Well, I did, you maybe stood for a second longer. But I just covered my face, covered it and lay there, waiting, waiting, then I got bored. Finally I thought, how much longer?, and peeked through my fingers... and there's just this ugly mug glaring right back at me!

Čurka laughed as if the whole thing was just a funny, pleasant experience. He was so good at doing that that only the girls called him an idiot.

– But the bottle? What happened to the bottle?

– You can't teach an old dog new tricks!

Per usual, they had bought their vodka in a plastic bottle. We drank from an entirely unscathed bottle, and the boys got ready to go:

– We're going to take another pass around the area, and then meet up at the bridge. That's where the real fight's going to be.

As they turned to leave, Arturiņš looked back at me:

– Have you thought about what we discussed?

It sounded good, like we were planning on stabbing the duke. I knew exactly what he was talking about, and answered:

– I have.

He didn't ask what I had decided, just waved and left.

But then I thought for a moment – maybe I didn't really want to. Why did I have to be in a band? Why did I need the extra hassle? And what if it didn't work out? And did I even know how to play anything? I didn't need anything more. There are normal guys out there who never think to start a band.

Then Death said:

– Should we start a band?

He asked it just like that, simple. I had to respond:

– We should. It's about time.

– You play the guitar at home a lot?

– Sure.

I couldn't contain myself, I had to ask:

– What'll you play?

– I'll sing, he sighed. I mean, I'd like to play the drums. But someone has to sing.

– Who'll play the drums?

– There's this guy... see, he could also just get us drums. But he wants to play, too. I think he's actually pretty good.

– No matter. Singing is fun, too.

– And you have a guitar? Is it electric?

An unexpected question. But he knows the answer already. Does he think I'd keep a thing like that secret?

– Yup.

– What? For real?

– Well, I don't have it yet. But I'm looking at getting one.

– What kind?

– A good one. A really good one.

It was so good that it wasn't worth talking about until I owned it.

– You have the money for it?

– Yup. I mean, not yet. But I've got a sure way to get it.

Death believed me, no questions asked. He must have assumed that tonight was a night for laying yourself bare, the world said it was so, and he had taken note and was expecting the same of me. He was right to do so, and I spoke only the truth.

– Well, then we better start soon.

Just then Zombie ran up to us, completely worked up.

– Where the hell were you guys?

The others materialized as well: Pūpols, Tonijs, Artūriņš, Čurka, Mele, her friend, Sammie, Ģirtiņš, DJ, a couple of metalheads I hadn't seen before and a pregnant girl.

Zombie shouted:

– Let's go dance!

But someone shushed him:

– Fuck, man, shh!

We all headed towards the road. The open-air stage was quiet. As we climbed up the embankment I asked:

– Where are we going?

And some unidentifiable voice replied: Home.

Home was on the other side of both rivers. Someone was standing on the opposite side of the road, and called out quietly to us:

– Where are you going you idiots? They're already waiting for you.

To myself I thought, well sure, someone's definitely waiting for us at home. Sammie called back loudly and with pride:

– There's thirteen of us!

It was definitely a sight to see when the thirteen of us showed up at the end of the bridge. Then I think we were spotted, and shadows started to move on the bridge – about thirty of them.

Our procession came to a standstill and someone, maybe Tonijs, asked:

– How many of them are there?

– More than us.

– But we have Pūpols, our budding pussywillow.

That, of course, came from Zombie, who was always cracking jokes. No-one laughed.

– What should we do?

– We're not going to make it across!

– They'll throw us into the river.

– But then what should we do?

The shadows were lining up diagonally across the bridge; every shadow had a smooth head and flowing legs (because they wore track-pants!), but I didn't care. I had already decided to just go along with what everyone else was going to do; I could cross the bridge, I could get thrown into the river; I could stay right here, in the silent open-air stage.

Tonijs spit onto the ground and said:

– Let's go around! The railway bridge!

– But that's so far!

– No it's not.

– Like five kilometres?

– Farther!

– Fuck off!

That was Pūpols. Tonijs wasn't offended.

– Then stay here.

And he turned to cross the road. Ten steps in he looked back at us and gestured for us to follow him. We all moved at once and walked to him. I hung back a little, turned to look at the silent stage, nodded, turned to face the bridge and stood completely alone facing the shadows. I couldn't tell if they saw me, by myself, a small and dark object on a dark road.

Then I turned and ran to catch up with my friends. Back off the road and into the reeds, except this time we walked forwards along the river.

Pretty soon we reached a fairly walkable sandy path. It was a pleasant walk, everyone asked everyone else for a smoke and for a drink, but no-one had anything left. I purposely kept my distance from Death; gentlemen need some space after sharing a close moment of friendship like that. I walked along with Mele and her friend, chatted about life, maybe even flirted with both of them. Maybe the darkness helped me, because it was pitch dark, everyone kept tripping on and bumping into each other. But no, it wasn't just the darkness. I had something now, something big, something all my own, and everything else was secondary.

Soon we had made it to the railway bridge. It's not easy walking along train tracks in the dark. And of course we walked right in the middle of the tracks; we weren't afraid of the train. We weren't afraid of anything. I shouted:

– Let's go back to that bridge!

Everyone laughed and shouted back:

– Yeah! Let's!

But we didn't go back, just kept walking, towards Jelgava. Finally the river was once again far below our feet; I threw a rock into it. I almost felt good. I was fifteen years old, I had a few friends, we had found another bridge, and all around us it was dark.

15

I kept that feeling for a long time. I listened to the most recent My Dying Bride album and said it seemed a little on the light side. I listened to Death's *Symbolic* and said it seemed a little too beautiful, a little too self-serving, wasn't it just purely aesthetic now? I listened to Moonspell's *Wolfheart* and shouted: what is this? *Excusez-moi*, but that's not black metal! It's shit! People, for shame!

I did all my shouting internally, though. Why should I tell anyone else, I knew perfectly well what I was and what had happened to me. It couldn't be stopped, big and exciting things were happening in front of me, and I couldn't do anything about that, either.

I was walking along Katoļu Street like some kind of pope and saw signs in everything. In windows, clouds, passers-by; everyone was acting too normally, like a bunch of conspirators in a novel when the main protagonist walks by. There was a large, yellow dog without a leash or owner trotting along in front of me. I kept about five metres back from it. The dog stopped at every tree. Obviously I couldn't walk past it, so I stopped when it stopped. Such a mundane path likely lead to big things.

I eventually came to the Cultural Centre. There were all kinds of people gathered outside it: jocks, thugs, teenagers, metalheads, girls and the media. I walked through the crowd with a feeling of total predestination, and I had to keep myself from waving to everyone, from looking to see if workers weren't already screwing a plaque to the side of the building: 'Jānis. Latvian *Perkele*. Was here.'

But they weren't here for me today, not yet. Culture was waiting for its time. Today they had set up some streetball hoops on Barona Street in front of the Centre, and they were holding a tournament. It was a youth tournament, and the winning team usually got a case of beer or a weekend at a sauna. Everyone else was milling around and there to cheer for their friends, or were just waiting for something to happen.

My friends were there, too. They were crowded in the best place along the court, drinking beer, everyone wearing a printed T-shirt, trainers and skinny jeans. Only Kārlis and his brother were wearing shorts. Their excuse was that they were playing today. The players on the other teams all had jock haircuts – only our boys had hair past their shoulders (Kārlis and his brother were playing with Artis, just some guy). While the rest of us tended towards a contemplative lifestyle, Kārlis and his brother were mad about sports. They usually beat everyone in streetball, and usually also swept in the triples tournaments. Their enthusiasm for sports had carried over from a time when they hadn't yet crossed over to the world of metal and melancholy.

They were warming up and fidgeting when Milēdija showed up. She didn't walk around the edge of the court, but crossed right through the middle, the sway of her hips almost enough to knock over the nets. Everyone warming up on the court just then made their shots, and the balls all got stuck in the nets. Milēdija walked up to Kārlis and kissed him.

This was almost commonplace now. Tedious, banal, boring. Then she came over to sit down next to us and said:

– Hey!

The first game started. Our guys were up against a team of weaklings. Pūpols announced that there was nothing to worry about, the other team didn't stand a chance; then he opened another beer.

– Hey! Death called out and waved to someone. I looked to see who. He said:

– Ģirtiņš.

And there was Ģirtiņš on the other side of the court.

– Man can he play the guitar! His fingers fly over his acoustic, sounds just like on the stereo. Then he slides up closer to the nut and plays a solo.

Then Death looked at me:

– Can you do that?

– You know what, no, I can't.

Regardless of how that sounded, it was the truth. I couldn't play any solos, just some strange muddle of sounds that I was rarely able to replicate. I would have said that much, too, but not here in front of everyone. Our musical project was still a secret.

What was up with the world? I'd arrived with blessings for everyone and everything. And what did I get in return? Just me, hiding behind my beer, wishing I were anywhere else. He didn't back down:

– Can you play any riffs?

– I don't know if it's worth getting carried away with solos and riffs.

– What?

– It's kind of an empty expression of technique. Black metal doesn't even have any solos.

– Mayhem do.

True, Mayhem had some killer riffs. I wanted to play like that. The ball rolled over to my feet; I picked it up and passed it to Kārlis.

Death seemed a little bummed:

– I just want to hear and make good music, okay?

And there you have it; he had everyone's attention.

– You guys have a band?

She asked that. She didn't sound that interested. I tried to shut the conversation down:

– There is no band. Not yet.

But Zombie's tongue had loosened up.

– You guys need an accordionist?

That's just what I needed, for someone to mock us, please, go ahead.

– I can play the opening to My Dying Bride, the one where Jesus is walking along the beach.

He was talking about the intro to 'Cry of the mankind', which was played on an electric violin – for me it was a personally very, very meaningful bit; I didn't want to joke about it.

– I'm being serious!

He was almost shouting. As if he wasn't joking this time.

– You guys know that I have an accordion!

But I didn't know. Zombie shouted over the court to one of his oldest friends, Kārlis.

– Don't I have an accordion!

Kārlis glanced over for a second, but then turned right back to the guy he was guarding. Death jumped in:

– You do, Edgars, I know. But an accordion is no good for metal.

I took pity, too:

– Why not? It could be interesting. An MDB cover with the accordion.

Death shot me a loaded, glib look, and then asked:

– Did you buy that guitar?

– Yup!

Death turned to look at me. The others didn't react much.

– What kind?

– A Gibson Les Paul.

This wasn't the time to think small.

– No fuckin' way!

It was an expression of excitement and awe, without question or a shadow of a doubt. Ģirtiņš had joined us.

– You get it at AT Trade?

– Where else.

– They're super expensive though.

I know, Ģirtiņš. Five hundred lats. The same amount you'd get for one fugitive.

– You can do anything with a guitar like that.

Yes, Ģirtiņš, you can. If you know how. And if you have the guitar.

– But that's a little mad. All that for one guitar? For the same price you could've got a decent Ibanez, a Death Metal pedal and even a drum kit from Mareks.

Death, why are you staring dejectedly at the asphalt like that? When have I had time to make it to Riga since our conversation, where would I have found the money to buy the guitar? Don't be sad, you'll get what you want.

Kārlis came over, grabbed a beer and drained it.

– What're you yelling about? I lost track of the guy I was covering, good thing my brother caught up to him.

– You not playing anymore?

– We won. The next game's about to start.

– And when will that be over? I'm out of beer!

Pūpols started to get cranky. The sunlight was blinding and creating strange reflections. It wasn't comfortable sitting here.

– It's this team, then the Lefties, then the Clearing.

Milēdija even knew the opposing teams' names. She was looking off into the distance. She wasn't even pretty. But that's exactly what I needed – to fall in love with a preoccupied and ugly girl. Alright, she wasn't exactly ugly. And fine, there wasn't any love there, either.

The fans started to shout:

– What d'you think you're doing!

– Idiot savants!

– Boys, get off the court!

– Morons!

– Assholes!

I looked out across the court, and there were my friends, the thugs. And true to form – going anywhere in the world according to their own rules, this time ignoring the parameters of the court and fully disrupting the game. A quick pass by the offense caught Kroģis on the right shoulder. He whipped around to the left, looking for his attacker. It's like that thing kids and thugs do – you come up on someone's left and tap them on the right shoulder. But this time his left side was flanked by the net post, and Kroģis walked on, not understanding why the offensive player and fans were jeering at him. Kandžejs wasn't much better off, even though his expression was one of cunning and awareness.

I watched as the approached and understood immediately. Crime wasn't a product of cunning, but of ignoring reality. He'd probably robbed a store thinking it was a vegetable patch, and had broken out of jail thinking he was just going to take a shower.

But now they came over and sat next to me. I was their purpose.

– *Davai*, pool?

I sometimes played pool with them in the Cultural Centre. Sometimes, when I didn't have anything to do and my real friends weren't around. I wasn't half bad, either.

They had obviously been circling the Centre, out of the loop of the day's events, a little confused why there were so many people out here, until they'd spotted me in a crowd of strangers and came to ask me to play.

– I can't, I have to watch streetball.

– What streetball?

– The game going on right now.

– Basketball?

– Sort of.

– Why? Do you play?

– No. My friends do.

– Let your friends play – come with us?

– I can't.

– What *can* you do?

I glanced around, cautiously, only at my immediate surroundings. Their eyes were steely.

Then Kroģis had a good suggestion:

– Let's go get some beers, then come back? It'll be more fun to talk him into it then.

– *Davai!*

They hurried off, again cutting right through the middle of the court.

– Who was that?

Did they really not remember?

– Some guys.

– Oh really?

– I didn't think that type really existed.

– Are they from the countryside?

Seriously, none of them remembered that they were the scary guys at the Villa that time.

Kārlis came off the court, panting, and asked us two questions:

– Who were those morons walking on the court? Is there any more beer?

And he sat down on the ground before anyone answered. I asked:

– How did it go?

I never asked 'Did you win?', so it would be less awkward for the other person to answer in the event they hadn't won. But he answered:

– We won.

Milēdija crouched next to us. She said something about the game, very calmly, in her way. Always so calmly, that it was almost unbelievable:

– Your third man is pretty good!

That bothered me; she was playing the expert in everything that Kārlis was into. He agreed:

– He is. We've played together a lot.

– I think he made more baskets than you did.

– I guess so, he had a good game.

What was her angle? Am I the only one who cared? But whatever, it didn't matter – I said:

– It's just a game.

Kārlis turned to me:

– You have to be good either way.

And she added:

– I like people who know how to do something with skill.

I don't know if she was being earnest, but it didn't matter anymore because her words were a quote from *Master and Margarita*.

– Maybe life itself is a game, Kārlis said. Anything can be. What's bad about wanting to be good at it?

– Nothing, I said.

– I'll play the game, you get the beers, cool?

His brother called to him from the court – it was time to play. Kārlis stood up and went to life. I stayed on the side-lines, resigned to observe.

I hadn't managed to see much of anything before Kandžejs and Kroģis reappeared with a clamour of clinking glass. Kandžejs started pulling out bottles of beer and passing them out to our entire row. Even a few people not in our group got one. Everyone opened the bottles their own way: with keys, rings, lighters. Someone's beer overflowed, and the foamy puddle trickled across the court. Kandžejs downed his beer in one and then turned to me:

– Coming?

– Where?

– To play pool.

I dropped my hands.

– I haven't finished my beer.

– So drink up.

– My friends are still playing.

– Don't you want to play yourself?

Everyone around us either stopped talking, or kept talking as if the question hadn't been asked. I felt Death's eyes bore into the back of my skull, and Milēdija's eyes on the left side of my neck.

Then she suddenly tapped me on the shoulder, and just as suddenly asked:

– I heard you're friends with some kind of thugs?

I was silent. And I felt the tiniest, tiniest bit pleased. But those thugs were sitting right here next to me. Kandžejs was blowing into his bottle like a kid. He wasn't wearing his black leather jacket, just a plain striped shirt. His hair wasn't shaved down anymore, but was growing out in ridiculous curls. Kroģis had finished his beer and was playing with pebbles on the asphalt and, even worse, was humming something that sounded like jazz. Right now they were not representative of the thug title. I understood that they were doing it on purpose, they were putting on a front, but this time I didn't like it. I was embarrassed by them. They'd screwed me.

I didn't answer Milēdija. And I couldn't answer her – they would hear whatever I said, they were right there. She didn't repeat her question. I looked at the ground, and she watched the game.

Kārlis shot too soon, didn't get enough spin on the ball, and it hit the back of the rim and bounced out. The tall guy on the other team got the rebound and passed it back to their sniper. Artis jumped and almost intercepted; he brushed it with the tips of his fingers, but it got past him. Artis fell when he landed, and their sniper was left unguarded – he shot and scored.

Now the other team was up by eleven points. That's a lot in streetball. Sometimes that's the total score for a single game. It wasn't clear how they'd gotten so far ahead.

There were only five minutes left in the game.

None of us was paying attention to it. Milēdija was the only one watching attentively, but silently. Her eyes shone and her lips were slightly parted.

Kārlis threw the traitorous ball angrily, despairingly, under the backboard. His brother caught it, shot it over the tall guy, and the ball spun into the net. Down ten.

The other team ran a slow, overconfident play and made a royal mistake – the guy dribbling hit himself in the foot with the ball, and the ball rolled away across the court. Artis, always watchful, grabbed it and took it back to the line. The other team reset their defence; the guy guarding Artis posted up by the free-throw line to block his path. But instead of taking the ball forward, Artis took the long shot. The ball hit the backboard with a crash and dropped through the net. Down eight.

The other team ran a great play, but missed the basket. Our guys got the ball back and Kārlis missed his shot, but he caught the rebound, faked out the defence, and passed it to his brother for the shot. Down seven.

The other team wasn't worried yet. They made a break for it along the outside of the court, but Artis caught on, stole the ball and turned it. The guy he'd stolen the ball from, a ginger, went after him, he didn't want Artis to get a shot in, but Artis was already two steps into his approach, already had his hands up for the shot, and the ginger was two steps behind him. He jumped when Artis did and slapped his arms pretty hard.

The ball flew into the seats and hit me right in the forehead. Whack, and my glasses fell into my lap. Everyone laughed. I passed the ball back with composure.

Two free-throws. You could even see red handprints on Artis' arms. Down six, down five.

How much time was left? Shouldn't the game be over already? A guy with a whistle and a watch checked and answered the ginger: No, almost a full minute left. This time he approached carefully; their sniper made the shot from a safe position, almost without jumping, and so Kārlis' brother blocked him pretty easily. He jumped, their sniper jumped, they collided, and the sniper fell to the ground and shouted: 'Foul!' but there was no foul, and Kārlis' brother passed it down to Kārlis, then ran down to the basket himself to receive the next pass. It was an easy shot from right under the basket, and the ball went in, even though their sniper had managed to get down there and push Kārlis' brother mid-jump. That was unnecessary, but he was offended, and his lips pursed with a sense of foreboding. I would've totally sympathised with him, had I been paying attention. Kārlis' brother made his free-throws. Down three.

Still they didn't panic. You need at least two possessions to get three points in streetball, but it was their ball and the game was almost over. But stay calm. The tall guy knew that it was impossible, there was no way they could make those shots in the time left, and that was that, while their sniper's brain was screaming at fate – no, come on, no way, that would be ridiculous! The ginger tried not to think. Our guys were thinking the same thing: 'It's just a game. If we lose, we lose.' The ginger advanced, stone-cold. Artis was on him immediately. Breathing in his face, groping for the ball. The ginger hated people who guarded this close. He bounced it to their sniper, who caught it, but instead of taking the shot passed it to the tall guy. The tall guy froze, thinking it was the smart choice, but then Kārlis' brother slapped the ball out of his hands. Everyone fell to the ground to get the ball. But instead of picking the ball up, Kārlis' brother slammed the ball with his fist, sending it bouncing to the end of the court, where Kārlis picked it up and made the shot. Down one.

The ginger's hands were shaking. He thought about hugging the ball, dropping to the ground and curling himself around it. But let their sniper do that. When their sniper lifted his arms to take the shot, the guy with the watch and whistle started to count:

– Three...

Their sniper jumped back from his guard and released the ball. It was probably the longest shot he'd ever taken in his life. The ball hit the backboard well away from the basket. Kārlis hadn't been expecting the shot to go that way as he jumped up for the rebound. The ball hit Kārlis so hard in the nose that blood gushed immediately out of both nostrils, fanning red across his shirt. But he managed to hold onto the ball.

The guy with the whistle said:

– Two...

Kārlis jumped and passed the ball over the tall guy's head, down to where Artis was already waiting. Artis jumped to catch the ball and, still in the air, took the shot.

The ball went through the basket like butter; the net swished like the longest skirt of the prettiest girl. Up one!

And the guy with the whistle called it:

– Time!

The other team didn't understand what had happened. Our guys were jumping up and down like crazy, hugging one another. The other team's fans were quiet; they were normal fans. Our guys' fans were silent, too, because they were not normal, and hadn't been paying attention to the game.

I was wondering what Milēdija cared about thugs, was she looking for some, was she in some trouble? She was off hugging Kārlis. No, lady, I need these thugs for myself. I turned to Kandžejs. He wasn't there. From the far end of the street, a police car was driving slowly in our direction.

16

One night I took my guitar and headed for the crossroads. I'd told my parents that I was going to go see Zombie. And I really had planned to meet up with him. I was hoping the thing at the crossroads wouldn't take long. I didn't really believe that it was going to happen. But I wanted to try. It was something completely irrational and black, and not really difficult. As Niels Bohr once said when someone asked him why he had a horseshoe over his front door: 'I've heard it also helps those who don't believe.'

All I had to do now was find the crossroads. I couldn't wait around with my guitar at the intersection of Rainis and Catholic Street. It would be safer near the church, but I could run into someone I knew. And I couldn't go to the intersection of Satiksmes and Tarktorisu Streets because it was crawling with thugs. I was more afraid of people than I was of Satan. I went to the intersection of Skolas and Pavasara Streets. It was a good area, significant street names and few people. Artūriņš even lived nearby on Plūmju Street. So if I ran into him I could just say I was headed to his place for a jam session.

So, the intersection at Pavasara and Skolas Streets. It was completely dark; there was a light somewhere along Pasta Street and the of a TV from a nearby window. I sat down in the middle of these crossroads, just as legend said you should. The road wasn't even asphalted here. I took my guitar out of the case my mom had sewn for it and sat. I was supposed to play something. If I didn't do it now, I wouldn't do it at all. It wasn't a big deal. I could do it quietly, no one would hear me. I started to play 'Sleepless', from Anathema's *Serenades*. I only knew about six measures, but they were repeated throughout almost the entire song. At the part where the was supposed to be a solo, I tried to improvise something and botched it. What now, should I try 'Sappy'? No, 'Master of Puppets'. I didn't make it very far. 'The Freezing Moon', yes. If only I could do the riff. But someone was coming, I had to stop for a minute. But the person stopped:

– What're you doing?

– Nothing.

– You playing the guitar?

– No.

He lit a cigarette; all faces look the black in the dark, don't they?

– You not allowed to play at home that you have to come do it out in the street?

– No, forget it.

My reply didn't make sense. I wanted to stand up, so I wouldn't be sitting on the ground in front of this stranger, but my legs didn't listen. He put down the box he had been carrying, and sat down on it. The cigarette illuminated his fingers, the skin looked like it had been painted black. Like Death's new leather jacket.

– And I'm just off from work. I'm a welder. Didn't even get the chance to clean up, everything's black. And I still have to get home. But that's all the way by the RAF centre.

– It happens.

This time I answered him like a human being. He glanced up at me.

– It happens for you, too? Welding all day and then dragging your ass home to a wife who's crazy?

I should've just offered him a cigarette. I hadn't noticed until now how cold it was. Not that a cigarette can warm you up, but it lets you shut off your brain for a bit. But he kept on moralising.

– Tough life you've got.

Strangely, he said that in a tone that was completely, totally devoid of sarcasm.

– Play something!

– Now?

– Why not? We're sitting, hanging out. A little music would be nice.

I set up a chord and strummed the strings. Maybe 'Freezing Moon' again?

– Play, play. Don't you want to?

I wanted to, so I played as best I could. The setting was appropriate, because it really was freezing, unnaturally freezing, and maybe that cold light wasn't from the TV in the nearby house, but from the moon.

The welder popped a half-smoked cigarette between his lips and held out his hand:

– Isn't that thing totally out of tune? Hand it here.

I gave him the guitar.

– So, what do you play?

– Black, death, doom.

My answer came in a polite whisper.

– What now? Black doom?

– Sure.

The welder rubbed his blackened cheeks.

– I'm more of a blues guy myself. Don't you want to play the blues?

– No, metal.

– Ah. Heavy metal?

And he picked his way through a Malmsteen-esque riff.

– No, no. Heavier than that.

– Pfft!

He set the guitar down.

– You need a different guitar for that.

– I know.

– You know where to get one?

– I do.

– You get that guitar and you'll be set.

– I know.

– So you know everything. Why are you out here?

– To learn how to play.

– Get that other guitar and then we'll talk. That's how the game works. You don't get something for nothing. You know where to get the money for it?

– Yes.

– And so? Decide! Decide what you're going to be!

– Okay, I whispered.

The welder stood up and walked away.

17

It was time. We had to get the ball rolling. I needed that guitar, and this is where my thug friends could finally come in handy. It was time for business, plain and simple. I just had to call the police and tell them that I'd found their fugitive, and then go collect the cash.

I was home alone. I crouched down by the phone, picked up the receiver, put my finger in the finger wheel. I'd long been fascinated by all these forbidden numbers, the ones you could only call in case of an emergency. Sometimes when I was home alone I'd dial only part of the forbidden number (read: I'd just dial the zero and then stop), feeling how there was only one move left between myself and the extraordinary. You weren't supposed to mess around with these things. Those of my friends who were gutsier than the rest did it easily and without consequence. Though the kid who called in the bomb threat to school that one time did get caught. I don't know what happened to him. But I didn't care; I wasn't about to do anything bad. What I was going to do was upstanding and commendable.

I picked up the receiver and dialled 0-2. Busy signal. Hilarious. What if I was being stabbed to death? I dialled again. I already felt bolder. It seemed logical for the line to be busy; there was always something going on in Jelgava, after all.

But this time someone picked up right away.

– What is it?

Did I recognize the voice? Could I have dialled up one of my friends with that two-digit number?

– Hello?

I had to say something, otherwise I was just breathing into the receiver like some kind of nervous girl. If I hung up, it's possible he'd think it had actually been a girl, but it wasn't, so I said:

– Hello!

As if he had called me. And he said:

– Yes, this is the police.

So it really was. But I asked anyway:

– Really?

– Yes, really! This is the police. What is it?

He was sounding increasingly annoyed and familiar. It was interesting. My heart stopped pounding in my chest. I had to say something, so I said:

– Never mind, it's nothing.

– What d'you mean, nothing? Who is this?

– Me?

– Yes, you!

This police officer was odd. I didn't know any other police officers who were like this. But this one, turns out, knew me:

– Oh, hey man, what's up?

It was Šolis! I asked:

– Šolis?

– Who else!

– What're you doing?

– I work here!

I hadn't known that. But when I thought about it, I think there had been one time when I'd made some scathing remark about the cops and someone, Pūpols I think, had mentioned that the hard-core metalhead Šolis was a cop. I hadn't believed him, and had laughed at him and promptly wiped the information from my mind.

– But how?

– Oh, you know. I came here to work right after I graduated. So they couldn't enlist me. Not a bad idea, don't you think?

What did I think – I wasn't thinking anything. I still had a few years to think about these things. I asked, to be polite:

– How's it going?

– Man, it's a mess! Hugo just called me because, hey, we've got a problem, they just arrested Gintiņš. For running from the cops. They've got him in lockup. So they call me all, what's going on? Why? What're you doing about it? But I wasn't even on duty at the time, you know?

– Yeah.

– Anway. So they're yelling at me – get him out of there! But what am I supposed to do about it. I go in, and yup, there he is. I ask, what do you want? He says, black tea!

Hold up, I had something to add to the conversation:

– Death ran into Morbid not too long ago in Riga. They're sitting quietly on a bench. Then Morbid goes: 'I'm still one and a half centimetres short!'

– With what?

– Death asked the same thing. Morbid says he's growing a stomach ulcer. Eating all kinds of paper, straight up, drinking lots of vinegar.

– That's nothing!

I hated it when people made comments like that when I told stories. But I didn't say anything, let them say what they have to say.

– Tontons was enlisted. He decided that he had to break his arm. But how? He asks Ernests to help. The two of them decide: Tontons is going to put his arm across the toilet seat. Ernests was going to jump down on his arm; that should break it. So they go into the bathroom. Tontons puts his arm down. Ernests backs up, takes a few steps and jumps. But Tontons' reflexes kick in and he instinctively pulls his arm back. And Ernests comes crashing down, breaking the toilet bowl and his ankle!

That story really was better than mine. I tried to think of another one.

– There was this one guy who...

– Alright, anyway, I've got to get back to work. Later! Metal.

– Later.

I remembered that Unholy had also had problems with the army. Their guitarist Jarkko Toivonen had served in the Finnish army while the band was on hiatus – which is why his brother, guitarist Ismo Toivonen, kicked him out of the band. Or maybe it was Ismo who had been in the army... All I know is the brother said: 'We don't have room for traitors'. No, wait, why would he say that? He said: 'We don't have room for slaves'. But what does that have to do with traitors? Why had I called Šolis? Oh, right, business. Never mind, I'd call back later.

18

A lot of people, maybe even everyone, have a day they're looking forward to. Some people count down the days to Easter break. There are even those who enjoy birthdays. For us, the concept of holidays and vacations was a moderately fluid one. We were waiting for something else, for a specific date to fall on a specific day: namely, Friday the thirteenth. Superstitious people were wrong when they said this day was no different from the rest. It was. Every time there was a Friday the thirteenth it was a metalhead holiday – Black Friday. I'd start to get anxious by the eleventh, much more than for my own birthday, which I had learned to emotionally ignore by that age to avoid the inevitable feeling of growing older. Time has no real meaning, time doesn't exist by itself, it's just a relationship between objects that move at varying speeds. Time is relative to these objects and speeds. What year was it? Ninety-five? Or maybe ninety-six? I don't know anymore. I didn't know back then, either. It didn't really matter. How long has it been since Kurt shot himself? Longer than between that moment and the day I was born. Finally, massive objects had appeared that moved at a different speeds, and time took on meaning, but lost its tempered fluidity. All I knew was that it was Friday the thirteenth.

Death, Zombie and I left on time, right after school. Black Friday was being celebrated in Riga, at the Robinsons Club. Everything went smoothly, no-one checked for tickets, and we got out at Riga's Central Station.

That's where the first significant event took place. There was an old man sitting in the square in front of the station. Right on the ground. He held out his hand, asking for money. Completely out of character, Death pulled out a twenty-santims coin and gave it to the him. Zombie asked:

– Are you insane?

– No, just pretty weak, the old man replied.

Zombie flinched, as if he hadn't thought that this pile of grey rags could talk. He apologized:

– Sorry, I didn't mean you, but this do-gooder here, he said, and pointed to Death.

Death didn't answer until were a ways away:

– I don't know. I suddenly got the feeling that that could be me someday.

– Moron, Zombie said.

I thought what Death had done was really admirable and deeply justifiable. Maybe that really would be him some day. If something extraordinary happens and we don't die young, then we'll be old men sitting on the ground, all alone. We won't give any orders and won't own anything. And if someone gives us any money we'll go straight to the liquor store and spend it all.

Which we already did now – we headed for the Latvijas Balzams store that was right across from the station. Back then it was a better bet to buy alcohol at an official retailer. If I remember correctly, we grabbed the usual, a 0,7 litre bottle of black-currant flavoured Riga vodka. What's more, we were short twenty santims to buy a chaser, even though we'd carefully counted out everything on the train in... Zombie was furious.

Then we went to hang out at Death's dorm. Yes, really, he'd just started college. The vodka burned our throats, and even Death questioned his earlier actions, and thought out loud:

– What is life trying to tell me?

Zombie chimed in:

– That you're an idiot!

But by the time we made it to the club, which was right next to the dorms, the vodka was going down smooth. As did the drinks we were offered by the other metalheads coming in from all over. There were people we knew and there were strangers, all of them sharing their bottles with us. Once we reached the entrance, though, the reason for their generosity became clear. The bouncers were patting everyone down and laying down some ground rules:

– If I find a bottle, I'm gonna shove it up your ass!

Everyone was helping everyone else empty their bottles before reaching the entrance, and then heading in feeling great. We followed suit.

I had finally made it to the Robinson. The legendary fortresses had surrendered to me one by one, and now it was the Robinson's turn. Though at that time I doubt Black Friday was really much of a legend. But I knew it was the biggest thing we had, and it wasn't that the world didn't know anything about us, no. It was we who didn't know anything about the world.

The place was packed. Even before we made it all the way in we could see tens of stages and bands. Now it was especially rare to see flannel shirts or patterned sweaters, but there were more famous people around. Over there was a young guy who went by Peksis. No-one knew who he was, yet, but he was sitting there, leaning forward and repeating:

– What're you looking at? Haven't you ever seen a punk before? What're you looking at? Haven't you ever seen a punk before?

Next to him was Morbid with his crooked, black beard. An unfamiliar, pretty girl stood behind him. Next to her was Sinister.

Death and I rolled up our sleeves and raced to say hello to our acquaintances. But I soon felt I was losing momentum. Then I noticed that one guy who's always having nightmares about the Middle Ages and was supposedly going to play bass guitar in Sinister's band. I went up to him and held out my hand. He accepted it, shook it, everything was good, he even smiled. I asked:

– How're things going with the swords?

Because he was always talking about swords and axes. But this time he stared at me like he had no idea what I was talking about. No idea at all. He started explaining in English that his name was Pauļus, he was from Kauna. But he looked exactly like the sword guy. The same long hair and ridiculous beard. He was here to see Nahash. In 1993, the Lithuania's leading black metal band had split to form two separate groups: Nahash and Pocculus (a ridiculous name, I said in Latvian). Both bands played some amazing black metal. I should come inside to join the others.

It was a lot darker further inside, the Lithuanian knew where he was going. I thought he would maybe introduce me to the band, or to all three of them, but no. People had formed a cosy nest on the floor next to a column – of leather jackets, beer, and a smiling girl. Her name was Živile. A ridiculous name, I said in Latvian. Pauļus asked me to keep an eye on the beer and the girl, while he went off in some unknown direction.

And so I found myself sitting on the ground with Živile. I drank their beer, and she smoked my cigarettes to keep things fair. I was especially moved when, before finishing each cigarette, she'd show me the stub and ask if I accepted its disposal. I've never again met someone with such refined manners. She was an all-around nice person, and we talked about important things, using a mish-mash of languages.

– Have you ever seen Nahash before?

– A little.

– They're amazing, she said, seeing through my lie effortlessly and without calling me out on it. They sing about witches. Is the beer good?

– It's good.

I decided it was my turn to ask.

But I failed at conversation. She took back the lead.

– Do you play in a band?

– Yup.

– Black metal?

– Mhmm. Kind of avant-garde.

– What's it called?

– Terrier Bitch.

– Ooh! Awesome.

My wildest dreams had come true in a single moment. Even if I really had a band, This is exactly how I would have told an unfamiliar girl about it. It was exactly like I had dreamed. I was dumbstruck by this sudden, phenomenal realisation. I sat and stared at Živile's lower lip.

Then Pauļus reappeared, and I gave him my seat and left. Živile half laughed, half smiled, and tossed her head in my direction, saying to Pauļus in their language:

– *Metalo viltis*!

Something was starting on stage, so I wandered in that direction. It was Heaven Grey, easy to recognise because they had a cello.

I made my way to the front row and thought about what Death

had said. The Lithuanians are our brothers, we should be able to understand their language. 'Metalo' could mean metal, in some declination. 'Viltis'... Maybe 'vilks', our word for 'wolf'? Wolf! A metal wolf, that's what I am in the eyes of our Lithuanian brothers. Jānis of Jelgava, known in Lithuania as the metal wolf. It's a little lame, but what can you do. But maybe it's not wolf? Maybe they had something entirely different in mind? Like 'viltnieks' – trickster? I didn't like how that sounded, but my intuition said I'd hit closer to the right meaning. Metal faker? Metal liar? My heart ached. I must truly be abnormal. But what do I care if some Lithuanians had unmasked me? No-one could take away all I'd gone through. But I hadn't really gone through anything, and probably wouldn't. It was all just in my head, all tricky and lies. The strongest were made of steel. I had imagined all of it. I was just pretending. Even now, I was pretending I was some kind of spy with a secret mission, looking for a hidden agenda. Whatever.

Heaven Grey started their set. The audience pushed me against the stage. No-one here was indifferent, everyone went all in from the first chords, letting loose some hard-core head-banging. I placed my hands on the edge of the stage for support and joined them. Now I was like everyone else. My hair was probably even long enough to hit the people next to me in the eyes. They don't know me. I could just as well be a genius. Or a murderer. Or a werewolf. It didn't matter. Maybe someone next time was a werewolf. Maybe everyone around me is pretending. But none of that mattered, metal.

I stepped over to the side for a minute. I was dizzy. I should find my friends. Wherever they were. But then Venom came up to me and said:

– Why hello and blessed be, so to speak!

– Is Dark Reign playing tonight too? I asked, even though I knew full well they weren't. Venom confirmed my suspicion, and his face clouded over. I asked:

– How come?

Venom grew even more sullen. Then he looked me in the eyes.

– I think they're trying to force me out of the band.

– What do you mean?

– Apparently I'm a little too abrasive. Invoke Satan too much.

He looked even deeper into my eyes.

– I made them, all of them. And they're just going to betray me. I can feel it.

I didn't say anything. Apparently my silence was somewhat commiserating, because he passed me his beer. I took a long drink, and thanked him.

– Don't read into it too much. No-one said metal was easy.

– Yeah, we'll see what's what, Venom sniffed and left.

Right after, someone wandered up to me and said:

– Remember me?

– Of course I do!

I had no idea who this person was.

– I crashed at your place one night.

It was the guy with the encyclopaedia of metal! The one who had run away from home. Before I managed to say anything, he asked:

– Are you wasted?

– No.

– I am.

I should've said I was in the beginning. I hurried to correct myself:

– I mean I am, yes.

– Then why did you say that you weren't?

– Like I have any clue what I'm saying. I'm wasted.

The reply satisfied him. We stood facing one another saying nothing. Misery started to play, a pretty decent group, Carcassy.

– Why did you turn me in?

I literally jumped:

– What? How did I turn you in?

– Well you wanted to!

– What d'you even mean? When?

Now we both looked confused.

– Well. You answered the phone, and you didn't say anything because I was there, right?

– Y-yeah.

– It was someone calling to ask if I was there, right?

– N-no.

He scratched his cheek.

– Didn't it seem weird to you that I was just gone the next morning?

I didn't really remember. I hadn't been paying much attention.

– I thought you'd just left.

– I ran away.

– Is that all you do?

– What do you want?

It was an unexpected question. I knew the answer, had a lot of answers to it, but didn't know which one to say first. He took a drink of his beer and asked:

– So you weren't going to turn me in?

– No!

– Okay, good.

He offered me another sip of his beer, and then took back the little that remained.

– Later!

And he left. But I got the feeling that it hadn't been beer in his cup, but something strange. I suddenly felt ill. Not from all the alcohol, but from all that information. I needed to find my friends. It was like some statistical anomaly – I kept finding myself in conversation with all these strangers, but I couldn't find my friends even if I systematically tried to. I tried to just wander around to run into them, but that didn't work either. What's more I could barely see anything anymore. I had gone back to the stage to where I had been during the next group, Dzels Vilks, and my glasses had gone flying off my face. I felt all fours to look for them, but it was dark, filled with stomping boots, broken bottles, and I was half blind. I stood up and rub my face. It was so easy to rub my face with my glasses gone. I was free. I was never going to find anyone. I couldn't go back home either, those glasses were expensive. Tonight I would run away, go on a grand adventure. Like him. Yes, yes.

I'd sit for just a minute before I left. I drag myself over to a wall and sat down among broken glass, my back against the brick. Much better. I tried to make out who was playing just done. Still Misery? Or Paradoxx? Or Terrier Bitch? I fell asleep without figuring it out. Like a tired child, or as if someone had hit me over the head.

Meanwhile, the concert – my dream concert – went on at full force. Dzels Vilks finished out their set; they played well, back then it was real music, none of this wind-wailing-through-socks-hung-to-dry sound they have now. Dies Irae, Infrogress and Apēdājs also played. But I wasn't analysing or naming genres, I was sleeping, and all this metal lulled me further into my dreams.

And while I slept, Death and Zombie were living the dream. They watched as Skyforger took the stage. It was a significant turning point in Latvian metal history. Pēteris, after the incident with the ghost-rifleman that time in Jelgava, had abandoned all thoughts of foreign warriors and had turned to Latvia's fallen riflemen. Grindmaster Dead had been disbanded, and Skyforger formed in its place, which played black metal and sang only about Latvian themes. In a heartbeat they had filled this niche that everyone else wanted to fill, and had become number one.

Pēteris had a real sword on stage; he swung it around wildly, the blade hacking into the low ceiling, raining down bits of plaster. His voice was like the sword, a deep, grating falsetto, like a stream flowing out of the throat of a stone golem, a sound that broke and ground you up in to the stream, carrying you away to who knows where, to spit you out here, to have the noble and heavy sound of the guitars crash down on you. Now and then you could make out some of the lyrics, like 'black' and 'clouds' and 'sacred'; it was how a concert should sound – gritty and real – and then the clearly-sung refrain: 'Symbols carved in stone!' It's amazing that it really exists, this hidden world they don't tell you about in school, don't write about in books.

That was how Skyforger introduced themselves. They would eventually become the most world-famous Latvian band of all time. And I didn't see it or hear it. I became a die-hard fan later, of course, and told everyone and myself about this, their first ever concert. What I didn't tell anyone was that, during their set, I'd actually been drooling and grinning like an idiot in my sleep, dreaming about twenty santims, the neighbour's old dog and a girl with Milēdija's body, Mele's friend's hair and Mele's unreadable expression.

Death found me during the last song. He shook me and said:

– Wake up! Skyforger is playing!

But I didn't get up. He said again:

– Please! Wake up! Please?

That touched me, and I answered:

– It's all good.

But I still didn't get up. I was so comfortable here, by the wall, among the cigarette butts and broken bottles. I understood that the concert was more important and that I should get up, but it was right over there, one step, one second, one blink away, I could do it whenever, so why not just stay here for one more second and maybe another. And so I sat until the very end of the last song, until the band left the stage to the sounds of a standing ovation. Then I opened my eyes and ears and said to Death:

– Hey! What's up?

After that came Apēdājs, I think. But everyone went into the corridor and talked about Skyforger.

– They're a bit like Immoral, no?

I nodded in agreement and even Zombie, who didn't really particularly like music, looked inspired.

– That was fantastic! Mele exclaimed. When did she get here? Her eyes glistened with tears, which was wild, but she could still see:

– Where're your glasses?

And then I remembered that my life was over and the world was a blur. Maybe Mele didn't have tears in her eyes; I couldn't see anything, after all. But then someone else joined our conversation.

– My band will be better!

I turned to face the cocky speaker, as did the rest of our group. I knew him, but couldn't make out who it was. The silhouette was definitely familiar, though. Someone asked:

– You're starting a band?

– Already have one. Just have to clear the ranks a bit. Kick someone out.

– What do you play?

– Black metal, obviously. But one-of-a-kind.

He had no shame, this unrecognizable acquaintance. I stepped closer to him, very close. I definitely knew him! Because of my confusion and total near-sightedness I came so close to him that he, and everyone else, fell silent. It probably looked strange, me stopping half a step away from him while scrutinizing his face.

My hair didn't stand on end only because it was so long. He was me. I was staring into my own face. I saw long hair, glasses and a perturbed expression. Those glasses – they were mine! That's why all the confusion! But beneath the glasses it was him – the pretentious guy from Riga, the one who I'd first met at the Stocks. He was dressed meticulously per usual, in his long, black, high-collared coat and shiny accessories I couldn't quite make out. He had obviously put on my glasses because they fit in with his getup. Maybe he'd found them on the floor, but maybe the pretty girl standing next to him had found them, or maybe one of the others form his entourage, who were all now glaring at me. I said:

– Those are my glasses!

I hadn't said anything funny, but his friends all burst out laughing. I didn't know why, but I knew it was at me. I felt the world turn back a lifetime, and I was once again a stupid little four-eyes.

The pretentious guy and his entourage turned to leave, but Ēriks was waiting behind them, leaning against the wall. He also had glasses, and not only knew everything and understood everything, but also had the prestige of an older metalhead. He took pity on me:

– Give him the glasses back.

The pretentious guy thought it over, then gave me the glasses. He became a warrior, while I grovelled. And he still didn't let up. He asked:

– Do you have a band?

I gave him the answer he was expecting:

– No.

And I put my glasses back on. He continued:

– But you're going to?

– No.

– But you want to?

I wanted to tell him: 'Do you have any idea what I've done to be in a band? That is, what I haven't yet, but would do? Could you become a traitor to be in a band? Could you betray a friend? Or maybe you've already done that? Do you think I'm just like you?' But all I said was:

– No, we don't.

Zombie brought the conversation to a close in his typical style:

– The only group activity we like is orgies!

And we trickled outside, where it was pitch dark, stumbling and bumping into one another. There were more of us know; some girls had joined our group. They even gave us money to buy alcohol from a lone kiosk, and then we headed back to the dorms. We had to get past the door man – in this case door woman, who was nicknamed the Terminator – so we stopped to collect ourselves so we'd appear nice and legal. One of the girls have me a scrunchie to get my tangled hair under control. We walked past the Terminator, all of us holding our breaths, avoiding eye-contact, and the scrunchie smelled like shampoo. As soon as we reached the stairs, we bolted up them like mad, again shoving and bumping into one another, and Mele's friend dropped her matches. She bent down to grab them, but I shoved her along. Death dropped his keys multiple times, but we finally made it in. We fell around the table, laughing. I'm not sure about what, exactly, but we laughed whole-heartedly.

Death started to drum on the table. He was a drummer, after all. Despite everything, he truly was a drummer. We started drumming, too, not really in rhythm with him, but we drummed so hard that the table lamp tipped over and broke. The room went dark, but Zombie had a solution: he lit his hair on fire and started to shake his head. The flame went out; he poured vodka over his head and tried again. It burned a little better, but reeked.

The door opened, and there was the Terminator. She illustrated her unwavering nature by ignoring everything around and simply asking:

– Did all the visitors leave me their IDs downstairs?

– Yes!

We all answered simultaneously. But she said:

– I don't have anything from any of you!

She paused for effect, and then turned around and left.

What did that mean? What were we supposed to do? Wait to be arrested? Either way, it got us to quiet down. But it was dark, because the hair had gone out, the lamp was broken and there was no overhead light. The conversation turned darker, too. Not too long passed before Mele whispered:

– Do you want to hear a poem?

And I said:

– No.

But Zombie hummed in a little voice:

– It's Black Friday, black things are going to happen, I feel it, all sorts of bad, black thinks are coming our way!

I added, in the same kind of voice:

– We'll have to slave away for seven long years!

And one of the girls, whom I hadn't noticed until now, spoke up in an eerie voice:

– Know what? I'm a witch.

That was honestly unsettling. Probably because it had been unexpected. Mele was the first to speak up, but the rest of us soon joined in:

– C'mon, cut it out, stop!

And the girl laughed:

– Alright, alright!

Death made his usual suggestion:

– Should we go to the woods?

I liked this idea.

– Maybe we should?

But where was there a woods around here? Death mulled this over, too, and said nothing. No-one said something for some time. Outside, the world had started to grow lighter again. Or else my eyes had grown accustomed to the dark. Near-sighted people see a little better in the dark than others. I saw that Death had fallen asleep in his chair, and that the unfamiliar witch was asleep with her head on his lap. Zombie had fallen asleep on the floor, naturally, right next to Mele's pretty friend, who slept with her head on his shoulder.

Only Mele sat by herself. And me. She was on the other side of the room, glaring at me. I suddenly felt sorry for this annoying idiot of a girl, who was so stupidly in love with me – couldn't she let someone else do that? I called to her gently:

– Tell me a poem!

But she didn't reply, just stared back at me with empty eyes. Eyes without irises. The hair on the back of my next stood up, but in the next second I understood that her eyes were closed, and what I'd seen was the morning light reflecting off her closed eyelids. I was the only one left standing. Why had everyone else fallen asleep? Of course, none of them had taken a nice long nap during the concert like I had. It was a little unnerving, like being the only live person in a wax museum; the morning light wasn't exactly cheery and hopeful, either, but a corpse-like blue. Everything would be set right if I could only have a cigarette, but I had no way to light one. One of the girls had dropped a matchbook on the stairs, but I was too scared to get up and go look. What if they all attack me? Death and the witch, all of them.

Death suddenly spoke, sounding like a real sleepwalker:

– Are we really not going to start a band?

I needed to roll my tongue around my dried-out mouth for a few moments before I could respond:

– I guess not. I could never get the money.

He responded:

– No worries.

And fell back asleep.

Outside, the sky had started to become bigger and warmer. I worked up the courage to turn my back to the room and look out the window. It was almost morning. I turned back and looked at them, my dear friends, how they slept, just like little kids, which they were, and no-one in the world was better than them.

I turned back to the window and saw the yellow grass of Ķīpsala, the mud that we'd soon walk through on our way to the train station – Death, Zombie, the girls, none of whom were mine, and me. Death – as silently as demon of the waterless desert, left undiscovered for centuries, completely unknown; Zombie – riding along regardless of the fact that the rest of us would be dragging our feet, he'd be riding, forever a restless spirit, the greatest jester that there has ever been. We'd walk along the canal, but not cross it at the bridge – we always crossed over two fat pipes that lay abandoned right next to it. We'd cross them this time, too, even though our legs would be unsteady and our heads dizzy, but it was never, ever out of fear, but out of the pure pleasure of walking across on these pipes. Once we make it across we'd stop. No-one will want to go further. The ducks swimming in the canal will stare at us. Zombie will shout:

– I don't want to go! I want to stay here and feed the ducks!
But we won't have anything to give them. And we won't have a santims
between us.

That place will stay in my memory. The mud, the canal, the pipes
and the ducks watching us reproachfully with their gentle, mysterious
eyes. Every time I pass by Ķīpsala, that same feeling will wash over me.

But I didn't understand that feeling back then, when I sat by the
window, staring into the future. I honestly couldn't understand if I
was happy or sad. I don't understand to this day.

And that's how Latvia's best-ever metal band was never born.

And with that our history of metal comes to a close.

III
POST-APOCALYPSE

1

It was only dark because my eyes were closed. The sun had been out for some time, I could feel it through my eyelids. But I kept them closed. I had just woken up; for a moment I didn't know if and who I was, but then I remembered everything, including that there had been a massive party the night before. It had continued until the moment sleep had descended on us, in that intangible border covered in dreams, there was laughter and deep conversations, and gazing at the heavens through smoke – I remembered all if it, but I still didn't know where I was. I hadn't yet opened my eyes.

I didn't want to open them. I could spend a little longer not knowing where I was.

That familiar feeling of being somewhere very far away. Now I was going to have to figure out where I was, say hello, interact, have breakfast and then get back home, which was probably all the way on the other side of the city from where I was, by bus or by tram, because it's late enough in the day that it would be silly to take a cab. I had absolutely no clue where I could be – probably in the middle of nowhere.

I finally opened my eyes – I was home! Actually at home. In my bed. The familiar ceiling overhead. The familiar trees outside the window, and behind the trees, the sun. It wasn't morning anymore, but midday. And, right – the party had been at my place. My birthday party. Now I remembered everything, except for the part where I went to bed. I got up and went to look around the apartment.

The first order of business was to make sure the bookshelf was still intact. By the looks of it everything was as it should be. No-one had dared to touch the old bookshelf. I pulled out one of the books and opened it to see if it was still old. 1695. My hear grew lighter. That always worked. I was soothed by these centuries that lay so silently in my hands and proved that time wasn't all that important.

But someone had taken out Latvian author Jānis Dāvis' *Plan for Jewish World Domination* and had put it back in upside-down. I wonder who? This book had perhaps the most intriguing title of all the books in the shelf, a bibliographical rarity. Though, who had needed J. K. Huysmans' *The Damned*? The book was shelved a bit crooked. Maybe someone had accidentally brushed against it with his shoulder, who knows, it was barely out of place. Everything else looked pristine.

The same could not be said about the rest of the room. Even though not a whole lot had happened last night. There was a black jacket – it wasn't mine – hanging on the back of a chair. There were empty glasses and bottles on the table, chairs, windowsills, all over. Some weren't even completely empty. The majority of the wine had been New-World Zinfandels and Cabernet Sauvignons.

The kitchen revealed more substantial signs of a party. The ashtray was overflowing and looked not unlike a hedgehog. Red wine had been generously spilled over the table and floor, and the midday reflected off shards of broken glass. The wines here were a little fancier, a rich German Riesling (even though it wasn't yet the season for white wine), a few Pinot Noirs and some jerk had unearthed my bottle of Corton-Charlemagne, which I had been stashing for a smaller party. Like maybe just me.

What was notable was the near-absence of any signs of hard liquor. I saw only one bottle of regular whisky, and a bottle of Bombay Sapphire. And those were only half-empty. What had happened to us? It wasn't that long ago, when Kārlis and I had been roommates, that the view the next day was totally different. Those days, the apartment would be littered with empty liquor bottles and unfamiliar women or at least one of our friends. Back then, Kārlis had just broken up with Milēdija. Thirteen years, and then it was over. We were once again single and wild.

But I guess he got tired of that carefree life. Me too. Everyone's becoming more sensible. All we really drink anymore is wine. And there are only a few broken glasses. And everybody took a taxi home. How many people were been anyway? There were more people here than were actually invited. There was even this one guy with a gigantic moustache, and a lesbian couple. And for all those people, only a couple of broken glasses and a couple of books out of place. I'm happy they were here. I'm happy for the years we've lived, that have made us so friendly and smart. The moustachioed guy and I had talked about grammar. About how Latvian orthography uses a lot of commas. In turn, I talked a lot about the makeup of France's Royal family. In France, a dauphin is the same as the Prince of Wales is in the United Kingdom. He didn't ask me about it, but I still told him.

The conversation in the kitchen was about how a reflective, intelligent person was, most likely, unhappy, or at least melancholy or depressed. I objected to this saying, girls, it may very well be that we're each reflective in his own way, but intelligent? It was Socrates who said that a wise man is a truly happy man. Have you no respect for Socrates? But do you know of any truly wise person who is happy? No, I don't. I noticed a little too late that I had offended everyone, whose only sin had been to be happy. But the girls kept on. You rely too much on authority. I rely too much on authority? Me? And what do you rely on? We see things for what they are. Oh, I see. I see things for what they aren't. Do you think all those idiots telling you how to live your lives think that they're looking at things the wrong way? No, they're convinced they're in the right, but they're wrong. And how are you any different? You all think you're right and that everyone else is wrong. Whatever, they said. I asked them what their combined age was. What does that have to do with anything? It's not like we're getting married. Okay, okay.

Now I think about how old I am. Just me. I remember everything clearly, except for the part where I went to bed and how old I was turning. I remember when the wine got spilled: a wide, dark stream, and all the guests cringed, but I watched as if hypnotized as it spread over the edge of the table and trickle down, dripping quickly at first, and then gradually slower. But now these clear memories reminded me the main reason why I had actually gotten out of bed.

Once I had taken care of that, I felt better. I tried to flush the toilet, but it didn't work. The handle worked, but there was no subsequent cascade of water.

Then I remember – it had broken last night. Each guest had his or her solution or advice to give, and so I had tried to fix it. Even though I'm no handyman, I still managed to do something, and even had a few pieces left over. But the fix, it turns out, hadn't been permanent.

What was I supposed to do now? I did what I usually did in those kinds of situations. I went back to the bedroom. The girl had just woken up, and I asked her what I should do. She thought for a moment, and then gave me the number for a plumber.

Perfect. All I had to do was call. But not now, when I had to leave for work. So I hit the street. It was the first day of spring – my thirtieth.

2

The plumber showed up on Thursday night, right on schedule. There he was, a regular guy, with his hair tied back in a ponytail and a bandanna around his forehead. He took his earbuds out of his ears, shook my hand and asked

— Where's the toilet?

I showed him to the bathroom and told him what had happened. He took off the tank lid, looked inside at what to me was an incomprehensible ocean, and let out a laugh.

— Yup... I'll see what I can do.

I thanked him ahead of time and left him alone. I went to the kitchen and sat down in a chair. As if nothing had happened. But it had.

Nothing had happened to me for about ten, fifteen years. I studied, worked, dated, broke up, travelled. I don't remember a lot of it. But what happened was to him, my plumber, who was currently in my bathroom banging around. I knew him. It was none other than Pēteris from Skyforger.

I hadn't listened to that music since my early teenage years. A couple of times during my college years, but less and less frequently and eventually not at all. I fell out of the loop, I forgot, I cut my hair. There was nothing left anyway – Dzels Vilks had deteriorated, Chuck Schuldiner had died and Grishnackh was released from prison. Only Skyforger and Pēteris remained. He hadn't given up yet, and still made good music. I still listened to them on rare occasion. I particularly liked the album *Latvian Riflemen*. If only I had known that I had been right there when Pēteris' relationship with the riflemen had begun... All I knew was that he was an idol, a monuments and cultural hero, the last bastion of Latvian music, the most famous Latvian musician in the world and my personal proof against the weight of the world.

I had never known him personally. That time at the open-air stage in Jelgava I had been a few bushes over, and after that had only seen him on stage or in the news. I'd heard that he worked as a plumber for the Daile Theatre. I had been amazed at how paradoxical it was – he was working in an institution that he was more famous than. I had never imagined that he would end up at my place, at my toilet.

I tried to decide what to do. There was an unusually clarity to my thoughts. The young me from way back when would want to talk to Pēteris of Skyforger. Which is exactly why I couldn't not do it now, not after I had broken all my promises and had become a slave, hypocrite, liar, swindler, pretentious and a snob – everything I hadn't been back then. I couldn't let the opportunity to talk with someone from that world pass me by.

I opened a cabinet and set out a bottle of Pouilly-Fumé and a regular little of Chateauneuf du Pape. It was a time when men could choose between white and red wine. I even cleaned out the ashtray and set it in the middle of the table.

I just hoped he didn't think that I was some crazed fan who had broken his toilet just to meet a famous musician. It was crazy, I was thinking like a teenager even though I hadn't been one for years.

But he was already coming down the hall. Instead of a sword he had a towel in his hands, and he was wiping them clean and said:

– I managed to fix it, it'll work.

And probably added to himself: 'Shit away!' That gave me some courage and I asked:

– Care for a drink? White, red?

– No. I don't like wine.

It was clear there wouldn't be any conversation – I had forgotten how to converse, I can only talk about people exactly like me, and now I'm someone else. But he asked politely if he could smoke. I pushed the ashtray towards him, and after a moment of smoky silence I asked:

– Do you remember that time that time, when you were still Grindmaster Dead, and you played at the open-air stage in Jelgava?

He smiled for a second.

– In Jelgava... Maybe. The open-air stage...where was that?

– Opposite the palace. On the other side of the river.

– I don't remember. But could be.

– It was one of the last Grindmaster concerts. You founded Skyforger not long after.

– I can't remember every concert.

– What year were Skyforger founded?

– Ninety-five... Why?

– Nothing, never mind. I was at that concert. Sometimes I remember the nineties. How back then... Back then things were different.

He nodded, but I thought – how were things different for him, his life is exactly the same.

– Remember pissing in the bushes at that concert, and Death said hello to you?

– I don't remember anything like that.

– Want a beer?

– I could maybe go for one.

He smiled serenely, as if he had anticipated this turn of events.

We drink a lot of unfiltered Valmiermuižas beer, almost everything that I had. We smoked and talked a lot – it happened very organically. Just like other true underground stars, for example, Dambis or Šubrovskis, Pēteris was as kind and open as a king. We talked about the ethnogenesis of Baltic peoples, the reasons for the Second World War and the shortcomings of the metric system, but most of all we talked about music. I watched him through the smoke and beer foam and thought – see, he had done it!

How had he done it? How had it been possible for me to say 'no' that one morning back in the nineties? Had I been scared then? Or perhaps lazy? Proud? How come I had left, but he had stayed? No, it wasn't that I had left – the world had ended! But maybe it hadn't? See, the world was still here and hadn't ended. He told me that they had their own club, Melnā Piektdiena – named after the Black Friday concerts – where all at the wildest bands from overseas come to play. Quality stuff. There was even an open-air festival for metalheads in Latvia now. I used to dream of that happening! Had they read my mind? I had imagined the festival would take place in the winter, in the woods, on trampled snow; but the one Pēteris was telling me about didn't sound bad either – in the summer, by a pond.

I asked him:

– Are there as many good bands now as there were back then?

He again smiled in his serene manner:

– Not as good as then.

And he got lost in his thoughts. I wanted to say – of course, I understand that there's one band that's still that good, you don't have to say it out loud, rifleman. But he said:

– Maybe that one band... Tabestic Enteron. They're maybe just as good.

– For real?

– Almost. Give them a listen.

– Will do.

How was I supposed to listen to them?

– Do they have an album?

– Well, no. Go to a show.

Yeah right – as if I would just get up and go. But he was on a roll:

– You've really never heard of them? I think they're from Jelgava.

How was that possible?

– Are they playing in the festival?

– In Blome? Probably.

– When is it?

– Tomorrow.

And then we went back to talking as if we hadn't spoken a lifetime, about the rifleman battles and how there were still bodies of fallen riflemen around Jelgava, how Pēteris altered his convictions, and how I altered mine, though I didn't know to what. I spoke less and less. I was trying to remember something. He stopped talking as well, and we both sat silent for a while. There was still some beer left (though not a lot), but he stood up to leave:

– I have to bike home!

And after a heartfelt handshake he was gone. I went back to the kitchen and took another small sip of beer. I felt the liquid do what it always does. Right, my toilet was fixed now.

I went into the bathroom and flushed. It worked – there was that waterfall sound. What's the largest waterfall in the world? I flushed again. That helped, right, the Guáira Falls. Pēteris had fixed my toilet. Pēteris from Skyforger. We all gave up, but he didn't. No, I wasn't going to shit in this toilet, like I'd planned. I took my keys from my pocket to carve the name of some band into the bathroom wall. What had been our band name? I didn't remember. I tossed the key into the toilet and went out, out of the bathroom, out of the apartment, and slammed the door.[4]

---

4 At the time I wasn't aware that the Guáira Falls, or the Seven Falls, had long ceased to exist. Poet Carlos Drummond de Andrade expressed his dismay at the destruction by writing: 'Seven falls passed us by, and we didn't know, ah, we didn't know how to love them, and all seven were killed, and all seven disappeared into thin air, seven ghosts, seven crimes of the living taking a life never again to be reborn.'

3

I decided to go to the festival. I didn't have anything planned that weekend anyway. I wanted to do something different. Something I hadn't done in a long time.

Friday after work I went to the bus station. I'd decided not to drive this time, even though I didn't own a car. I never learned how to drive. Someone else was always driving and offering to give me a lift. But no-one else was going this time. So I went to the bus station and asked for a ticket to Blome. That's where the problems started. It turns out there were two Blomes. Which one was I going to?

– Where are both Blomes?

As if the answer to that would help.

– In the same direction, basically. One's closer, the other a bit farther.

– Give me a ticket to the farther one.

I went to the platform, satisfied with my choice. I'd chosen right – there were already a few groups of long-haired, lanky boys and girls in all black. They were sitting on rolled-up sleeping bags with tents on their backs. Should have brought something like that with me, too? It hadn't even occurred to me. In the end it wasn't the most important part. I was going to observe, not sleep.

Almost as soon as I got onto the bus, a group of three girls addressed me, almost in unison:

– Excuse me, sir, is this your seat? We have seats five, six and seven.

I waved my hand, sit, and went to the back of the bus. They're the kind I need to watch. Uniformed morons. Sheep who can't find their seats without asking for help. We had to deal with people like them in our time, too. But now this: 'sir'. 'Sir'. I was only used to hearing that from businessmen and professors. I only wanted police officers to call me that. In turn, if taxi driver or maintenance guy accidentally addressed me informally, I wasn't offended, and felt a secret joy in the depths of my heart that there was still a youthful part of me. But now the youth was referring to me as sir. And the type of youth... It wasn't worth my time to go on this trip. But the bus had already pulled out of the station, and so I did what I usually do when I'm confused and/or trapped on public transportation in-transit: I took a book out of my pocket.

It's like the book was boring on purpose. I stared out the window and pretended that the landscape was filled with the plots of interesting books. Someone was lurking behind those bushes, trailing someone who was on this bus. There's a man sitting on the bench at this stop and he's not looking at us. What's he thinking?

The group sitting behind me was growing increasingly loud. I had noticed them when getting on the bus; they were from that initial group. Two girls in all black and two long-haired boys. It was like an illness, like wearing a uniform. Were they afraid of being singled out? They weren't all entirely alike, though; I started to notice a certain order to things. The shameless trio of girls up front were sitting quietly, their backs straight. This was probably the first time they were going to something like this. Towards the middle of the bus sat a lone thirty-something metalhead with glasses; I was maybe similar to him, except that he was fat, and had maintained his long ponytail and sour expression. He had probably participated in a lot of events, but was still an introvert and stuck to his very select group of friends, none of whom were with him now. And finally there was the group behind me – the loudest group, and they were getting even louder. I wasn't even paying attention to what they were saying, but then one of the girls called:

– Come sit with us!

I waited for a bit to see if she called to me again, and I was surprised   – how had they figured me out? I'd hadn't looked the part in a long time, and I was holding a boring book. I'd been able to slip past the front lines unnoticed, but couldn't fool the oracle in the back row. I went to join them. Signe, Ella, Ilmārs, Justs. Strange names – and they told me they were already drunk. Ella was the only one who denied it, but Signe told her:

– I know, you say that now, but as soon as we get off the bus you're going to fall over. I know how much we've had to drink.

And they showed me how much they'd had. One 0.3-litre bottle of vodka, with just a sip left at the bottom. Between the four of them. It became clear that my travel companions were very nice. And by nice, I mean young. They couldn't handle any more vodka, and offered me the last of it, which I drank in four seconds.

Ilmārs remembered that he had a 1.5-liter bottle of a mixed drink with him. With my help they finished that off quickly. The girls remembered that they had wine. Oh, I said, oh! What kind of wine do young women buy? And by god, it was Martini. Girls, that's not wine. But I said nothing, and drank it politely – a disgusting beverage – and then that was gone too. Too bad, because I was just starting to feel a buzz. And already loved my new friends. They really liked me. Signe put her hand on my shoulder. I had just gotten a buzz, we were on our way to a festival, and behind us was nothing, nothing at all, just us, people who met on the road, the perfect kind of human contact – being almost strangers who don't need anything from each other. I felt so connected to our word, the real world, and so confident that, after accidentally making eye contact, invited the fat metalhead to come sit with us. We introduced ourselves – his name was Imants, and he had a little bottle of Riga Black Balzam with him.

Then a woman up front asked if we were headed for Blome. All the passengers know where we were headed. I already felt like the leader of the pack and answered that there was no need to panic, because we needed the Blome that was further away. We had just passed that one. How had we missed it? Imants said that he had known which one to get out at, but also hadn't noticed it. Meanwhile the other passengers were saying:

– Yes, yes, you have to get out here!

We asked the driver to stop the bus and spilled out of it next to the ditch. There was only the road, the forest and the ditch, and that's all we needed. Imants said he'd get us to the festival; he made a call on his cell phone; there'd be a car here in a minutes, and we believed him and we laughed because we knew that'd we'd be able to get anywhere.

And we really did make it. It only took a second for me to lose sight of my new friends. They had to go pitch their tents and whatnot, and I was left by myself, with no supplies, and so it took me longer to get in. I found an entrance where they were supposedly letting people in, but also maybe not. A few long-haired festival goers got in, but a few of them were stopped by security and sent away, and they left wordlessly and headed for the nearby field. Then I understood – you couldn't bring alcohol into the festival grounds. Those who weren't let in had gone to the field to drink what they'd tried to smuggle in. Some of them ended up passing out in the process. The field was apparently meant to serve that exact purpose; I laughed, but then suddenly remembered that I had a bottle of whisky in my pocket. I wanted to try to get in, but the security guards looked serious, twice as broad as they were back in the day. Although I couldn't have taken them on back then, either. But what did that matter if I was simply a respectable person. I walked down to the field.

I joined a nearby group, took a sip of my whisky and offered it around to the others. The first metalhead carefully accepted my bottle of Jack Daniels, then looked at me and asked:

– Are you headed for some kind of VIP zone?

Very funny.

The whisky disappeared quickly, but the conversation didn't go anywhere. I asked:

– What're you all most looking forward to this year? What band?

– Tiamat, I guess.

– Hah, there was a band with the same name back in the nineties. Pretty decent doom metal.

– It's the same band.

I laughed:

– No way. There's no way they're still alive.

– It is!

I let it go. Kids, they don't understand the weight of time. I asked something else instead:

– What about Tabestic Enteron?

That got some mixed reactions:

– Those guys?

– They're shit.

– No, come on...

And one of the girls came to life and said:

– They're crazy or something.

My heart ached, and I asked:

— Where are they from?

— The looneybin.

— From Jelgava or somewhere.

I continued:

— From Jelgava? Who's in it?

— Faun, y'know? Pussy Grinder, y'know?

— Ah. Right, of course.

But I didn't know them. Not Faun, not Pussy Grinder. Then someone else asked:

— Are you from Jelgava?

— Yes! I answered earnestly.

— So you know Jana, then?

— Jana... Tell me something about her!

— Well, she's sixteen...

— No. Then I don't know her.

The Jack Daniels was finished. The metalhead closest to me pulled a bottle out of his clinking sleeping bag and handed it to me. It was a bottle of Hektors. And it was just as sweet when I was a kid. Just as cloying, and just as detrimental. I'd had enough to drink, and went to the festival grounds.

There were metalheads all around me, but I didn't know anyone. It had been over ten years since I'd left the scene. But I observed it all with an anthropological curiosity. First of all, there was an unusually large number of girls. In the nineties, it was rare to find women in alternative society. Today, here, it was like a mass parade of models. Back then the girls had dressed just like we had, in ripped jeans and a T-shirt. Or in long skirts... But here it was like a carnival! Black lace, costume jewellery, sparkles, powder!

It was clear I wouldn't know any of them. I looked at the guys; they looked about the same as we had back then. All of them with long hair, heavy boots and colourful T-shirts: Burzum, Amorphis, Skyforger and a lot of groups I didn't recognize. I looked into their faces, searched, and there, that guy looked like Cips, that one like Nose, but it wasn't actually them. Maybe they were all dead. Or maybe none of them came here anymore. One guy looked like Peksis, but it couldn't possibly be him. This guy's mohawk was more colourful, and he was heavier-set than Peksis. As I watched him, a girl wandered out of the crowd, waved to me and walked determinedly towards me. I thought I knew her from somewhere. Long, long ago, but my memories feel so present that it could've been only recently... It was Signe, the drunk girl from the bus, whom I met an hour ago! She flung her arms around my neck and said:

– Where were you? Where were you?

Seriously, I thought, where had I been? What had I been doing this entire time?

Signe and I were going somewhere. She must have been leading me. I didn't say anything, but then she asked:

– How old do you think I am?

I looked at her carefully. I was never good at guessing ages. I guessed:

– Eighteen?

Thinking that it was always better to guess too low; girls always love a compliment. Signe laughed with pride:

– Hah, people always guess I'm older. When I wear makeup I can pass for twenty.

I tilted my head; for some reason I felt younger than her. We'd stopped in front of a beer tent.

– Great idea, Signe, wonderful.

– Right?

I bought four beers so we wouldn't have to wait in line again and we went to sit in the grass. What now? I raised my cup to my face, but how long could I hide behind it? Signe stared off into the distance, her eyes bright. Who knows what she was thinking.

– What do you want to talk about?

– What do you mean?

A maddening counter question. I had never known what to say when people answer with that, and I didn't know what to say now, either.

I had completely forgotten why I had come here. And then I looked up and, shit, there was Venom! Was it really Venom? It was, but he was bald now. And a little rounder. But it was that same sullen expression;

no one else in the world had that face. There was no room for anything run of the mill in that face. I turned to Signe:

– Excuse me!

And I went to Venom. He remembered me! Or else he was used to being approached by strangers now and then. We didn't hug, but he said immediately:

– Well, what do you think?

– What?

He gestured to the stage. I listened for a moment; it wasn't half bad. It was almost old-school. But they were no My Dying Bride.

– Not bad. Who are they?

– Frailty, obviously.

I had absolutely no idea who they were. Now that I'd already failed I could continue on with the conversation normally:

– Do you still do anything with the metal scene?

– Yeah, I'm into journalism. We're making a documentary about Skyforger, with three cameras. An article for a magazine. That kind of stuff.

– Cool.

– I've left all the nationalist organizations, though. There's no discipline, nothing. I got sick of it and left. All of them.

Now he peered at me closely:

– But I'm feeding my tiger. What about you?

I really like this expression of his. He repeated:

– What about you?

– Me?

– Yeah.

– Nothing.

– I see.

We were both silent. I thought about my tiger. What was it? How was I to feed it? I said to Venom:

– Alright, I have to get back to the lady, shit.

But Signe was gone. I went to look for her by the beer tent. I got a beer and a whisky, and looked around at all the girls. Too bad; all I saw were tits and ass – how was I supposed to recognize Signe? It was easier to recognize girls back in the day. Shouldn't I be home with my girl, anyway? My phone vibrated; she was calling me. I didn't hear what she said, it was so loud there, so I just spoke into the receiver:

– Everything's fine. Everything's fine. You know me.

And everything really was fine. I just kept on going back to the beer tent. A sort of calm had taken over me, and I dozed off a few times right there on the bench. Some guys said I could go sleep in their tent if I didn't have my own. Was it already time for bed? I turned down their offer:

– Sorry, boys, but I'm accustomed to a certain level of comfort.

And I fell asleep right where I sat. My dream was filled with wonderful music. It sounded familiar, as did all things beautiful. I didn't want to ever wake up, I didn't want this music to end. It sang:

Do you dream of me?

And I murmured through my drooling, yes, yes, yes.

Even though I fell asleep on a bench, I woke up under a tree. Right in the festival grounds. Some girls walked past and asked:

– Where are your glasses?

I ran my hand down across my face; really, where were they? My head cleared immediately – they were Dior brand. I looked up. My glasses were hanging from a low tree branch. Old habits die hard. I put my glasses back on and went to find breakfast.

There were already people outside the food tent. I ordered a huge omelette and went to sit down:

– Good morning!

– Good morning to you!

– The morning's as good as he who gives it!

Like we were old friends, even though I knew no-one. One of them asked me:

– What did you think of Tiamat?

– Hm?

– They were good, right? It was great that they played some stuff from the nineties.

Ah, right. Like that old song: 'You awake – and it's true.' It really was the same Tiamat, still alive and kicking, and it was them who I'd heard in my sleep. It hadn't been a dream. I shouldn't have been afraid to wake up. I only needed to open my eyes for the dream to become reality.

But no-one around me was interested in my dream-like tragedies. Despite the early morning hour, the table was already crowded with half empty glasses of beer, and the others started to sing quietly. They saying happily, earnestly, without exaggeration, but they didn't know the lyrics that well. I finished my omelette, finished my beer and joined in, modestly and with reservation, at first only letting my voice be heard when their choir forgot the end of a line, but soon they were all following my lead because they wanted to sing and someone finally knew most of the words. It was better than nothing. When we sang:

> My brother died in the war,
> But I hear him ride at night...

The guy sitting next to me, my unfamiliar brother, shirtless and with a long beard, cried himself silly. I looked at him in disbelief – this tough-looking ironman was crying over schlager music. But he just kept on wiping away his tears while the table next to ours finished the song; they had fallen behind us by almost an entire verse. Wiping the last of his tears, the man clapped me on the back. I felt moved as well, and ordered him a beer and some garlic toasts. I was surprised by how good the food was here. The omelette was pretty decent, and the garlic toasts were quite garlicky.

Then I felt it starting. The desire to push people away, to be macho, to have respectable friends and to be the wise guy. All of these were things that had stood in my way so I wouldn't find what I came here looking for. And now I felt the strong desire to throw my money around. It started out so innocently – what's more innocent than ordering a beer and bar snacks for a crying stranger? Even the Good Soldier Schweik had done that. But for him that had been the last of his money, and it had been the right thing to do. But I had a lot of money left. And I wanted to prove it. I had shaken off the kids; now I was surrounded by men who sang, men who were closer to my own age, but I didn't have long hair, didn't have anything. I was a stranger, and what's worse, I was a traitor who had served the enemy for years, and now here I was, at a celebration, hopelessly trying to pass as one of them, and now I had lay down the only weapon the unworthy could wield, behold, I can buy garlic toasts, garlic toasts and beers all around!

Theoretically there may have been a bit of solidarity in it all, of the prodigal son returning. Maybe that's why I so sharply sensed how awful it all was – the fear of authority and the joy of being praised, and all that money. I had to get rid of it. Our table piled up with empty glasses. Here they had the pleasing habit of not clearing off the empty glasses, also you could see the damage done. I'd quieted the traitorous feeling in my brain and focused on drinking, but I felt myself sobering up with each glass. It can happen. The rest of the guys were warmed up from the singing and had turned to conversation. A Russian guy brought up the question of nationality. They're usually the ones to start that one. The Latvians, maybe more online. But this guy got right into it, and asked loudly:

– So what if I'm Russian?

– Who cares. No-one said anything about it.

I tried to be the voice of reason. It was true, no-one had brought it up at all.

– I'll have you know that my grandfather fought in the battles for Latvian independence!

And he looked at each of us in turn. No-one said anything, because there was nothing to say. I was the only one who spoke:

– How nice. Respect and honour to your grandfather.

Everyone chimed in, well, of course, yes, of course. But someone on the other end of the table suddenly turned the attention to me:

– But who are you?

I didn't hear the question because I was thinking about something else. Well, not so much thinking about something else as looking somewhere else. There was a woman sitting on the neighbouring table. She was wearing a T-shirt and thong underwear, and was sitting with her back to us. She fit into the overall setting quite well, and maybe it was this quiet, unobtrusive presence that pulled me into existential contemplation. I stared at her ass like I was watching two planets collide. Or like an idiot. And then the question came again:

– Who are you?

I gave a start; I'd been caught, I was flustered. I didn't know the answer to the question. And I was tired of the question. I scratched my forehead with a two-lat coin and said:

– I don't know.

I stood up and went for a walk. Who was I? Without long hair, without a tiger. There were no advertisers or French aristocrats who would recognize me. But hadn't Signe recognized me? She hadn't asked who I was. What had she seen in me? Where was she now? I couldn't see her. And I was still unable to remember something. Something was niggling at my brain. Who was I? What was I looking for here?

I started to notice that people had been running into me from a single direction. There was some kind of movement happening. Everyone was nudging me towards something. Or else they were the ones going somewhere, and I was just getting in the way. Then I heard music. And it was really good music! Could it be? Morbid Angel or Demilich? Anything was possible here. Now I was hurrying ahead of everyone. I worked my way up to the front of the stage. But no, I didn't recognise the guys on stage. They looked like totally normal guys, except that they were dressed like clowns. One in a dress, one doing tricks, while the guitarist was wearing nothing but a thong. I'm dead serious. That's what they looked like. But the music, the music was amazing. I couldn't believe it myself. I said: 'Brain, no tricking me this time. What are they singing?' And I listened to the lyrics:

You can't stomach our shit-stained balls,

But all you taste is rhubarb,

Sooner or later I'll be your astral whore.

It wasn't bad. Not bad at all. There was a hidden poetics in it, believe it or not. And then the final verse:

And you'll massage my little rosy balls,

You'll be my friends, we'll go hand in hand

To a place where the sun doesn't set and birds sing Judas Priest.

I just want to be happy.

I almost started to cry, no joke. Just like that metalhead at the breakfast table and the song about the brother. The final solo was just perfect, too – tiu-riu-tiu-tiu! Once the song was over the audience started to chant what I had already figured out:

– Tabestic Enteron!

– Tabestic Enteron!

Isn't this why I'd come here? It must be. Now I looked at those clowns in a completely different light. Especially at the guitarist in the thong underwear. It wasn't the outfit that caught my attention this time. It was... It was Arturiņš from Jelgava. One hundred per cent, without a doubt. He was in a band now. Why hadn't he waited for me? I get why Pēteris had started Skyforger without me – it was because he didn't know me. But Arturiņš, why hadn't he waited?

When it seemed like the concert was nearing its end, I left the front row and made my way to the beer tent. I pushed my way past the losers just hanging around, and didn't even glance at the girl who was still sitting on the table. I bought six beers. Five for Tabestic Enteron and one for me. I wanted to raise a glass with my friends, the accomplished musicians. I had forgiven them. I was a great enough artist that I could value art more than I valued myself. And there they came, no longer visible to the public, discussing among themselves how their set had gone.

I approached them with my bouquet of beers. I handed it to them and said:

– A gift, dear musicians, from a long-time fan of metal!

Next to Arturiņš was a beautiful woman. She looked at me, then at him and asked that same question:

– Who's that?

But Arturiņš, or rather, Pussy Grinder, looked at me and said:

– That's my friend! Always older and wiser than me.

4

You must think that I was done after Blome. But oh, far from it. The scar had reopened, and I couldn't sleep. I still hadn't found what I was looking for, still couldn't remember some very important thing. It was in the past, the important things are always in the past. But the past is a mystery. There's a great part in Plato's *Theaetetus* about a bird cage. Remember, where Socrates and Theaetetus are discussing memory. Is it like a wax tablet in which all the events of our past are imprinted? Some go deeper, some are more shallow, the imprints grow duller over the course of time, are smoothed out, and eventually we no longer remember what once was. How many people came to Black Friday in 1996? According to the written record, 800. But an eight can look so much like a three... But no, says Socrates, our memory is more like a bird cage. And the birds aren't docile chickens, but wild, vicious birds. If you put your hand in the cage they'll start to rage, thrash against the bars, up and down. You can try to catch hold of one, but you don't know which one it will be. You pull it out and look; did you pull out the memory of a mysterious girl, or of an epic failure? You try to catch hold of another one, but birds aren't just animate objects, but fragile things, you can injure them, and if you do it will never be the same again, and they're easy to kill. The meanest ones peck your fingers, and then you're the one running away. The beautiful ones are the hardest to coax into your hand. Tired of being pecked and desperate to catch what you know, but can't see, you press your face against the door to the cage, and then you just give in and stick your whole head inside their bird kingdom, and they attack you and tear you apart.

I didn't know where to continue with my search, and then I got a call from Kroģis. The same old thug friend of mine. I didn't even know he had my phone number, but I wasn't too surprised – I'm sure he has his sources. He called to tell me that Kandžejs was just back from Ireland. I sort of remembered, right, he had gone to Ireland around ten insane years ago. Probably still on the run, I thought. Kroģis had run into him, and they thought – maybe all three of us could get together, play cards or something. Just like that. Something in this sleepy, peaceful world of the present had been set into motion.

Soon enough, as unbelievable as it may seem, the three of us really were sitting together at an outdoor café. The sun was shining and Zane (our server) was all smiles. I had chosen the place, because they didn't know their way around Riga. And there they sat, these two men, who had been so mysterious that at times it had seemed as if I had imagined them. It was so strange to see them sitting at a table with fancy glasses in their hands. Kroģis hadn't changed a bit, though he was maybe a bit wider. His expression was just as grumpy as always, and a few more timid people at the café gave our table a wide berth. Kandžejs was a little broader than before, and was just as real, drinking unfiltered beer and constantly fussing:

– Get one for yourself, it's on me!

– I already had one.

– You don't want another? See, I've got cash, have another!

– I haven't even finished this one.

– Drink, drink up! I have the money, we'll order more. Drink!

Kroģis said nothing; he had become the quintessential manifestation of his own qualities and, it seemed, had stopped speaking altogether. But no matter, Kandžejs spoke enough for both of them.

– I drank Guinness in Ireland, but we don't have it here.

– What d'you mean they don't have it!

– You mean we do?

– Well not here, but at Suns, and in the Irish pubs.

– We have Irish pubs?

– They're all over the place.

– Can we go there? We'll take a cab!

– I don't want to go to some dumb Irish pub. I don't want Guinness, either. Can you make it without it for a little longer? You'll be back in Dublin soon enough, you can get it there.

Kroģis opened up a pack of cards and started to deal.

– I live in Limerick, not Dublin.

– Very interesting.

– I can tell you about the house I have there, too.

– So tell us.

– I have a garden, too, with roses...

– I was kidding. I don't want to hear about it.

– Well then what? Should we go play pool? We can take a cab. I played in a pub in Dublin once against Ronnie O'Sullivan. Beat him three to one.

– I don't believe you.

– Oh well.

I waited for them to blow off their steam about Ireland. After the second beer things calmed down, and I asked:

– Do you remember that time in Jelgava?

– I remember, I remember. We got lost in the woods and stole a boat, of course.

– I meant the time we were watching my friends play street ball.

– Maybe. I don't remember.

I understood it wasn't time yet. I focused on the game. I made a lot of mistakes, and had to deduct myself points. I was always the scorekeeper.

– What do you do in Ireland?

– Nothing! I have an Irish job now, which means I do nothing, just get paid! I play Unreal Tournament at work, I'm already on level five.

– I only play Tetris at work, and I'm on level thirteen.

Jesus, I thought, what are we doing here? Bragging about who has the easiest job. Kandžejs and I, like true friends, had always some level of competition between us, but now I thought – enough. Just then he called, and in his typical style – by turning his head and saying: 'What a risk, what a risk!' Of course, he had a decent hand and, of course, won, claiming it was a crazy heroic feat. I wanted so badly to get good cards, so I could show him how it was done, without talking, with a poker face, but I kept getting useless cards, and I made a lot of mistakes. Kroģis had already given me one of his looks. He had been the one who had taught me how to play all those years back, and now he watched my performance like a disappointed coach, probably thinking I'd wasted all those years letting myself go. I wanted to make him proud, but I never got the right cards. But Kandžejs got them, and eventually my frustration got the best of me and I asked:

– What exactly were you in for?

I needed to know. But he just trumped my hand and lamely replied:

– What I was in for last night? Why don't you ask your mom, she knows.

– No, I mean that time in the nineties. What were you in for?

– Where?

– What do you mean where?

– Well, where?

– In prison! In the Jelgava Pārlielupe Prison.

– Sixty-two.

He had the annoying habit of counting points during the course of the game, thus announcing his victory. Then he turned his attention back to me:

– What were you saying?

– What's wrong with you? I'm asking, why were you in the Pārlielupe Prison that one time?

– Ah, me, in prison?

– Yes!

– For kicking your ass at cards, that's why.

– I'm serious. Tell me, please?

– What do you want?

I looked into his eyes and saw earnest confusion.

– You used to always talk about prison... Folklore, stories...

– Sure, I liked the subject, the music... You talked about metal all the time, but were you actually metal?

– Yes!

– Hey, metal, are you going to finally play like a person?

That reprove came from Kroģis. I'd completely screwed up my hand. He discarded the junk cards and added:

– He was never locked up anywhere. You out of your mind or something?

Kandžejs howled with laughter:

– You honestly thought that I'd been in prison?

– Well, no, I mean... To be honest, yes.

– How old was I back then? Fifteen?

– Older... You were older than me.

– Okay, so seventeen, maybe.

– But how… You drove a car!

Now both of them were laughing.

– You thought I was some hard-core criminal, but that I would never drive a car without a license, right?

– But the car, it was black…

– That was Igors' car, my sister's boyfriend.

They were positively shaking with laughter. I took the cards, shuffled and started to deal, but Kroġis grabbed my hand. I stopped, collected the cards, shuffled them again and gave him the deck to cut. I tried to get a hold of myself and re-join the world. But there was more. Kandžejs stubbed out his just-lit cigarette and said:

– Oy, oy, oy. She's coming. Look sober.

A very attractive woman approached our table. She greeted everyone like old friends. I looked at her face, and I'll be damned, but it really was her – it was Mele, good old Mele. We had both changed enough that we could honestly say to each other:

– You look great.

– You mean not fat anymore?

Some things never change; this question was just like the old her. Then she explained:

– I used to eat a lot to piss my dad off. All he wanted was a pretty daughter.

And now he had one. Her teenage curves had stayed in all the right places, and I couldn't stop staring. It really was her – who would have thought! I turned to my newly ex-cons:

– Do you all know each other?

– Oh yes.

Kandžejs gave Mele a lecherous look. She answered coolly, casually:

– We ran into each other not too long ago, when he first got to town.

– But how did you first meet?

– Weren't you the one who introduced us?

– Was I?

I wrinkled my forehead and rubbed my cheeks. I couldn't remember, but maybe it was possible. It turns out anything was possible. Kandžejs said:

– Yeah, yeah, yeah, that one time, remember? At least I think so. That time in Jelgava – and he became animated again – Nellija, can you imagine it, this one was convinced that I'd escaped from...

I put up my hands:

– Stop! Stop! Everybody freeze!

I turned to Kandžejs:

– Did you pay already? You have to pay for the beer!

He immediately rushed in to pay his tab, pulling notes out of his wallet as he went. I turned to Kroģis:

– Do you need to go to the bathroom?

He considered everything with an equal amount of seriousness. Even then he thought for a moment and then said:

– I suppose I do.

And then we were alone. She immediately grew sullen, just like she had a hundred years ago. I don't think she had been faking it. I sat there fidgeting just like I had back then, and I'm an honest person. More likely the mask had been everything that had happened in the meantime. And even if not – for just a moment we were just as we had been back then, without pretence. I said:

– So?

And she replied:

– So what?

– When did you two meet?

– Meet who?

– That ex-ex-convict.

– Who's that?

– Kandžejs.

– You were the one who introduced us. We ran into each other not that long ago. It's not like that. We just talked about the old times. I wanted to go back there for a little bit, to be close to it again. Back then I'd been totally in love with someone in your group.

And she smiled brightly. My heart ached for my missed opportunity. I could I have known that she would turn out so beautiful. She had noticed me. I said:

– I knew.

She wasn't too surprised:

– Really? Did Gatis know too?

– No. I didn't tell anyone.

And she smiled wickedly:

– Too bad. Now it seems like it would've been better if he'd know.

That was where I started to get confused:

– Why?

She was confused too:

– What do you mean why?

I tried to concentrate:

– Why would he need to know...

– Because I wanted him to know. But how could I tell him. You remember what I was like.

I concentrated even harder:

– Who were you in love with?

– You said you knew!

– I forgot.

– With Gatis! You all called him Death.

I burst out laughing.

– What's so funny?

How could I not laugh. The two respectable citizens returned to the table and sat down. I asked them:

– Who are you? Who am I?

They paid no attention to my questions; they'd already grown accustomed to them back then. But back then I'd had a far better grasp on what was going on.

Kandžejs and – alright, okay – *Nellija* were getting ready to go somewhere and began saying their farewells. But Kroģis suddenly grew pensive:

– Hold on... I just remembered something. Who was it with?

– What then?

– Or who was it who told me... You, Jānis?

– Told you what?

– The story about the two guys in the dump...

– What are you talking about? Calm down.

– Someone told me that story...

One he had his mind on something, he was immovable. We sat

down to listen.

– It went something like this... One of the guys had a gun.

Kandžejs made as if to interject, but stopped himself. Kroģis continued:

– He went out to the old Jelgava dump to practices shooting. There wasn't anyone there, usually. He got there early in the morning, not another soul in sight. He pulled out his gun, and then spotted someone. But it was the same guy. Also with a gun, also come to the dump to practice shooting. They both spot each other. And are both frightened! And they both wanted to shoot – they were very particular about that – and suddenly they're advancing towards each other! But then they both dropped to the ground and hid. Just lie on the ground and froze. So the other wouldn't see them. There's no way of telling who the other one is. He probably wants to shoot you. And you can't move, because if you move, he'll shoot you. And they're both thinking this very same thing. So they lie there, not moving. For a long time. Because what in this situation can change? No-one else comes to the dump. It's an old, abandoned dump. And so they lay there all day.

– And they're still there now!

Kandžejs couldn't resist. Kroģis continued, unwavering:

– And so they lay there until night fell. They both tried to stay awake, and couldn't figure out what to do. They both think: how foolish, how stupid. Maybe I should shout 'truce' to the other guy? Let's get up and leave? But then what if he shoots me anyway? But then someone else does show up, someone without a gun. Some girl. She wants to learn to play the flute or recorder or something. But she's too embarrassed to practice at home. So she's come to the dump, and doesn't see the two guys; she sits right between them, takes out her flute and plays. I think that must've been the most batshit concert there ever was. Who told me that story?

– Why are you telling it now? Kandžejs asked. Kroģis cleared his throat; it had to have been the longest he'd ever spoken in one sitting:

– I don't know. No reason. Alright, let's go. Have to go back to the wife and kids.

Kandžejs glanced at the score sheet:

– Don't worry about paying me my winnings, you can keep it.

Kroģis glanced at the score sheet as well. And asked:

– What did you do?

I was still in the throes of his story. I looked at the score sheet. They had all screwed me over so badly, what more did they want? Usually I was good at keeping score. But this time the events of the day had proven to be too much for me. I had given everyone positive-points. Everyone had won. Kroģis shook my hand:

– See you around! Learn how to count!

– Later!

– Later!

– Later!

5

As long as all the important things that had happened to me wasn't just a figment of my imagination, I decided that it was time to write them down. I wrote for seven days and nights. I spent several years working this way.

When I had finished, or as close to finished as I could get, I needed to make sure that I hadn't screwed anything up. While the ink was still drying, I went to the Rare Books and Manuscripts department of the National Library. When I didn't find what I needed there, I bribed the librarian with a kiss to let me into the secret literature section, the so-called Special Collections section. There I found a volume titled *Complete Catalogue of Metalheads*. It wasn't hard to find Death. The catalogue included his last known address and telephone number.

We sat on a terrace along the river. Some guest house in the Jelgava area. Death set aside the last roll of parchment paper and sipped his tea. He thought for a moment and then said:

– It's all true.

I nodded in agreement, it really was. Death, who once again went by Gatis, put down his empty cup and asked:

– But why do all of this? It's all over. Have you been back to Jelgava? The gypsies don't live by the Shittery anymore. The Pārlielupe Prison is being torn down.

– The physical things aren't what's important.

– What else? The open-air stage is gone. Your Tabestic was disbanded while you were writing this. They must've really been good. Now it's all gone. No ideas, no mission.

I shook my head, without knowing why:

– It can't all be over.

– Maybe it isn't.

He walked over to his sound system and put in a CD. John Coltrane's *My Favorite Things*.

– I only listen to jazz now.

But he shot me a look over his shoulder and added:

– And sometimes Meshuggah. Meshuggah is too good not to listen to.

I didn't know what that was. Thrash? Death?

– Thrash, he said. But we've changed too. Have you not?

And how, my friend.

– But why didn't you write about First Frost?

What more did he want from me?

– What's that?

– You don't remember? It was an incredibly important event. It was a landmark for a lot of people.

No. Wait, wait. I started to remember something... It was after the end. When we had already decided not to start a band. Right?

– It was the Sinister concert. The first top-quality death-metal concert in Latvia.

I remembered it now. Strange, I had almost forgotten all about it... We went to that concert. Just that one last time, because Sinister was playing.

– Man. Back then it was like, if we didn't make it to that concert, then

everything would be meaningless. We had to get there no matter what.

– It was snowing horribly, even though it was only October. I was waiting for you guys at the Ozolnieki station. You were seriously late.

– It was seriously snowing, and we were on our way already, and the train was going as fast as it could. We were stuck at the Sugar Factory station for at least half an hour. We'd already polished off half a bottle of Merkurs.

Meanwhile, I'd been waiting on the Ozolnieki station platform. The station building was closed, and the snow just kept falling down on me. The train was delayed, and maybe wouldn't come at all. I was by myself on the platform. Maybe I should walk home. But I couldn't do that – what if the train pulled in and I wasn't here? They couldn't go to the concert without me. I think I felt almost elated when I spotted the headlights of the train tunnelling through the psychopathic snowflakes. I scrambled onto the train. Snow fell from me as I walked through the train cars, as if I were a little piece of the outside world that had stepped in to a homey, rumbling room. They were in the second-to-last train car, and Death called to me:

– C'mon, sit. Why are you so nervous?

I sat down on the seat, which happened to be right above the radiator. They had saved that spot just for me. You couldn't handle it for too long, believe me. But for now it was just what I needed. I didn't get to sit there for too long anyway – as soon as I had started to turn from a snowman into a waterfall, they wanted to have a smoke, and so we went out to stand between the cars.

We smoked, we drank, but we didn't go back inside. Death said he didn't want to be around people, and so we stayed right there, between the cars. The train stopped in Cena. Death leaned out to check whether any conductors got on and Zombie, of course, pushed him out. He only just managed to jump back on, and got a little worked up. When the door slid closed, Zombie kicked it back open. Death asked:

– You going to throw me out of it while it's moving?

– No, it's just so we have some fresh air. We're going to keep smoking.

Though, that is quite an idea...

Snowflakes rushed past the open door, but I wasn't worried about it. We were going to the Sinister concert, and we had left the world behind. Everything was going well, we weren't going to get kicked off the train. As soon as I thought these words, Death said:

– Conductors got on the train in Cena.

– What? Why didn't you say anything?

– I didn't have time, and you were too busy trying to kill me.

Zombie peeked into the train car.

– No-one's coming yet. Let's make a run for it at the next station.

Death was sullen:

– The next station is Olaine. It's the worst station. If we don't make it to Sinister I'll never smile again. We should've just bought tickets this time.

– Shut up.

Zombie peeked again in to the train car, but they were coming from the opposite direction. Except that they weren't conductors; they were five *gopniks*.

– Oh! Look what we have here!

We said nothing.

– What's up, Rapunzels?

We said nothing.

– You have to get off the train, see, the door's already open!

– After you?

– What?

And he punched Zombie. Even though I was the one who had spoken. Zombie lunged at him, but one of the other guys, a really broad one, grabbed him with some kind of sambo move and threw him to the floor. Then there was an awkward silence. Just to keep up the conversation, Death asked:

– What's your problem?

– What?

– What's your deal? Why are you creeping around and starting shit? No-one wants you around. People can't stand the sight of you. You're already the real outcasts, is that what you want?

Then the guy punched Death, too. Then gestured to the others – let's go! He looked offended, and they left.

Zombie stuck a finger up one nostril, pulled it out and looked at it. It was red.

– What happened here? Did we just get our asses handed to us?

I lit a cigarette and explained:

– That's how it has to be. We're their enemies. It can't be any other way. That's our only chance – to be their enemies.

Death said:

– I think you're full of shit.

Then the door opened and I jumped, but it was someone else, with hole-punch and uniform hats. There was a woman in their group, and she said immediately:

– You can't smoke here.

I tried to save face:

– We're very sorry, we'll take care of it right away...

But the men shouted in unison:

– Tickets!

And again we were quiet.

– Tickets!

– We're just going to Riga.

– Out!

The train stopped. It was the Olaine station. Death said:

– We can't get out here. We have to get to the Sinister concert.

– Out!

And we got out. The woman shouted after us:

– And get a haircut!

They watched us to make sure we didn't jump into a different car. Other offending parties were sent off the train, too, muttering to themselves. Then the doors closed. The train rolled into motion, giving off a blast of blue sparks, and pulled away. Was it even worth waiting for the next train in this blizzard, on this particular night? We didn't know. Death indicated with his head to the group of people at the end of the platform.

– It's them. Our friends.

– What friends?

– The guys who just kicked our asses. They must've gotten kicked off too.

– Let's get out of here.

And we left.

– They're following us.

– Go, go, go!

Where were we going? We didn't know. It was still about twenty kilometres to the concert. But we didn't care; we walked along the train tracks. It was tough going, the tracks were slippery, and the ties weren't set at comfortable intervals. Visibility was bad – that is to say, visibility was non-existent. That's probably why we chose the wrong set of tracks to follow when we came to a split. That is to say, we didn't choose anything, we just walked on without speaking. Zombie soon grew bored.

– At least it's not snowing!

Although it was snowing, and cataclysmically so. No-one laughed at his joke. But he kept on cracking them.

– It's nice and cool out, so at least my lip doesn't sting!

I asked with genuine sympathy:

– He get you good?

– Half-way decently.

And added fatefully:

– You never get anything.

– Who, me?

– Yeah. You never get involved all the way. Isn't that right, Death, he never gets hit?

Death nodded.

I stopped. This was insane. I had gotten used to being insulted. I had learned to stop caring. But now, suddenly, tonight, in a blizzard, and by my friends. It wasn't the time or place for serious discussions and appropriate behaviour. So I did what I would never have done before that moment. I turned around and headed back. With giant steps. It was hard walking along the tracks, and the ties broke my rhythm, just like they had going the opposite direction. And now the snow wasn't blowing into my face, but onto the back of my head. And I didn't have to keep stumbling into someone. I walked alone, again, finally, as always. All this time, for all the Nirvanas, the metal – death, doom and black – I had walked with them, hadn't fallen behind a single step, but it turns out, I wasn't for real. In order to be that I had to go alone. Completely alone. Even the frozen moon wasn't visible through the curtain of snow. Somewhere in front of me were my enemies, ever closer, and my friends ever farther away. Then, through the blizzard, Death's voice:

– Moron! Hey moron? Where'd you go? We'll never make it to Sinister this way!

As if we could still actually make it anywhere, as if we weren't completely lost and, even if a train did come our way, we were nowhere near a station, we're somewhere in the wrong direction, we're going to freeze to death, don't they get it? Am I the only grown-up one here? The only sensible one, the only cautious one? That is, the only weakling? Someone had managed to infiltrate this group of guys who would never grow old, someone who's always been here, a little, trembling old man. How could I ever start a band? Enough, enough, I have to head straight into my black destiny, to finally be fully birthed. And I went, and the snow wasn't falling in my face anymore, and I could see what was happening in front of me. There they were, like two little trees on a swirling white backdrop.

This is where my memory gets hazy. I asked Gatis:

– What happened after that?

– How should I know? You'd turned around to go back like some kind of idiot. And by the time we realized what was going on. I still don't really get what happened.

That's right, exactly, I'd turned back by myself. I saw some people, they were there, like two little trees. I thought maybe it wasn't the skinheads, maybe we hadn't seen clearly in the dark, maybe it was someone else entirely, friendly and familiar people, but as I drew nearer I saw that it really was the skinheads. They sneered, baring their teeth when the spotted me. I didn't speak, just adjusted my gait a little and planted my left foot out in front of me, shuffling towards them little by little in a boxer's stance. The skinheads didn't fully understand what was happening, but they knew what they had to do. The leader, the one who had already hit my friends, came forward and swung at my face. But my face wasn't there anymore; I had taken a half-step to the left, dodging him. His fist punched through snowflakes, and I hit him with a right-hook. His legs twitched as he rolled over in the snow. A second skinhead came at me, but he was already terrified and had his fists up to block his face. I hit him in the stomach, and he whimpered and crumpled to his knees like an alcohol-soaked sponge. I saw the flash of a knife in the third one's hand...

Gatis interrupted my memories:

– We got there maybe a minute later. Right, yes, it was soon. You were

standing there, so were they.

Right. My memory corrected itself immediately. It hadn't gone exactly like I had just said. Yes, they were really standing there like little trees, and yes, it was really the skinheads. Their leader asked:

– Where did you guys go?

I didn't know what to say.

– We were following you, we thought you knew where you were going.

We knew, stranger, we knew.

– Where are we now? We're all going to fucking freeze here!

He sounded genuinely concerned, and the others chimed in:

– Yeah, what are we going to do?

They looked so scared that I almost started to giggle, I could barely hold it in. Gatis added:

– Right, I noticed that too. They'd practically pissed themselves.

– But so I didn't get punched in the face? Again?

– I don't know. Your nose was bleeding when we got there.

– Really?

– Really.

I stifled my laughter, and remembered why I'd come back to them, my saviours. I said:

– You're a bunch of morons.

– What? What? Speak up, will you, I can't hear because of the blizzard.

I cleared my throat and spoke again, louder:

– You're all pigs!

It occurred to me that pigs weren't inherently bad animals, and I amended my statement:

– You're a disgrace to your species!

The skinheads looked at one another.

– What is he saying? What?

– You want a knuckle sandwich?

– What?

I went right up to him and shoved him.

– What's wrong with you?

He must have really thought it was all some misunderstanding. What was I supposed to do now, what?

– You little shits!

And then someone finally punched me in the nose. From the side. I didn't see who; it was a blizzard, after all.

It wasn't even that bad, it was a dull feeling. I felt a bit dizzy, but that's all. And my nose started to bleed , my upper lip got wet. At first I thought it was snot, but no. It was Pūpols-esque.

Then you guys got there, my friends. I was convinced you had really left me, forgive me.

– Where would we have gone?

Zombie said:

– Good evening, gentlemen!

He saw my face:

– I see you haven't wasted any time!

And he hugged me. The skinheads were talking amongst themselves:

– It wasn't me!

– Or me!

– Well then who hit him?

– I don't know, I didn't see!

– I wasn't us!

But Death had already moved on:

– Fuck, but how are we supposed to get to the Sinister concert? Hasn't it already started? It probably already started! How could this happen – we missed Sinister!

The skinheads reached a deeper level of stress:

– What... is that?

– What did we do?

– What is up with tonight?

But then a voice came from the darkness, a girl's voice:

– There is no Sinister concert.

The skinheads jumped, but Death asked:

– What you mean? No concert for us?

– For anyone. They never showed up. They panicked.

The voice came closer; it was Mele.

– Where did you come from?

– We were on the train, too. We were going too.

And there really was a group with her. Anything could hide in this blizzard. Like maybe all of Jelgava. But Death asked:

– But what's this about Sinister? How do you know?

It was a good question. But Mele held up a shiny object in her hand.

– I got a call!

It was a Motorola StarTAC. The model didn't mean anything to us; we just knew it was an important object. At that time it truly was. The skinheads were now standing at attention.

– What were you told?

– That Sinister were too scared to come to Latvia. They're not here.

– For real?

– Yup. They got scared. They never showed up. So no concert.

– So we didn't miss anything?

– There's nothing to miss.

Death lifted his face to the sky, which kept snowing down on us, and said:

– Thank you, God!

And he hugged me and Zombie. Someone else joined in, but I don't know who. We laughed happily, what else were we supposed to do? I had become someone, and nothing in this world happened without us, and we had defeated our enemies.

Gatis nodded his head:

– Yup, that's how it went.

– How could I forget? I was surprised.

– We'd been drinking. And then drank some more.

– But it happened like we just remembered, right?

– Yes, yes. Or maybe they were scared off by your thug friends... didn't you say something like that once?

– No, no, no.

– But how did we make it back that time? We didn't stay there.

– I don't know. That I really don't remember.

– Ah! That girl must've called Kārlis. He came to pick us up with his parents' car. He was really pissed off. In that blizzard! Kārlis, who else.

– To Kārlis!

– To Kārlis!

We sat in silence for a moment.

– But all that... What was it for?

– What do you mean?

– I mean, what did we learn from it? What did we gain from it?

– Honestly?

– No, lie to me!

– Yeah?

– No, tell me truthfully.

– I don't really know. Maybe we didn't cross over to the other side.

– But maybe we should have? Maybe then we'd be more successful members of society?

– What's with you?

– Supposedly nothing. But real life suddenly doesn't seem that serious to me. All that stress over jobs and our place in the world. That's not what we learned.

– Well, we were morons.

–Yup. Total idiots.

And we laughed.

Zombie came out onto the terrace; he went by Edgars again now. He'd gained some weight, cut his hair short. He saw me and said:

– Oh! Blondie!

He took my hand and shook it firmly, and looked me in the eyes. We hadn't seen each other in years, but he broke the ice of time, distance and the past all in his first question:

– How's the sex life?

END